Rivers Last Longer

Other Books by Richard Burgin:

Novel: *Ghost Quartet*

Stories:

> *The Conference on Beautiful Moments*
> *The Identity Club: New and Selected Stories and Songs*
> *Stories and Dream Boxes* (with art by Gloria Vanderbilt)
> *The Spirit Returns*
> *Fear of Blue Skies*
> *Private Fame*
> *Man Without Memory*

Novella: *The Man with Missing Parts* (with Juan Alonso)

Nonfiction:

> *Jorge Luis Borges: Conversations* (Editor)
> *Conversations with Isaac Bashevis Singer*
> *Conversations with Jorge Luis Borges*

Rivers Last Longer

Richard Burgin

Texas Review Press
Huntsville, Texas

FIRST EDITION, 2010
Requests for permission to reproduce material from this work should be sent to:

Permissions
Texas Review Press
English Department
Sam Houston State University
Huntsville, TX 77341-2146

Acknowledgements:

For their generous help and support I'd like to thank Chris Cefalu, Edmund de Chasca, Doreen Harrison, Paul Ruffin, and Eric Miles Williamson.

Cover Art: Ian Darragh, " Figure at a Window" 1984, acrylic on canvas. 76cm.x56cm. Image courtesy of private collection and www.ian-darragh.com

Cover Design: Doug Hagley

Author Photo: Valerie Dixon

Library of Congress Cataloging-in-Publication Data

Burgin, Richard.
  Rivers last longer / Richard Burgin. -- 1st ed.
     p. cm.
  ISBN-13: 978-1-933896-45-8 (cloth : alk. paper)
  ISBN-10: 1-933896-45-0 (cloth : alk. paper)
  ISBN-13: 978-1-933896-46-5 (pbk. : alk. paper)
  ISBN-10: 1-933896-46-9 (pbk. : alk. paper)
  1. Male friendship--Fiction. 2. Man-woman relationships--Fiction. 3. Murder--Fiction.
4. New York (N.Y.)--Intellectual life--21st century--Fiction. 5. Suspense fiction. I.
Title.
  PS3552.U717R58 2010
  813'.54--dc22
                              2010004554

Rivers Last Longer

For my beloved son Ricky

1

The shirts lay across his bed like souls in purgatory waiting to be judged. He was staring at them about to make a decision when he suddenly saw an image of the King with his mother and him. It was more than thirty years ago, just before the King went to New York and left them forever. They were all in the tiny kitchen of their Brookline apartment where the King was laughing while he told a joke. He was a tall man and when he gestured with his arms, it was like a giant bird spreading its wings.

A moment later the image went away. He didn't want it to, but that was the way memories were, of course. Since Jordan, he'd been thinking about his father quite a bit lately, Barry realized. It was also surprising that sometimes he still thought of him in the way he did as a child—as "the King," no less, in spite of what he ended up doing.

He returned to his task of choosing which shirt to wear to the White Dog tonight, although, if he was honest with himself, he already knew which one he'd pick, knew it before he removed them from his closet. It would be his silver wine-drinking shirt from Italy, but somehow he felt compelled to conduct this "contest" anyway. He put on the silver shirt in the living room where there was better light, then stared at his desk in the corner where he should have been working. Sometimes, his desk seemed to be waiting to pounce on him like a tiger. He had an even larger desk in his New York apartment filled with even more papers, but it was best not to think of New York now. Instead, he looked at his new, much smaller Exton apartment surrounded by generic furniture and hundreds of books but bereft of a single truly personal possession. Well, there was one, of course, that was very personal, that he'd brought last weekend from New York. It was his mother's fur coat, which he'd hung carefully in the hall closet. She alone should provide a link between New York and Exton that he otherwise wanted to keep rigorously separate.

He opened the sliding door of the closet, looked at the coat again, then finally put his face against the brown fur while he slowly inhaled until he felt her presence enough that he could speak to her in the silent way he usually did. Perhaps a half minute later he reached into her coat pocket, felt some paper, and was surprised to find a letter from Elliot, written more than twenty years ago. Moreover, wedged into the letter was an old photograph of the two of them in Harvard Square when they were somewhere in their late teens. He read the letter quickly then reached into the other pocket and found a photograph of his mother and him on the beach at Cape Cod. In that picture he was nine years old, Barry thought, certainly no more than ten. How had this happened? The only conclusion was that in those days after his mother's death—when he barely seemed conscious—he must have constructed the beginnings of a miniature museum of sacred memories that he decided to put in her coat pockets. He felt tears come to his eyes as he took the letter and photographs and placed them in the bottom drawer of his desk.

He walked to the other side of the room, put on some more clothes, but soon returned to the desk to read Elliot's letter again, this time more slowly. It started normally enough, segueing after three lines into yet another installment of their Bill Evans vs. Thelonious Monk debate with Elliot (ever the romantic) arguing for Evans as the greatest jazz pianist. By page three the argument finally shifted to who was the world's best filmmaker, Scorsese or Kubrick. It was odd how important it seemed at that age to identify "the best in the world." The best novelist, the best poet, the best country to live in, the best city, the best dessert, the best painter, basketball center, halfback, and symphony. He saw now that part of the reason for these mental jousts was just the chance to match wits in a relatively unthreatening way, since they never argued about who was the better writer or athlete between the two of them.

Finally he put the letter back in the desk, amazed at how palpably real Elliot still was to him, and shocked to realize how much time had passed—six years—since the last time he saw him. Strange world where the missing, like his mother or Jordan, his father or Elliot, were so vivid while the people in his so-called present floated by him like uninterested ghosts. He saw an image of Jordan then as he'd first seen her on the street and shuddered. Had his past and present gotten inadvertently mixed up like clothes he'd unwittingly removed from the wrong dryer and was now trying to wear? Jordan would never leave him, of course, but neither would his father—who had wronged *him*. But even though his father had chosen to disappear and had robbed or otherwise conned him each time he found him, his father was still present. And even though he had chosen not to see Elliot any more six years ago, after their fight, Elliot was still present too. Really, it was different with Elliot than with his father (whom he'd now written off completely) though for a while he hadn't seen that. Elliot had even sent him letters and occasionally tried to call him over the years. And this last week or so, as he thought more about him, he'd started sometimes calling Elliot himself, though he'd always hung up shortly after Elliot answered, just as he had a half-hour ago.

He was standing in front of his mirror fully dressed now, adding a few insurance dabs of cologne, when he suddenly remembered a dream he'd had a few nights ago. In that dream he looked in the mirror, saw a wolf, and woke up screaming. Jordan was in the dream too. Dreams were like the last attempts to contact the missing, he thought. But what if you did find these missing people? Would your dreams then find new people to contact? It was something to think about and later, perhaps as early as tomorrow morning (depending on how things worked out at The White Dog), he'd think about it more and reach some kind of conclusion. Meanwhile, he definitely needed a woman tonight. Even if he didn't get one, the attempt alone would at least get him through the night, provided he didn't do anything stupid again, which he'd absolutely promised himself he wouldn't do. Then when the woman issue was over, one way or another, he'd call Elliot and this time actually talk to him. It was evil not to follow through on good ideas.

Amazing how easily it happened. The woman who sat next to him at The White Dog asked him to pass the salt and soon they were talking about margaritas. He was on a pleasant vodka high and she seemed to laugh at everything he said. When she asked him where he was from he said, "New York, Boston, Europe." (It turned out she was from Doyleston, PA, of all places.) She said, "Are you really from Europe?"

"I'm from everywhere, capiche?" More laughter. "So tell me your name, s'il vous plait?"

"Susan. Pretty all-American, huh?"

"All-American, maybe, pretty, definitely," Barry said, looking at her closely.

She smiled, blushed actually.

"So, Susan, what do you like to do when you're in Philadelphia?"

"Oh, you know, girls just want to have fun."

"Well, you're about the most fun I've had in years."

"Really? Thank you." She looked closely at him then. "I like your shirt," she said.

"I got it in Rome."

"It's really cool."

"I think you're cool," he said, putting his free hand just above her knee. She didn't seem nervous or surprised, merely acted as if his hand wasn't there.

"Tell me what Rome is like," she said. It was funny how a woman could continue everyday conversation even as someone she'd just met had put his hand near her crotch.

"Rome is...*sui generis*."

She looked at him blankly.

"One of a kind, unique," he added.

"Oh. I thought you were speaking Chinese or something," she joked, as she finished her drink. "You don't know Chinese, too, do you?"

"No, not Chinese, I'm afraid. I've never even been to China, though I'd like to. I was even talking about going there with someone recently."

"Your girlfriend?" she said, half teasingly.

"No, with my mother actually . . . ." He stopped himself then, for several reasons. First, he wanted to keep things light, and then also, he couldn't bear to talk about her to anyone except Harvey because Harvey's own mother had died, too, or to Elliot (when he'd call him later tonight), because besides his father, who he would *never* see again, Elliot was the only person in the world who knew her well.

"So what happened," she asked, "why didn't you two go?"

"Something came up . . . but maybe we'll go to China, what do you think?"

"Sure," she said, laughing. "I wouldn't even know how to order food there, though. I wouldn't even know what to eat."

"I'd tell you what to eat," he said, smiling.

"Yah. I bet you would."

He laughed, then signaled to the bartender for more drinks, feeling they each needed one more.

"Where I'd really like to go is Paris," she said. "Paris is like my dream city, based on what I've read about it. Have you been to Paris, too?"

"Mais oui. Paris est très jolie. I'll take you to Paris then."

"Really? You must be kind of rich if you can go to all these places."

"I do all right."

"What did you say your name was?"

"I didn't. But it's Gordon," he said.

"So what kind of job do you have, Gordon?"

"I'm fortunately in a position where I don't have to have a job."

"You don't have to work?"

"No," he said, shaking his head and at the same time moving his hand an inch or two up her thighs. "I work on my life, basically, and I write books."

"I can't even imagine that. So whenever you want to you can just go to different places?"

"Something like that. My only problem is I'm kind of lonely, at least I was until I met you," he said, as his hand went a few inches higher.

Shortly after that they left The White Dog together. She was genuinely high, he was sure of that, and was walking unsteadily towards his car, almost leaning on his shoulder, when he first kissed her. "Where are we going?" she said in the car, half slurring her words.

"To Wonderland."

"Wonderland? Is it in Pennsylvania?"

"It is tonight."

"But I don't even know your name."

"Don't worry, you're in good hands. After all, I'm the mayor of Wonderland."

She laughed again and closed her eyes and a few minutes later ostensibly fell asleep. He looked at her more closely then, not fully believing she was asleep. She was good-looking enough, but there was something inauthentic about her that he'd sensed as soon as he started talking to her. It wasn't about how she looked. She wasn't overly made up, or dressed up and her breasts were too small to be artificial. It was something in her personality that was missing, and she knew it and tried to cover it up. At the next light, when he thought she really was asleep because she was snoring, he opened her pocketbook and looked at her ID. "Susan L. Hunt" was her name—but Alice Love Hunt sounded better. He kept her ID, put the pocketbook back and drove on to Exton.

"Where am I?"

"You were asleep. I just woke you up."

"Really? I must have passed out. I'm sorry."

"That's fine, I didn't mind. It was kind of peaceful, though I'm definitely glad you're awake now."

"Why were you driving so long?" she asked.

"Was it so long? Come on, open your door, let's get out."

Outside it was extremely dark and she could hear the wind blowing through the trees around the parking lot. He walked around the car and took her hand.

"Where are we?"

"Wonderland," he said lightly.

"I believe it," she said. "We must be way out in the middle of nowhere."

"When we were in Philly you only thought it was night. Now you know what night really looks like."

He opened a door at street level and they walked into the apartment.

"Jesus Christ, it's even darker in here. How can you see?"

"Because I'm Mayor Bat, the mayor of Wonderland."

"OK, Mr. Mayor, could you turn on a light?"

"Do you know Thelonius Monk, the famous jazz musician? Anyway, he said 'it's always night or we wouldn't need light.'"

He walked straight ahead and turned on a dim lamp at the end of the living room.

"Wow, I've never seen so many books before. It's like you live in a library."

He laughed as he went into the adjoining kitchen.

"You want something to drink?" he said, opening the refrigerator, "or would you like something else?"

"Yes, sure."

"Yes, sure, what?"

"Yes to both of them," she said, laughing and following him into the kitchen. "I need to get back into a Wonderland kind of mood."

He looked at her, struck by how skinny she was (in the bar he thought she hadn't looked that thin) although she did have a figure. "OK, Alice, I'll see what I can do."

"Hey, who's Alice? You don't even remember my name, do you?"

"You're Alice in Wonderland, aren't you?"

"Oh, OK, I get it," she said, taking the glass of vodka and tonic he'd poured her and immediately beginning to drink it.

"So which character are you, the Mad Hatter?"

"I'm Lewis Carroll."

"Who's he? I don't remember any Lewis Carroll."

"He wrote the book. He was an Englishman who liked little girls, especially a little girl named Alice, so he wrote a book about her."

She took a big swallow of her drink until it was practically gone. "So you think I'm like a little girl?"

"Not at all," he said. "You don't look like one and you don't kiss like one either. Come on, finish your drink."

"Why aren't you drinking?"

"I'm gonna smoke with you. It's not easy being Lewis Carroll."

"I'll bet."

They were in the bedroom, where there wasn't much light either, smoking a joint. He felt slightly embarrassed by his room, which he suddenly realized didn't have any personality. There weren't any pictures anywhere, or even a TV. Just a regular kind of bureau and bed table where the ashtray was, a mirror on the wall, and more bookshelves. It looked more like a nondescript motel room (except for the books and CDs) than someone's bedroom. He thought he would explain about just having moved here but then she asked him about the walls.

"Yes, they're soundproof. I've never been able to master the art of sleeping, so I need all the help I can get. Here," he said, handing her the joint. "Finish it."

She took the joint and inhaled. The thing about drinking was people usually laughed a lot because things suddenly seemed so light and funny, but when they smoked pot, especially right after drinking, it was often like going down a slide and landing in a serious and silent world where the quiet could sometimes lead to bad thoughts. He knew he would have to talk soon otherwise they might both start to get paranoid.

"Can I tell you what I'm thinking?" he said.

"Yah, sure, I'd like to hear."

They were lying on his bed with their clothes on, so far not touching.

"I was thinking about what things in the world are really poetic and I came to the conclusion that the most poetic thing in the world must be the love between a father and his son, especially when the son is young, like seven or eight years old."

"What about between a mother and her son?"

"No, then it's too sexual, all that Oedipal stuff ruins it. It may be more intense, it almost certainly would be more intense and deeper, too, of course, but not really as poetic as a father's love which is much more elusive and mysterious and so in that way more poetic, capiche?"

"What's *capiche* mean?"

"It means 'do you understand?' It's an Italian expression."

"Are you Italian?"

"No. I don't look Italian, do I?"

"No, I guess you don't."

"So what do I look like, what nationality, I mean?"

"I don't know…you look like the mayor of Wonderland."

"Is that good? Does it turn you on?"

"I wouldn't have kissed you if it didn't."

"But you haven't done that for a while."

"You could do something about that," she said, as she moved closer to him.

Alice was asleep again, or pretending to be. It was a few minutes after they'd had sex. Of course it was insulting in a way her "passing out" for the second time that night but he could see the humor in it, too, if he tried. At least he thought he could. The first time she passed out in his car was odd, too, but he definitely hadn't remembered her drinking or smoking enough in his place to pass out a second time. Maybe she'd taken some drugs he didn't know about or maybe there was some mechanism in her brain that made her fall asleep whenever an intimate situation arose, or at least pretend to. He thought the latter was where the truth really lay. In any event, there she was pretending to sleep again, just as earlier she'd pretended to have an orgasm. It was so exasperatingly obvious and to cover up her lie she'd quickly transitioned from fake orgasm to fake sleep.

Lately women had been tricking him a lot one way or another. There was Marianne and the whore in Madrid and then Jordan, who had more than tricked him. It was the essence of humiliation, he thought, the very essence, and yet it had happened again tonight, this time while his mother's coat was only a few feet away.

At any rate, nothing objectively "bad" had happened. There was no reason why *he* shouldn't sleep, yet he was feeling increasingly awake because of the skinny zombie beside him in bed who only now, to judge by the authentic sounding snores he was finally hearing, was actually asleep. He'd been wondering if she was a zombie for a while, but now that he'd had sex with her he knew it was true. That's when he felt the emptiness inside her, that there was nothing there but her need and a bunch of tricks to make sure that need was minimally fed. It was pointless to agitate himself by thinking about her, he knew that, but he couldn't seem to stop. In fact, he was getting more and more irritated with each snore Alice was releasing. It was time to wake the little zombie actress up and at least ask her some questions, like why deceive someone by *pretending* you were sleeping? Did she think a man of his experience couldn't tell the difference? He heard her recurrent snore and then the old Everly Brothers' song in his head, "Wake Up, Little Susie." Just before he woke her he sang to himself, "wake up Little Zombie, wake up."

2

"Hey, what are you doing?" she said.

He was sitting on her, fully dressed, except for his shoes, one knee pressing hard on each of her biceps. It was about twenty minutes after they'd had sex, maybe less.

"Come on, get off me, it hurts!"

He didn't answer, just looked at her, although it was dark enough that she propably couldn't be sure exactly where he was looking.

"I mean it, it really hurts. Get off me—it's not funny," she said, trying to move him again without success.

"In a way I think it's quite funny."

"Gordon, I want you off me now."

He shifted his knees slightly but it still hurt just as much.

"Come on, you're hurting me and scaring me."

"Two things you would never do to me, of course."

"Get off!" she screamed until he covered her mouth hard with his hand.

"Don't do that again or it could get a lot worse," he said, lowering his hand until it was near her throat. "Learn to communicate softly. Whisper."

She looked shocked—too shocked to speak. There was at least one moment in every woman's life when she felt this, he thought, and this was hers.

"Are you completely unaware of how much you've hurt me tonight?" he finally asked.

"No, yes. I'm unaware, what did I do?"

"What did I do? What did I do? Poor Alice hasn't a clue," he said, removing his hands from her neck but putting even more pressure on her arms.

"Jesus Christ, will you get off me?" she said, trying to move him and then starting to cry.

"That won't help you either. Your crying will only make things worse. Crying and all your emoting and manipulating won't help you anymore. No one will hear you anyway. Remember what I told you about the walls?"

He could actually see her trying to remember. Then she looked like she might get hysterical.

"What did I do?" she said. "What did I say that hurt you? I'm sorry, I can't imagine what it was but I'm truly sorry."

"I'm sure you are…now."

"I don't understand what I did or why you won't tell me."

"What would be gained by my telling you?"

"So I could apologize."

"And what would be gained by that?"

She looked puzzled for a second, like she was trying not to cry.

He became excited again. It was like his excitement was chasing his anger, but his anger was stronger, his anger was still the faster dog. "Do you think all you have to do in life is utter a little perfunctory apology and then you can get everything the way you want it?"

"No," she said. "No I don't."

"Do you think that if someone you know killed your mother, then said to you 'I'm sorry, I apologize,' you'd respond by saying, 'OK, I understand, now we can be friends again'?"

"No, of course not."

"Well, then I guess you do understand."

"So what can a person do if they hurt someone by mistake?"

"The best thing they can do is not make the mistake in the first place, capiche?"

"Yes, I understand," she said, trying to look ashamed, hoping probably that that might appease him, although there was also the possibility that she actually was beginning to understand, he couldn't dismiss that entirely. "Are you beginning to understand now?" he said.

"Yes, but what can I do? I mean, I'll do whatever you want. Just don't hurt me."

He looked at her face. The anger dog was slowing down but the excitement dog wasn't even moving now, as if it had lost the trail.

"I'm going to give you a second chance," he finally said.

"Thank you," she said softly.

"I'm going to make a Kierkegaardian leap of faith and give you a second chance, but you have to do exactly what I tell you."

"Yes, yes, I will."

He got up then and she moaned a little. "Stay still, till I say you can move," he said, as he got off the bed and began searching for his shoes and then his keys in the dark. It reminded him of a time when he played hide and seek with his mother and the King and he asked for a flashlight before he hid, which made the King laugh. It was a moment he would always remember.

"Come on," he said, "let's go."

"Where are we going?"

"Right here," he said, taking a few steps with her while he held her with one hand and turned on the bathroom light with the other.

"The light is so bright," she said. She seemed embarrassed to be naked in front of him, he thought, maybe because her breasts were skinny or because she probably remembered the unfortunate tattoo on her bottom, which she tried to cover with her hand.

"What are you going to do?" she said.

"The question is what are *you* going to do. And the answer is: take a bath. That's not too difficult, is it? Go on, pull aside the shower curtain and turn on the bath. Come on, turn the faucet on more. You want this to end soon, don't you, but it can't end till it begins."

Her hands were shaking on the faucets making it difficult to adjust the temperature. First she made the water too cold, then too hot. It was as if her fingers had turned into centipedes. Finally, she thought she got it more or less right, probably too hot but still the best she could apparently do, and then she turned on the faucets full force and waited while the water roared.

"All right, that's enough. Turn off the water and get in now, and while you're in there I want you to think about what a bath is."

"What it *is*?"

"What it means. Think about purification and the chance to emerge a new person."

She was lying in the tub now, instinctively covering her crotch, looking both scared and confused.

"Based on how aggressive you were in the bar I'd say you have a lot to purify."

She nodded, still trying not to cry.

"Look at me while I talk to you. You were attracted to me in the bar, weren't you? It was you who pursued me and made this night happen. Am I correct?"

"Yes."

"How attracted to me were you?"

"Extremely. A lot."

"But that's not a good reason to start flirting and then get in a car with someone you don't know and go to their home, is it?"

"No."

"And that's something you've done before, I'm sure. You use men like a drug, don't you, so you can feel better about yourself in the short run. But that's very bad behavior. And it's bad for the man, too, because you don't know him, just like you didn't know me. You may think you do but you don't. And what happens when you don't know someone well is you can hurt them very easily."

She nodded. "Yes, I see that now."

"Now I want you to wash yourself with that bar of soap very thoroughly, including your private parts, especially your private parts. Go on, put the bar of soap inside your pussy and wash out every speck of me."

"Yes," she said. "I'm doing it."

"I'm going to keep watching you to make sure you do."

She started washing herself while he stared at her. Then he took a step closer, till he was right next to the tub.

"You're not washing yourself vigorously enough."

"Sorry, I will," she said, doubling her speed.

"Put the soap inside yourself and scrub. Are you going to make me do it?"

"No, I'll do it," she said, washing harder.

He leaned over so he could see better and noticed that while she was washing she was clearly thinking of something.

"Stop thinking," he hissed at her, making her shake again. "I can hear your thoughts and I don't like them. Just keep washing yourself."

"OK."

"Harder."

"It's starting to hurt."

"OK, stop," he said. Then he pulled the plug and the water began to drain. He didn't say anything as he continued to watch her with a nondescript expression.

"What are you going to do?" she said, looking oddly small in the empty tub.

"Don't worry. I always have a plan. You really don't know where you are, do you?"

"No, how could I? I passed out in the car and then it was so dark and when I asked where I was you didn't tell me."

"No I didn't. It's lucky for you you drank so much that you passed out. Lucky for you and in a way unlucky for me because I'd like to drink now, but I can't because I have to drive."

"I'll drive, if you want me to," she said hopefully.

"No," he said, laughing a little, "that would be difficult, given my plan for you."

"Why? What are you planning to do? Are you worried that I'll tell someone about this?"

"Should I be?"

"No, no. What would I tell them?"

"Exactly."

"I made the decision to sleep with you."

"How was the sex, by the way?"

"Fine."

"Fine?"

"Great. Probably the best sex I've had in years."

"In years?"

"I meant *ever*. It was the best sex I've ever had in my life."

"Really? That's strange. And here I thought you were faking and lying the whole time and making a fool of me. You should be grateful to me then for that experience and now for what I have to teach you about consideration and purification."

"I am grateful," she said weakly, thinking that she'd probably been too stoned to fake her orgasm as well as she normally did.

"All right, now get out of the tub and dry yourself off. I'll be watching you every second, of course. Then you'll get dressed and we'll go."

"Where? Where are we going?"

"Ah, don't expect answers to every question, otherwise I *will* start thinking you're a little girl."

She dried herself quickly and looked at him indecisively, not knowing what to do with the towel.

"Put the towel back on the rack," he said, knowing that she hoped she could wear it.

"Oh. OK," she said, taking it off her body slowly.

"Are you still scared? Be honest."

"No, yes. I'm just a little confused and anxious."

"Would it help if you prayed?"

"Excuse me?" she said.

Then he opened a cabinet door, took out a bag and removed a gun that he was now pointing at her. "See this?" he said.

She stared at him. She looked like she'd been electrocuted, he thought, her eyes almost popping out of her head like Little Orphan Annie's.

"Don't shoot, don't, please don't," she repeated, holding up a hand.

"Calm down. All right? Just calm down, tout de suite. I just showed it to you, that's all, OK?"

"OK."

"OK, that's better. Would you like to pray now, would that help?"

"Here? You want me to pray here?"

"Yes, right here, right now. Get on your knees and pray for what you want out loud so I can hear you."

He could see her shake a little. "The floor's cold," she said.

"Go on," he said, standing over her and still holding the gun with one hand and something else behind his back with the other.

"Dear God, I pray…"

"Wait a minute. Hold the phone. Who's God? Are you sure that's who you want to pray to? Does God come over to your apartment to visit you? Does God ever invite you to dinner or take you for a drive in the dark to the suburbs?"

"What should I say? How should I do it?"

"Pray to me, Gordon. At least you know I'm real."

"You want me to pray to you?"

"Yes."

"OK. Dear Gordon," she said in an uncertain voice. "I pray that you won't hurt me and will take me home tonight."

A flash went off, then another. She looked up and realized he had photographed her while she was praying. He put the camera behind his back in some kind of bag he was holding and said, "Guess what? I've decided to grant most of your prayer. Nothing bad will happen now if you continue to cooperate, capiche?"

"Yes. I'll cooperate. Whatever you want."

"All right," he said, taking her by the hand into the bedroom where he turned on an overhead light. "Get in your clothes now, tout de suite. And by the way, the picture looks like it will turn out well. Do you want to see it?"

She didn't say anything. She looked at the floor, where most of her clothes were in a tangle. When she finally put her shoes on she said, "You're not going to shoot me, are you? You're not going to kill me?"

"I already shot you," he said, pointing to the camera and looking at her with an expression that was meant to feign shock. "How many times do you want me to shoot you?"

He shut off the light and began leading her by the hand out the door, still holding the gun as they got in the car.

"There's nothing for me to worry about, right?"

"No. Nothing. Absolutely nothing."

"You don't know where I live, and by the way, I don't live here."

"I didn't think so."

"I don't even live in this state. And also, in the tub, you washed out every trace of me."

"I also don't know your last name," she added.

"Guess what, you don't know my first name either."

She looked like a tremor passed through her and he felt reassured and continued. "But I know your name, Susan L. Hunt, *and* where you live, as well."

"How?"

"While you were sleeping I took your ID from your pocketbook. I'm going to have to keep that, I'm afraid."

Again he saw her tremble like an insect had just crawled across her face.

"I'm not going to tell anyone anything ever. I just want to go home."

"And you will get home, eventually."

She repeated his words right after he said them as if she didn't trust what she heard.

"Are you still wondering what else I have in my bag?"

"Yes."

"Well, one of the things in it is a blindfold that I'm going to have to put on you and tie it a little on the tight side."

"But it's so dark anyway. I'll keep my eyes closed, I promise."

"Since it's so dark it won't make much difference. But I recommend you do keep your eyes closed while the blindfold's on. It will make it much easier for you."

"OK, whatever you want."

"I want you to promise me."

"I promise."

He put the blindfold on in silence, then said, "It's a shame."

"What?" she said quickly.

"That we got off on the wrong foot. That you hurt me. I think we could have become friends."

"Yes," she said softly.

"I've been thinking some more about poetic things, and I have to change my conclusion. I think the most poetic thing in the world is friendship just because you're not born into friendship like you are into your family. Because both people have to choose to be friends. In fact, after you leave, I'm going to call my best friend in all the world, although I haven't spoken to him in a long time. His name is Elliot, and tonight I'll finally call him after all these years."

"That's great. I know what you mean about friends—I agree with you completely . . . . So, Gordon, where are you planning to drop me off?"

"It won't take you long to get home. Don't worry. You have enough cash in your wallet. Trust in Gordon."

"I don't understand."

"I'm going to find a nice outdoor train stop for you. One where there aren't many cars or people, not at this time of night, and you'll get a train to Philly before too long."

"Can I take off my blindfold now?"

"I'm afraid you'll have to wait till I drop you off for that. By then I'll be long gone—just a stranger in the night, an eidolon. Oh, and by the way, I borrowed this car from out of state. You'll never trace it."

"I won't try to. I never saw the license plate. Never saw it."

"No, I don't think you did. And I don't think you'll try to trace anything else either. I think you realize that you've learned a lot from me and that you'll behave differently in the future. And I don't think you'll ever forget me, either."

"No, I never will."

A moment later the car turned and began circling slowly until it stopped. Then he reached across and opened the door. "Well, I've got something to do now. I have to call my best friend. Now don't make a sound or take off your blindfold until I'm gone," he said almost tenderly. Then he half helped her out the door. She tried to stand still on the ground but fell down on something hard and gravelly. He waited until she stood up and took a step towards the station before pulling away into the night.

It was like driving away from a car wreck, like driving away from madness, he thought. Because it *was* madness to try to help people like her who couldn't be helped—zombies, addicts—addicted to humiliation. One ended up being the fool, being the truly humiliated one and in his case having to live with the terror of being potentially punished as well. He began reviewing the events of the evening over and over like watching a videotape. Supposing someone saw the whole thing, he asked himself, what was the worst thing that had happened? He hadn't hit her and god knows he hadn't raped her. He'd pulled a gun on her (an empty gun), that was true, but he'd only done it to make her listen to him. To get her attention. With zombie people like that, what other way was there? And she had listened, so perhaps he'd made a difference.

He had to stay focused, not tilt like his mind was nothing more than a pinball machine. She had reassured him over and over that she wouldn't tell anyone and he knew that was true. Besides, what could she say, what did she know? Nothing. Nothing to the ninth power. He merely had to concentrate on the image of nothing. "Being and Nothingness," as Sartre aptly called it. A patch of air above an empty lake. Nothing. "Nada y pues nada" as Hemingway called it. "The Night of the Living Dead," as Wes Craven called it, or was that another director? There were getting to be so many directors these days, more directors than writers. He thought of Jordan and a shock ran through him so strong it made him close his eyes for a second.

He'd call Elliot soon, once he got back to his apartment and had a drink or two. Finally, he'd call Elliot after all these years and that would make him feel better, he was sure.

3

Elliot answered the phone in time, but once again the caller hung up without identifying himself. When he *69ed the call he heard, "The sea whispered me," a line from Whitman delivered, incongruously enough, by a mechanized voice. It had to be Barry then—who else? Two nights ago when the same thing happened he heard some lines from Frost, and Whitman and Frost were two of Barry's favorite poets. Even before he'd heard either message, Elliot thought (hoped) it was Barry and had actually talked about it less than an hour ago with Annette, during yet another of their too-long coffee house dialogues. Yes, Annette and he never had any trouble talking. He wondered if by now they qualified for the *Guinness Book of Records* for "Most words exchanged between an under-forty heterosexual man and woman without any form of attempted sex." Half an hour before they finally left the coffee house (after his progress report on how he was recovering from Linda, who left him six months ago, and Annette's last bit of griping about their department head), he'd mentioned the hangup calls he'd been getting.

"Yah, I get those all the time," Annette had said, flipping back some of her black lustrous hair, hair he'd sometimes thought about. "I think, by now, Philadelphia should be in the phone fetishists' hall of fame."

He'd smiled but said nothing.

"So who do you think it is, some long-lost love maybe?" she'd asked. "Maybe Linda?"

"Not exactly. I don't want to speak to her again anyway. I think it's more like my long-lost best friend, but maybe that's just my wishful thinking."

"You mean Barry, the guy you've been telling me about lately?"

"I could be wrong, of course, but I think it's him."

"This is the guy who won all that money in a court case and led you on about starting a literary magazine and then got mad at you when you asked him about it?"

Elliot nodded. "It's more complicated than that. It was his mother's money, not really his."

"OK, whatever, but why do you think he'd suddenly pull an adolescent phone prank on you? How do you know it isn't just some ex-student who didn't like the grade you gave them?"

"I'm an easy grader. No one's ever complained. I should probably be in the grade-inflation hall of fame."

Annette laughed. At least they were good at making each other laugh from time to time. "OK. So how do you know it isn't just some kid or weirdo who picked your number at random?"

"I did think that at first, but then the calls started to form a pattern."

"So, weirdos love patterns."

"They were all late at night and Barry stays up later and sleeps later than anyone I know."

"So, weirdos love late night, too—it brings out the inner Halloween in them. Besides, how many years has it been since you've talked to him?"

"Six."

"He's probably on all kinds of anti-depressants by now, like everyone else, and falls asleep in a mildly cheerful mood at 10:30 every night."

Even when he told her how he'd *69ed the last call and heard the lines from Frost, she managed to explain it away. Why did she so often try to thwart his hopes? Was it all part of "the kit" she used to make herself sexually off limits to him, as if she instinctively knew just what to say to prevent him from ever making a move, while simultaneously keeping them platonic friends forever?

To her credit, though, she did ask him how Barry and he became friends, perhaps because of her momentary guilt for dampening his spirits. Yet, as he remembered it now, she did seem to also convey some genuine interest so he'd told her how they were each trying to be the starting shortstop on their eighth-grade team until the coach finally decided he should start instead of Barry.

"When he announced the starting lineup a little before game time, I looked at Barry a few seats away on the bench. He looked so absolutely stricken I felt my heart melt. 'Congratulations,' he said softly. Well, that was it. There was something about that incident I couldn't forget."

"Love at first vulnerability," Annette had said smiling. . . . "So it just took off from there, from your baseball bonding?" she'd added, with her typical tinge of sarcasm, another crucial component of her kit.

"Something like that," he'd said. "I guess it's fair to say I could appreciate his sensitivity while secretly feeling a certain sense of superiority," he'd added, with a self-mocking little laugh.

"That's a neat trick. How did you feel superior?" she'd said, flipping her hair again in the same way she had a few minutes before.

He should have said, "I didn't feel superior, I just felt I had superior luck." Instead, he told her about growing up in a very big white house that he used to think of as a castle with professionally successful parents (his father was a pianist and professor of music, his mother, a professor of literature) and a smart older sister. But Barry was the only child of a young divorcée who lived in a little apartment in one of the few unfashionable parts of Brookline. With some financial help from her brother, who was a fairly affluent lawyer, she'd raised Barry alone since he was seven or eight.

Annette nodded, but he felt she didn't really understand it, which wasn't her fault because even if he'd talked about Barry for nine straight days, he still couldn't have explained the essence of their friendship, any more than he could have explained his own childhood either.

He leaned back an additional notch in his recliner and closed his eyes, and he could hear his father again, explaining how a passage in a Beethoven sonata should be played to his students on the top floor of the house with the door half open, which allowed Elliot to watch or spy on him—he was never sure which—since his father could have closed the door if he didn't really want to be observed. Below him on the second floor in her study, his mother was practicing a lecture she'd be giving in New York. Sometimes he would race down the row of waterfall stairs, as he thought of them (or slide down the banister) to watch her practice her lecture, but most times he preferred watching his father practice or teach, perhaps because he spent less time with him and he always seemed the most mysterious person in the house. Later, when Barry got to know him he agreed that his father was both "mysterious and cool."

It was odd, he was born in a castle or a castle-like house and for the rest of his life would remember it and try to unravel its mysteries. Yet he once lived in the house quite unselfconsciously accepting it as his simple friend with its four floors (counting the basement) and twenty-one rooms, and its high, circular windows that looked out on the playground and indeed all of Brookline so that it seemed he could survey the entire town. The front and back yards were just as important as the house, of course. In the back yard in front of the sunroom with its stained glass windows was the large outdoor patio surrounded by a gray cement wall (like a moat), ideal for snowball fights, he remembered, that he sometimes had with Barry at the beginning of their friendship. The front yard also had high wooden fences and a row of trees on each side protecting the yard from the neighbors. It was by these fences in the spaces between the trees that the flowers bloomed, red, yellow, pink and blue flowers, preternaturally bright like he'd never seen before or since. There was also a trellis draped with roses and lilac bushes that grew under his mother's window and a narrow cement path the same color as the patio wall that led down to an alley in back on which he used to sled with his sister, Michelle. He played other games with her in the backyard, too, mainly baseball and badminton, until she went to high school and then he had to simulate them for a while with his imaginary friends.

He was lonely at times, once Michelle stopped playing outside with him, but he was beginning to like music more, thanks largely to his father, and was beginning to write little stories, encouraged mainly by his mother. That made him feel different from a lot of the kids at school (as did his house itself, of course) and it was a difference he mostly enjoyed, although he was then too old for his imaginary friends and hadn't really made any at school with whom he could share much.

And then Barry came into his life. It began with the school baseball team and soon spilled onto the playground with its endless games of basketball and football. But unlike his other friends, Barry and he shared music and literature, too, and most of all their fantasies and dreams. At fifteen or sixteen at the latest, they each admitted that they wanted to become writers and to be at least as great (and famous) as William Faulkner. They were calling each other every day by then, sometimes skipping school to listen to Thelonious Monk or Bill Evans or to Mahler symphonies in Barry's apartment on Tappan Street, while his mother was out working.

For the rest of his high school years they had a kind of friendship in paradise, only occasionally interrupted by something from the outside world. One such interruption was when he found out Barry scored 80 points higher than he did on the English part of the SATs which meant Barry would get into a more prestigious college. It took a few days to snap back from that, but then came a more serious shock when Barry lost his virginity first. Still, he was much too close to Barry to have a petty jealousy disturb things for any length of time, not when there was the latest issue of *Downbeat* to discuss, or the latest movies by Herzog or Woody Allen to argue about.

Then Barry *did* go to a more prestigious college in Ohio, while he stayed home and went to Boston University. Once again, Barry was far from insufferable about it, as if there were something too innocent in his nature to realize his advantage. Barry was in his anarchistic phase then, very much under the influence of Henry Miller, and repeatedly said college was the last thing he wanted to do, that all he really wanted was to go to Paris (as Henry had) and "become a great writer."

Still, it was surprising, like a dream really, to see him knocking at the back door of his house a few months after Oberlin started, having hitchhiked all the way from Ohio and vowing never to return.

It was the first outward sign of a fissure in Barry's life, but he was far too happy to have Barry back in the castle to think about that then. At the time he viewed it as yet another example of Barry's flair for the dramatic surprise, and so paradoxically, in that sense it wasn't really that surprising. What was surprising was that his mother, Roberta, didn't force him to go back. He didn't know exactly what her reaction was, only that Barry stayed home with her that year.

Barry did return to college the next year, but to New York University at the Greenwich Village branch. If he had to live in America, then it had to be in New York. Brookline, in fact all of Massachusetts, was "too small and provincial" for a writer with his "concern for the world." This time Barry stayed in school for a year and a half before quitting in a rage, though he continued to live in New York supported by Roberta and his uncle. He never learned what went wrong exactly, though he tried to talk to Barry and Roberta about it many times. Barry had been doing well academically (Roberta said he was offered a university scholarship) but he began fighting with his professors or intermittently losing his concentration in class. At night he'd suffer from insomnia. He seemed to love New York, but how could he enjoy it when he couldn't sleep? Roberta called and pleaded with him to talk Barry into going back to school.

"Elliot, you're his best friend. He'll listen to you. His uncle is going to wash his hands of the whole thing and then he'll never be able to get a degree."

He'd call Barry and give him all the standard arguments for finishing college (which he only half believed), but as he expected, Barry wouldn't budge.

"If he doesn't straighten out, he'll never get a job. Roberta can't support him his whole life," his mother said. But getting a job, despite occasional threats from Roberta and his uncle, was literally the last thing on Barry's mind. Not only did he still worship Henry Miller, he'd discovered a bevy of contemporary writers and artists who lived in Paris. It was both the most natural and imperative thing in the world, as he saw it, to escape "the absurd contradictions and crass materialism of America" and move to Paris where one might walk down the street and bump into Beckett or Foucault. By next September, Barry moved. Elliot could remember it all, now, how things slowly began to collapse—his uncle no longer supporting Barry, Roberta taking a job in the insurance industry to make more money, her faith in Barry still absolute.

He came back to the present with a jolt. Someone was yelling outside—a wolf-like kind of yell. Elliot got out of his reclining chair, then heard the sound of tires screeching. Walking quickly to the living room window, he looked out at Walnut Street at the same corner where just a little while ago he'd been standing with Annette while they waited for her cab. He couldn't see anything now but the street lamps and the cold ghostlike buildings half visible behind them. The street was strangely quiet as if an invisible funeral were taking place.

He went into his kitchen, opened a beer, and walked back to his chair, placing the bottle on a small table next to it. After a few sips he thought of Annette's hair flip (the way she did it the second time) and started free associating. Two hair flips. "Played Twice," a tune by Thelonious Monk that he and Barry used to listen to. Debussy, who his father said always repeated his key musical ideas but was an important composer anyway. The first time he made love with Lianne twice, still the love of his life, with whom he and Barry had once spent so much time in Harvard Square at cafes or going to movies. (He'd been a little jealous at times because Barry was a natural flirt, but was almost sure nothing had ever happened between them.) Barry's telephone call—if it *was* Barry—would probably come a second time tonight because Barry was a little on the obsessive side and always did things at least twice if they didn't happen right the first time.

He put the beer down on the table, walked into his bedroom, turned on the lights, and opened his bedroom closet. On the top shelf, resting on a couple of unlucky shirts, was his "memory box"—a large, clear plastic box, perhaps four by two feet, that had once contained a train set and other toys from his childhood. Inside it were photographs of his parents and his sister, as well as some letters from them and perhaps a half-dozen girlfriends (from different periods of his life) for most of whom he had photographs as well. Some of these pictures, like Linda's or Lianne's, were still too painful to look at, so he'd hidden them underneath the box scores and accompanying articles of his high school newspaper that chronicled his modest success on the school basketball team.

It was among these pictures that he'd saved his only photograph of Barry (now faded and curled at the edges) of the two of them standing by the lake near his parents' summer home in the Berkshires. For a number of summers when they were teenagers Barry used to visit for a week, and he guessed that in this photograph they were about sixteen and trying to look cool and serious, though both were grinning slightly in spite of themselves. Underneath that single photograph, however, was a stack of letters, postcards, and several early publications of Barry's that took up more than half the box.

He looked through some of the letters briefly then returned to the photograph. He supposed he was better-looking in a conventional way but Barry's face was more striking, commanded more attention as if always demanding a response. As he looked at the picture more closely he was somehow surprised to realize, again, that they were exactly the same height. He looked once more at Barry, then finally put the memory box away. It was getting late, even by Barry's standards, and he no longer believed he would call, at least not tonight. For a moment Elliot saw himself alone in his shabby apartment, a struggling academic and barely published writer starting therapy for the first time in his life because his girlfriend left him, dreaming of his childhood and a lost friend and worst of all, since he loathed self-pity, feeling sorry for himself.

He lay down on his bed, but almost immediately after he fell asleep the telephone rang.

4

Elliot picked up after the fifth ring. Later he remembered that the phone felt almost weightless, like a tiny leaf or a few grains of sand. It was well after midnight.

"It's Barry. Long time no speak."

"Barry . . . how are you? *Where* are you?" he said, his voice shaking a little.

"I guess we're both nervous," Barry said.

"It's just been so long," he said.

"I nearly called you a lot of times, but I lost my nerve. Then I finally found out you were in Philadelphia."

"I *tried* to call you lots of times, but I didn't know where you were. How'd you know I was in Philadelphia?"

"I heard a rumor that you were teaching there. Then I met a former female student of yours once in a bar. I spent most of our time together asking her about you."

"You go to bars?"

"Just once in a while when I need to remind myself that I still have a dick."

They both laughed then Barry said, "I'm really sorry for what happened with us . . . and for some of the things I said to you."

"Me, too," Elliot said quickly. "I wish it were just a nightmare that had never happened."

"So let's just pretend that it never did. I've learned to do that about the bad things in my life. I've learned to kick them out of my mind as if they never happened."

"I wish I could do that. That's a real art."

"Not that I can do it all the time. But I'm getting better at it."

There was a silence and when Barry spoke again his tone had shifted. "There's something I need to tell you, Elliot . . . my mother died. It was six months ago so I can deal with it now. I've learned to deal with it. Of course it's completely changed my life, but I don't want it to dominate our conversation now. I really don't."

Elliot felt tears spring to his eyes while he said how sorry he was, and asked how it happened.

"It was her kidneys. You don't think about a kidney, you know."

"No, you don't."

"But they failed her. Collapsed. It was very painful and sad, of course, I guess it was a little after that that I started going to bars," he said with a quick laugh. "But we were able to control her pain near the end and she died a beautiful death."

Barry talked about her for perhaps another minute and then no more, though her presence hovered over the rest of the conversation. At least for Elliot it did, to the point where it was difficult to remember, even now, when he was trying to reconstruct the conversation.

Roberta was dead. He heard the line from the old John Lennon song: "My mummy's dead / I can't get it through my head." In all the scenarios he constructed about Barry's fate over the years he never imagined Roberta dying. He'd even had a dream a week ago where he bumped into her in mid-town Manhattan near the old Coliseum Book Store.

In the dream she was still strikingly pretty, in a white fur coat with her carefully coiffeured black hair, and her green eyes under a stylish pair of sunglasses. Physically she had aged, if at all, in very subtle ways.

"Don't turn away, Elliot. Come on, give me a hug. Let's forget the past, we can forgive each other, can't we?"

They embraced and soon were seated at a nearby coffee shop.

"So, how's Barry?" he finally said.

"You'll see him tonight when you come to dinner. I'm cooking for all of us in his new place."

"Where are you living now?" he asked, but then he'd woken up before getting the address.

"Where are you living now?" he'd heard himself say to Barry. He was aware that he had been talking while he remembered the dream and wasn't sure what he said.

"In New York. Beekman Place. Do you know it?"

"It's kind of a wealthy neighborhood, isn't it, way over on the East Side?"

"That's it. My financial situation has improved quite a bit, of course. I've been living here for almost three years. My mother had the bottom apartment, which she loved, and I had the top. We'd traveled around in Europe and the States a lot. You've heard of the wandering Jews, right? Well we were setting a record. And then we finally found a place we both loved but then came the bad kidneys. Now I'm still upstairs and rarely use the other place at all. When you come to visit me you can stay there."

"That sounds nice."

"I'd thought about renting it but couldn't bring myself to do it. Now that we're in touch again I'm glad I didn't. Cause it's perfect, don't you see? You can always have a place to stay when you're in New York now, capiche?"

The conversation changed and Barry began asking him some questions about his life.

"You're still writing, I hope?"

"Yes, not that you'd know it by visiting anyplace as mundane as a bookstore or a library."

"Well, I've read three of your stories in magazines I found in bookstores, though nothing in the last few years."

"That's been about half my published output."

"They were very good," Barry said, "*very* good."

Elliot felt himself smile broadly as if his facial muscles were powerless to constrict.

"Thanks," he said, wondering if now would be a good time to ask Barry about *his* work. He was still afraid of saying the wrong thing, but, of course, if they were really going to be friends again one couldn't behave like that no matter how careful one wanted to be.

"What about you?"

"I published a book in France with a small press," Barry said quickly, "and I'm putting the finishing touches on two different books that will be coming out soon."

"Really? That's impressive. What are they?"

"One's a collection of literary essays, the other is more theoretical and deals with . . . the aesthetics of film."

Was it true? He'd caught Barry in "publishing lies" before, though never confronted him with them. He noticed that Barry hadn't given the title or publisher of either of the books, still Elliot tried to kick the question out of his mind. It seemed almost sacrilegious to be thinking about that now that he was finally talking to Barry again. Besides, he knew Barry had the ability to write books and wanted to more than anything else in the world and that in itself made it true in a way.

"What's happening with your school?" Barry said, ostensibly changing the subject just in time.

"What's happening is that they'll be getting rid of me for sure in two years at the most and possibly in one year."

"You didn't get tenure?"

"It was never even a tenure-track job. It was always a terminal job with an eight-year ceiling. I've already used six. I have academic cancer, so I have two years left to live, tops."

Barry laughed a little. "So why not beat the putzes to it?"

"What do you mean?"

"Why wait around to die? Why not seek your fortune elsewhere?"

"Well, of course, I'm going to be looking at the M.L.A. job list in the spring and apply wherever there's a position. I'll have to."

"That isn't what I meant. Why not get out of Philadelphia where that little school is mistreating you? Has it really done so much for you?"

"It's not a question of that."

"Sure it is. It's your *life* that we're talking about, right?"

"Exactly, and my point is where would I go, what would I do?"

"Come to New York and stay with me for as long as you want, or at least until you get a job. Like I said, you could even have your own apartment so there's no way we could get on each other's nerves, and it would cost you literally nothing."

"That's really kind of you and generous, of course, but I've got to be a realist and keep my job as long as I can, don't you think? Besides, everyone wants to live in New York. New York teaching jobs are the hardest to get in the world."

"But there are other things you could do in New York besides teach. There's a whole publishing world that you're more than qualified to flourish in. There are lots of writing jobs too. And there are a ton of private schools, where you can teach right in the city. At least think about it . . . why are you laughing?" Barry had said, half laughing himself.

"Because my lease is up in a month and I really could do this. Which, of course, isn't to say that I should or will."

"But why shouldn't you? You're still young enough to take chances. My whole life has been a chance."

"True, but, I mean you obviously have some money."

"Believe me, I take other kinds of chances, all the time. There's no life without risk, right? Anyway, couldn't your parents help you?"

"They would, but I couldn't ask them."

"Well, I can certainly help you," Barry said. Elliot said he couldn't accept that either, then fell silent and began to think about Barry's idea for the first time. Was it possible that everything Barry said made sense, the deepest kind of sense that he desperately needed in his life?

"What are you really clinging to in Philadelphia? Is there someone you're in love with there?" Barry said.

"No."

"Is there something there that's really helping your writing career?"

"I have no writing career."

"Do you love your apartment? Is that it?"

"It has a good location, but it's overheated and there are bugs."

"Let's see, you could stay in Philadelphia with the bugs where you don't love anyone and where no one is helping your career and wait to get fired, or you could live rent free in your own terrific New York apartment with your best friend in the world one floor above you. Do the math, Elliot, do the math. Stay in Wonderland or stay with me. At least say you'll visit and see what it's like."

"That I will definitely do," he said. And then a moment later they began talking about movies and a few minutes later began arguing about books.

5

He had slept when he'd least expected to and he had dreamt about the King again. "The Lord giveth and the Lord taketh away," he said to himself as soon as he woke up. It was only a twenty-minute sleep so he must have dreamt right away, as if his sleep was merely a ruse to force him to face his dream. Yet little had happened in it. All he remembered was playing chess with his father outside in some kind of park. He was young and didn't know how to play but was afraid to tell the King. A simple dream, yet after he went over it he immediately began pacing in the living room. It was some time after 3 a.m. and outside his apartment New York was quiet. Sometimes when he paced he believed that by sheer repetition he could erase a thought or memory. Other times, especially when there was more than one thing he was trying to erase, it didn't work. An overload of anxiety trumped pacing every time, and tonight was definitely an overload situation. Even though he'd finally broken through and called Elliot, he was feeling more anxiety than usual and had to acknowledge that the call and Elliot's imminent visit was creating a substantial, if unspecified, anxiety of its own. No wonder he intermittently interrupted his pacing to drink more vodka from his glass on the kitchen table.

Still, he was glad on balance, very glad, that he'd called Elliot, who was hardly his biggest problem. Right now his most important need was to get to sleep (his dream-filled nap merely made that more difficult) and he knew the only way to do that was to treat his anxieties sequentially. The first part was targeted at erasing the things Love Hunt said and did that hurt him. The next would be targeted at his anger for what he did to her. Although he'd been both high and stoned and never would have done it otherwise, he knew he still couldn't forgive himself for pointing his gun at her (though it wasn't loaded). Taking her picture was one thing—he needed that for his own protection—but he'd crossed the line when he took out the gun (loaded or not) and he believed in lines he shouldn't cross—without them there was chaos.

He was upset at other things, too, like the Harvey situation. Harvey was his quasi-friend who managed a bookstore in the Village. "The Harvey Situation" was something he had to act on in a matter of hours and would require a firm decision. But he couldn't bear to face it yet so he continued to pace without any thoughts at all and for a while, like a kind of diversionary dance, it worked. It was just as this time ended that he became aware in a different way than he had before of his mother's empty apartment—which was now his—on the first floor directly below his, almost as if the apartment was alive in a vague, restless way.

He didn't believe in "The House of Usher," of course, nor in ghosts of any kind. Not really, though he thought about them a lot. The dead were the dead and houses were houses and could only be alive metaphorically. Yet he also felt that as long as his mother's apartment remained empty this situation with these sounds would continue. But what was the alternative? He knew he couldn't bear to sell it. It was as if his own apartment on the second floor was his conscious mind but his mother's apartment was the unconscious below it, propping up everything—so he continued to pay the two rents.

Lately he'd been thinking that one day he would live with a woman he'd fallen in love with in his mother's apartment—that that would be the solution to the problem, but given the state of his love life lately it seemed more like a fantasy than a solution. Now, in a matter of hours, his mother's apartment was going to be invaded by Harvey and some members of Harvey's family and though it was only supposed to be for a night, who knew how long they would really end up staying? It could even overlap with Elliot's visit (and he didn't want the two of them to meet), forcing Elliot to stay upstairs with him. How had this happened? How had Harvey become his "friend" (though he would never be a friend the way Elliot was). It was only because Harvey's mother had died too, so he found him useful to talk to. It was Harvey who suggested he go someplace new for a few days, after his mother died, to a place that wasn't "saturated with memories of your mother" as he put it. Harvey said he had gone to Utah and then to Santa Fe after his mother died and claimed that it helped.

"It's not as if your grief will disappear, Barry, but it will do some good."

"I don't want to go far," he'd said. "It would be too hard."

Harvey nodded. He was the sympathetic type. Harvey was only a few years older but had a fatherly aspect to his personality that allowed him to give advice in a natural, convincing way. There was also one other quality of Harvey's he especially admired—his superior sense of geography. He remembered the lunch they had at a Japanese restaurant in the village. When Harvey discussed a possible trip it was as if he'd placed an elaborate map of the United States on the tablecloth that not only had all the states in their correct positions but how long it would take to get to each one from New York.

"There's a two-step process of elimination we need to follow,"

Harvey said, tugging at his prematurely gray beard. "First, we need to select a place that isn't too far away. Second, it needs to be a place you haven't been to with your mother."

He had told Harvey about all the trips he'd taken with his mother after she got her money, money that was now his. He'd told Harvey about his missing father as well. Actually he'd told Harvey quite a lot but, of course, he'd also kept a lot hidden.

"I think we need to add a third condition," Harvey said. "I think it needs to be a place that's not only new and not too far away, but also one that has impact. A place with some real impact sights."

A number of places was proposed and eliminated: New Orleans, Kansas City, and the Outer Banks in North Carolina. Finally Harvey brought up Chicago. He spoke of it with great enthusiasm and precision as if he was making a presentation at a conference—especially when he described the beach. "It's in the middle of the city and it's startling, surrealistic, like seeing the sand and ocean in the middle of Fifth Avenue."

There's no ocean in Chicago, he'd pointed out, but Harvey said Lake Michigan was so big it looked just like the ocean. "Wait till you see the beach surrounded by the tallest buildings in the city. I swear you've never seen anything like it."

Harvey was the persuasive type, too. Because of his ability for generating spontaneous enthusiasm, Harvey had convinced him to go to Chicago—which was where he'd first crossed the line. Even though the woman, Mariane, was literally old enough to be his mother and perhaps was even richer than his mother and even though it was she who picked him up on the beach it was still wrong, or at least weak of him, to sleep with her and then, of course, taking the fifty or so dollars from her pocketbook while she was asleep afterwards was atrocious. It was just because he was crazed with grief, he told himself.

He winced as he thought of it and stopped pacing to drink more wine. He wanted to call Elliot again to tell him this great idea he'd gotten a few days ago about actually doing the magazine together the way they'd once planned. Why not, now that he had the start up money, but his mind wasn't free enough yet, there was a pressure build up, a blockage which he thought must be this Harvey business he had to deal with in a number of hours.

Harvey knew he had two apartments though he hadn't told Harvey the effect it was having on him, and hadn't told him about his apartment in Pennsylvania, either. Nobody knew about that. Three days before meeting Love Hunt, Harvey called and asked if he could stay at his place on Friday night. It seemed Harvey's brother and his brother's wife were visiting from the Midwest and Harvey's own apartment was too crowded for the three of them. Also, Harvey wanted them to meet him, so Barry ended up saying they could all stay and hoping for the best, even though he knew there was no "best" in this situation.

But it wouldn't really be a *big* deal, he tried to tell himself—nothing that should keep him from sleeping. He'd give Harvey a key, welcome them all, explain a few things about his mother's apartment to Harvey and then leave them alone for their family time, telling Harvey to take the key with him before they left. The next morning or early in the afternoon he'd come downstairs and clean. They was all adults so there was no reason to expect too much of a mess. Of course, there would be a certain smell behind—every family had its own smell—but if he opened the door and windows and washed pretty thoroughly and sprayed everything with air freshener it would eventually go away.

All and all it would not be so terrible. Besides, Harvey had been decent to him, kind even, and he owed him this favor. He felt a kind of clearing then in his head that tricked him for a moment. Then a new, far stronger blockage rose up with a vengeance. It was Madrid, of course, where he'd gone just a month ago, without consulting Harvey (why would he after the Chicago fiasco?) and besides he didn't want anyone to know he was there. It was preposterous to have been in such a beautiful city as Madrid without his mother (like a fairy tale with a wrong ending). She, who always believed in him, who loved him with her whole being and was sure he would one day be a famous writer–but there he was walking in its biggest park without her but with her money in his pockets. She not dead even six months and he walking around with enough money to last the rest of his life without even a sibling to share it with or a father (who'd left him and his mother over thirty years ago—the better to try and con the world). There was no wife either Barry thought, nor cause to give it to—not with what he knew of the world. Maybe the magazine—with Elliot—but he hadn't gotten that far in his thinking yet. So far he was giving it to random women. He was traveling to places, ostensibly to see the sights but wound up chasing after women and getting into trouble.

Once again he thought that in a new place, things would be different, the same thing he thought when he went to Chicago. It was strange, he was in New York now pacing in his living room in shrinking circles, remembering everything, but he was also in Madrid. His mother was dead but he was still stepping on leaves in Retiro Park looking at the boats in the lake, the children playing by the water and towards the end of the park the drug dealers from whom he wanted to buy pot or something stronger.

While he walked towards the dealers he began to pace (as he was now in New York) as he always did, at least since his mother died. It began with her kidneys—he thought of a kid's knees, a child's knees because he had always loved her knees and had often kissed them when he was a child. He took her to the hospital with her failing kidneys and it was as if she'd gone inside a cave or some kind of awful fun house that swallowed her.

He visited her every day and sometimes stayed all night. Other times he walked the streets of New York at two in the morning all the way back to his apartment. Each day she got weaker like a softening cloud blending in with the eventually indistinguishable air. Still she held his hand, she said things to him he'd never forget. At the time, he told himself she'd died a beautiful death.

Afterwards it was like having a heart attack in his brain. He thought the only way to escape it was to leave New York, then after his experience in Chicago, to leave America itself, which in many ways had mistreated his mother and therefore mistreated him. But he had to hang around to settle various financial matters. He wondered now that he had come into a lot of money (the same way his mother had inherited hers), if he'd suddenly hear from his father, but so far he hadn't.

When the money matters were finally settled he went to London. He hoped to begin living differently in London. He hoped to finally begin writing a novel—he expected it—thinking the city of Shakespeare & company would inspire him, that his talent and imagination would finally be free now that he no longer had to worry about money. But nothing came to him. He wrote an image or two. In one week he wrote only half a page. He thought of his mother and his father and his uncle, too. He felt rudderless and victimized, even by the money, as if its secret purpose was to force him to realize once and for all that he wasn't a writer, would never be famous or known for anything at all. That it was all a colossal illusion. It scared him and it made him angry. He began drinking at night and he had a couple of bad encounters with women he met in bars. One ended with him screaming at her before she ran out of his room.

He went to Madrid, thinking maybe things would be different there, and began carrying his mother's urn with him in part to share what was beautiful in the city, in part just for the company. Madrid *was* beautiful, heartbreaking really with its fountains and cafés and its endless avenues of flowers and statues. The city itself was a work of art—he knew that—but it was also menacing as if while he walked through it, it was also walking after him. Part of it may have been political—they hated his government, the way it invaded Iraq and occupied it—he couldn't blame them for that—that was part of it but not all of it. He was an interloper with filthy American money. Behind the warm smiles and friendly words he felt targeted, like the city was preparing to mug him. Some of this was irrational, he knew, but still he walked quickly with his urn in hand and looked over his shoulder while he walked as well.

He also continued talking to himself the way he was now in New York, often improvised pep talks to convince himself that he wasn't a fraud and would soon start writing. Between talking to himself and talking to his mother it got pretty complicated sometimes. He also remembered that he began to go to bars but his Spanish wasn't very good and he couldn't bear to talk to an American. He was afraid to be away from the urn too and carried it everywhere with him, once even to a bar. Then he worried that he'd drink too much and leave it in the bar or else on the metro.

Eventually he gave up on the bars and he left the urn in his hotel room and took the metro to Sol. It was like the Times Square of Madrid, and he started to walk the streets looking for hookers. The buildings were yellow and white and faded pink with black iron grills on the balconies. The streets were thick with people and very hot and humid. He started to see the girls then, half undressed in tight fitting shorts or jeans, many of them tattooed; a surprising number of them fat. He bought one who seemed to have a simple face. Again it was difficult to speak to her in either English or Spanish. He wanted to take her to his hotel but she insisted, so far as he could understand, on hers. He was afraid to go to her place—who knew who else would be there or might appear later. He wound up paying twice as much to get her to go to his hotel.

She took off her clothes right away. She was dark-skinned although not exactly a black woman. She had a tough, vacant expression; protruding teeth which perhaps explained why she kept her mouth closed and didn't smile. There were some indecipherable tattoos on her shoulders, stomach and left buttock.

He looked at her and didn't think he could do her. He began thinking about the urn again but when he thought of it, it was like a bar of gold, floating in space—untouched by anything else on earth. Meanwhile, the girl was looking at him and spoke to him sternly in Spanish. He spoke back sternly too, and she suddenly bent over completely naked in the middle of her room thinking that he wanted to spank her. He did want to hurt her in some way, although her life or even just her mouth seemed punishment enough. He looked at her bottom, sad and vaguely muscular at the same time, and then he spanked her, several times in succession.

She straightened up and turned around to face him with the same look in her eyes as before and told him how much money he owed her, in Spanish, then, eventually, half in English.

"Fine," he said (he could actually watch and hear himself say things then as if he were a character in a movie). "I'll pay you."

Then he pushed her shoulders and forced her down on the bed underneath him. She looked too frightened to scream and a moment later he was sitting on her, right on top of her skinny tattooed arms, then up to her face, the way he would sit on Love Hunt a month later.

He gave himself a lecture about never doing that again because it was wrong and dangerous. He'd made the hooker cry and when he finally let her go she ran into the night barely remembering to take her money. She'd tell her pimp and he might come back and break his legs or even kill him.

He began pacing in ever-narrower circles. Then he realized there was not even time to pace. He threw his things together—he was moving as fast as a cockroach or a frenzied wasp. When he checked out of the hotel only twenty-six minutes had passed since the whore left yet it still felt as if her pimp could appear any minute.

Madrid suddenly seemed like a small city. He told himself there were many other hotels, of course, in other parts of the city but he didn't listen to himself, wasn't really listening. He imagined the pimp had seen him get into the taxi and that he'd follow him to any hotel and wait, pay off the concierge, then send a couple of goons to his room to do the job there. He told the driver to take him to the airport. He looked at the urn he was cradling in his lap, which he would now have to put back somewhere in the maze of his suitcase.

"Why didn't you stop me?" he said to his mother. "Why didn't you stop me?"

It could have been any city. It was simply a question of which plane was leaving first that he could still catch. His "police" told him to take the first available plane and he listened to them. It was a flight to L.A. It could be a lot worse. Get on it, his police said. Get on it no matter what.

On the plane he remembered that Santa Barbara was only an hour and a half north of Los Angeles. He'd gone there with his mother once after she got her inheritance for a short vacation. He remembered columns of sunlight shimmering on the water, the backdrop of the mountains and the elegant courthouse illuminated in lemon colored light and all the palm trees and flowers on State Street. She was happy there and would appreciate going back. He remembered in his hotel room in Santa Barbara she'd noticed some food that had stuck to his lips. She wet a face cloth and wiped it off. She had washed his face in Santa Barbara. It was a memory he would never lose.

Santa Barbara would be a good place to cool out; he would sit on the beach and feel the wind. Maybe he'd climb a mountain. He would swim, of course, let the waves crash over him. "The sea whispered me," he said to himself over and over on the plane.

When he arrived in L.A. he was more tired than he thought, too tired to rent a car and drive to Santa Barbara. He was exhausted and just wanted to sleep—he could drive to Santa Barbara in the morning.

It was the middle of the night. He took a cab to Hollywood and checked into a Motel 6 using his fake I.D. because he was still nervous, and paying in cash. He took the urn out of his suitcase and placed it under his bed and then he made an effort to sleep. He took his clothes off and got under the covers. He felt bad about the whore in Madrid and kept replaying the whole scene with her. It occurred to him that it might be much worse than he, at first, remembered. That maybe she hadn't run out screaming but was still in the hotel unconscious. His mother was shocked and angry—angry that he'd bought the whore and then shocked at what he did to her. Then he remembered that he couldn't be sure what his mother felt, since she was dead. So he really couldn't be sure, and yet he knew.

He took a tranquilizer—one of the pills they gave him after his mother died, but he couldn't sleep. He had an erection that he couldn't get rid of (he could never bear to masturbate, it made him feel profoundly defeated), so he got out of bed, put some clothes on and hit the streets.

Perhaps he'd outsmarted himself going to Hollywood where all the hookers were when he could have simply stayed at a hotel near the airport, especially considering how tired he was. It was surprising that he didn't realize what he was doing at the time, that he was able to sneak it by his own police.

He was on Sunset Boulevard, then he was walking past Hollywood High School. Soon he saw hookers everywhere. It was prime time for them. Without a car, though, he had a handicap. They'd think he was a cop or else figure he had no money since he was searching for them on foot but he kept pursuing them anyway.

He took a side street off Sunset and followed a young black girl. She was not dressed as outrageously as the others but he could still tell she was selling. When he got closer he saw her face looked like a wounded animal's. He decided to call her Bambi, in his mind at least. She had big, liquid, still innocent eyes that he remembered even now as well as he remembered his mother's face. That shouldn't be possible but it was true. Life was cruel that way. It was like his mind was a maze filled with hundreds of conflicting tunnels and passageways and at the end of one of them was a secret switch that determined which faces he remembered and which ones he forgot, and Bambi had found her way through the labyrinth and pressed that switch. While she was there, she pressed his videotape switch as well so he'd always have to watch and hear what happened with her. He might not have to watch it for a day or two or even for a week but eventually he *would* have to watch and hear it simply because she, or something else—some ghost or spirit—had pressed the right switch in the dark.

He finally approached her and looked at her face trying to determine how old she was.

"Hello officer. How are you tonight?" she said.

He laughed a little. "Pretty horny thank you, only I'm not a cop."

"Really?"

"Yes, really. Why do so many girls think I'm a cop?"

"I don't know. You just look like one."

And you look just like Bambi, he said to himself. Now that he was closer he could see she was no great beauty but she was pretty in a way hookers usually aren't. There was a softness to her face.

"What you want, then?"

"Excuse me?" he said, though he had heard her.

"How can I help you, mister?"

"In so many ways," he said. "So many ways, so little time."

"You want to date me, is that it?"

"Yes I do, but please call me Gordon," he said.

"OK, Gordon, what did you have in mind?"

"I have to know in advance everything I want to do with you? Where's the spontaneity? Where's the romance?"

She laughed. "That's not the way it works. Haven't you done this before?"

"Oh yes. I'm just in a funny mood, capiche? And I'm glad I am because it made you laugh and you look even prettier when you laugh."

"Thank you, that's very nice. We need to talk money up front though, capiche?" she said with a little smile.

"Touché. Have you been in Italy?" he said, thinking more likely Italy's been in her.

"Something like that. So what do you have in mind, Gordon?"

"You want me to make you an offer you can't refuse, or at least one you can't refuse at two o'clock in the morning."

"Something like that," she said, smiling again.

"OK. How about two hundred dollars for an hour? Will that cover most things?"

"Yah, *most* things. Where do you want to spend time with me? You got a car?"

He told her that he didn't have a car at the moment but that he did have money, some of which he took out of his pocket to show her. To her credit, she barely looked. He went on to tell her that yesterday he'd been in Madrid and had to get out of there in a big hurry—all this to explain the no car situation and also why he was staying at a Motel 6.

"That's fine," she said. "We can go to your hotel."

Already he knew he wanted her for more than an hour and he tried to calculate how much he could actually spend on her; five hundred, six hundred tops.

"Can you tell me your name?" he said, as he started walking.

"Jordan," she said, in a matter-of-fact voice that made him think it really was her name, and so he stopped calling her Bambi to himself.

"Jordan? After Michael Jordan?"

"Not even close."

"After the country?" he said, trying to remember where Jordan was and whose side they were on politically.

"After the river. Rivers last longer than countries."

"Longer than athletes too. Is that your goal . . . to last a long time?"

"Why not? If I last long enough I figure things'll get better and I'll come out on top in the end."

He felt unaccountably nervous then. He wished he didn't but he did. He felt other things too but he mostly felt nervous.

"So, Jordan, let me ask you if you happen to have something I can get high with. . . . I'll pay you for it of course."

"How high you wanna get?"

"Pretty fucking high."

"All I have's some weed and some sleeping pills."

"Whatever. I'll pay you for the weed."

"That's cool. I just have two joints so you can have one but I want you to pay me for my time before you smoke, all right?"

"Here," he said, taking a hundred dollar bill out of his pocket. "Here's a hundred dollars for walking down the street with me. Can that be a deposit?"

She laughed a little and waved her hand dismissively. "Put your money back in your pocket, man. I just want you to pay me when we get to your room before you get all messed up with my weed, OK?"

"Fair enough."

"Speaking of your room, when we gonna get there?"

"Sorry about that. It's not too much longer—just a couple of blocks."

At the next corner another hooker nodded at Jordan and said, "Hey girlfriend."

Jordan smiled and said, "Hey" back. He decided that he couldn't really imagine her life.

When he got to the Motel 6 it didn't seem like his room, it was more like a place he was visiting in a dream only this time he was visiting it with someone else. This feeling was heightened because he entered from the street without any one from the motel seeing him. It was exciting, but it was making him nervous and he began to pace.

Jordan asked for her money then. He knew she was going to and he knew he was going to pay her but it hurt him anyway. Also, he couldn't help feeling a little angry which made him still more nervous.

"Where's that joint, can I have it now?" he heard himself say.

She produced it like a magician from some hidden opening in her skirt. Hookers always had more exits and entrances to their clothes than he could imagine.

"I don't have any matches," he said, and a moment later she produced a match from another secret place. He admired how calmly she lit it, he found the confident expression on her face exciting. It was sharing space with her vulnerable expression as if they were uneasy roommates in a double bed.

He touched her finger as he took the joint and inhaled. Immediately his erection came back to him. It was as if it was impossible to be in this room in a Motel 6 without an erection. He inhaled some more and thought vaguely about starting a hotel called Hotel Erection based on the same idea. A lot of men would check into that hotel.

"Let me have some," Jordan said, taking the joint from him. She was a little too confident. She would have to find out who was really boss. He took the joint back from Jordan and inhaled some more. It was very strong, maybe mixed with something else.

"I want us to forget about time," he said.

"OK," she said. She sounded like an angel—it seemed possible—so he smoked some more.

He began looking at her smile then, at the structure of her lips and mouth. It looked like a kind of pristine tunnel – like the first thing he'd ever seen. He felt drawn to it and wanted to kiss her but was afraid she wouldn't want to.

He was done smoking now. He was very stoned and when he closed his eyes he didn't know where he was. He refocused on her tunnel/mouth and soon felt drawn to it again. He moved closer and kissed her and she didn't stop him. She looked strange, almost shocked, when he saw her again but she didn't say anything.

"I really want us to forget about time," he said.

"All right," she said. He put his arms around her and realized that they were both naked but it seemed almost too trivial to bother having sex. He looked down at himself and realized that his erection was gone and that his underpants were off, but for once he didn't care that a woman saw him without it. He felt accepted by her and by himself—it was hard to remember why he ever worried about it.

He felt dizzy then and lay down. He closed his eyes but felt even dizzier so he opened them again, not really knowing where he was. "What's in this stuff we smoked?" he managed to say. She shook her head, said she didn't know.

"Can you lie next to me?" he said, "I think we should stay close to each other while we're both so high."

She didn't say anything or at least nothing he heard or remembered but she did lie next to him. When he touched her arm she seemed to be vibrating or else just trembling a little. There was a difference. If she was vibrating it meant one thing, but if she was trembling it meant another. He decided that this time it was going to end tenderly—that he was going to stop the pattern of which the whore in Madrid was only the latest, if most extreme example. If he was really free, as he believed he was, he could do it.

She looked at him and nodded. He remembered that he never had intercourse with hookers, that it was too dangerous, but he could only half remember why. Then he remembered that hookers never kissed him or let him kiss them but she'd already kissed him—something he found very touching. He kissed her then and when he closed his eyes he couldn't really remember what a prostitute was.

The light around him grew lemony as if his motel room had its own little portable setting sun. He became extremely curious about this person he was kissing so strongly but also felt he knew everything about her at the same time. He wanted to tell her that it was all fated —he'd come from Madrid and happened to take the flight to L.A. If he'd arrived at the airport ten minutes earlier or later he would have gone to New York. He hit the streets, her street, because he couldn't sleep. If he'd taken his pill ten or twenty minutes earlier he might have fallen asleep and never met her. But they did meet because it was all fated, just like his mother's kidneys were fated to fail and he was fated to be alone and do something important in the world—once he got his woman addiction under control—nothing else made sense, why even spend the money he had now if he didn't do something important, something great that would make him live forever, like the literary magazine.

He was inside her now and looked directly at her face. "My name's Barry," he blurted. She looked puzzled for a second and then smiled.

"Barry Auer," he added, as he continued to penetrate her. He kept on doing her but stopped himself before he was going to come. He didn't want it to end so soon and more importantly he wanted her to come too.

He began sucking her, half remembering that this was something he never did with prostitutes but was no longer sure why, or (again) what exactly a prostitute was. She had been sucking him for a while at the same time but he stopped her, sliding down on the bed and just devoting himself to her. He put his heart and soul into it, until he was in a world where nothing else existed but his mouth and her. He sensitized himself to her moment-by-moment responses and made the appropriate adjustments. He was consumed by the desire to bring her pleasure.

When she got really excited she started producing a sequence of exotic sounds. It was as if each person carried around their own hidden music, which only the right musician could reveal, and that music was as individual as their fingerprints or speaking voice. It was the music of their sexual soul and he wanted to hear hers before she heard his.

He kept building her music. It was a lot like building a fire which he learned to do at the camp his mother sent him to years ago before she got her inheritance. It was the one thing he learned to do at camp and now he was doing it again because it was all fated.

Just as her fire was at its peak he went inside her again and felt her writhe and come on his dick and then and only then—watching her face the whole time—did he try to come too.

"I'm not Gordon," he said just before he came and made his own music—more uncontrolled than he'd imagined it could be. And then the two fire musicians collapsed into each other's arms, and for a short while just held each other.

They were an unlikely couple, but it didn't matter. He could figure that out later, the point was he had traveled across the ocean to meet her. He had fled from one dangerous world to another—he with his urn and his ten thousand memories of his mother and now he wasn't alone anymore.

He gave her hand an exploratory squeeze. She didn't squeeze back but she let him hold her hand. She didn't say anything either. She was very still, as still as a corpse. He wondered vaguely if he had killed her but that made him think of Madrid—that perhaps the hooker there had really died, had run for a while after she escaped from him and then had a heart attack or just died from what he did to her and never even left the bed.

"Jordan," he said, "are you all right?"

He looked at her and saw that she was sleeping. Should he feel insulted? He felt a mix of anger and tenderness. Her sleeping could be a sign of how powerful the experience had been or else simply indifference. He needed to find out though he was reluctant to wake her, there was something fascinating about the transition from writhing woman in heat to corpse-like body in repose; something that mesmerized him.

He propped himself up on his elbow and examined each part of her. It was a young woman's body—the breasts were so firm—she was probably in her early twenties, maybe younger. She had shaved a lot of the hair around her genitals but left a little in a kind of heart shape. It looked nice. She looked kind of sad while she slept, serene but sad—which, he had to admit was a little disconcerting.

"Stop sleeping on the job, bitch," he muttered to himself. He was aware that his transcendent feelings had left him and he looked at the ashtray hoping to find part of a joint. There was about a half-inch of one of them left, next to the still flickering candle—like a low flame in the bowl of death, he thought. His mother was in her bowl and soon enough he'd be in his. He'd read an interview with a writer once who compared the bombing of Hiroshima to human life in general. He said he couldn't see much difference between the two. "Life is Hiroshima only stretched out a little." If that's all life was, why did people, including himself, get so hysterical about death? Was it just biological programming? When he tried to remember his life there wasn't really that much to it—sometimes it seemed like two instants—his mother washing his face in Santa Barbara (but he wasn't in Santa Barbara, why wasn't he?) and the last time she looked at him in the hospital in New York.

He smoked the remainder of the joint as quickly as he could and got another buzz again, almost instantly. Suddenly he couldn't bear to be alone and he shook her shoulders until she woke up.

"What's up?" she said.

"You passed out. I didn't want to be alone so I got you up."

"Oh, OK. That's cool. Good high, huh?"

"I'm still high, I smoked again."

"That's cool, it's all good. Hey, Gordon, can I use your bathroom?" she said, already half out of bed.

"Go ahead," he said, pointing to it. He watched her nice pop-up ass as she walked to the bathroom but he was mad that she called him Gordon. She must have been really stoned when he told her his real name, but still, he'd said it twice. Didn't she listen to anything he said? That was extremely insulting, soul-killing, really.

He was angry, but he still missed her while she was in the bathroom. She seemed to be in there an extraordinarily long time. When she came out she looked half dressed, which was another shock since he hadn't noticed her carrying any clothes.

"Hey, what're you doing?" he said, putting on his underpants as he got up from bed. "Why are you getting dressed?"

"It's getting late. I've got to get on my pony."

She was already half in her short little purple skirt when he reached her, grabbed both wrists and threw her down on the bed.

"You're not going anywhere. What do you think you're doing leaving me now, when I'm so stoned? What about all the things we said to each other?"

Finally she looked a little non-plussed, finally a crack in her confidence. "You only pay me for an hour man, I know I've been here almost two."

He dug his nails as hard as he could into the palms of his hands and his arms shook like he was having a seizure.

"How can you do this to me?" he screamed at her.

"OK, calm down, man."

"My name's not *man*, bitch."

"OK Gordon. Calm down and don't be calling me *bitch*. No need to."

"My name's Barry. You weren't listening to me, were you? You were just lying and manipulating my emotions and now that you've got your money you're leaving me in the state I'm in."

"How long you want me to stay?" she said, looking at him seriously.

But it was too late to talk. He had already jumped like a praying mantis, screaming and covering her in her bowl. She was screaming but it was a muffled scream because she was underneath him and what did a scream mean in a Motel 6 anyway. And then the scream stopped and he stopped too—got up from her, stared hard in the dim light at her and to his horror realized her flame was gone.

He didn't remember when he left her and got out of bed. As breathless and inert as he was then, it was hard to say which one of them was more dead. "It was an accident," he muttered to himself. "It was an accident." Then he wanted to scream again but of course he couldn't risk drawing attention. So far he didn't think anyone had seen him or probably heard anything either—not this late. Besides, Motel 6 residents were not exactly known to be community watchdogs.

He knew already what he had to do—it came to him like a vision. The first thing was to leave her in the room and get a cab on the street. The next thing would be to find an all night car rental. Then he'd have to get rid of his fingerprints and give the body a shower. Probably he would have to do all this in the dark but there was still time for that and to put the body in the car before it was light.

Thinking about all this he noticed that he was pacing and then had to make himself stop. It seemed that he was born to pace.

…He was on the street again, walking towards Sunset. He had made a decision but it wasn't really a decision because it was all fated. He got a cab on Sunset and told the driver to take him to the nearest car rental that would still be open. He thought he'd have to go to the airport but the driver took him to a place only ten minutes or so away. He remembered that he gave him a five-dollar tip.

At the car rental he was nervous for a moment but he reminded himself that no one suspected anything, that they only cared about money. Then his lines came to him easily as if he were reading a script. They accepted his Gordon ID without a thought, let him pay in cash and gave him very good directions back to Sunset.

Once in the car he thought only about getting to the motel as fast as possible. His mind cooperated the whole time, he was not even aware of himself.

It was much more difficult in the motel, however. It was awful to face the body and even worse to wash it and the sheets in the shower. He felt himself about to buckle then. He was actually sobbing for a while, but he stuck to the task, he did it.

It was past four when he finished washing it and wrapping it in the wet sheets with a sock on each hand. Then he opened his suitcase, took out a scarf he'd bought (but not opened yet) in Madrid and wiped every inch of the room at least twice. At twenty past four he opened his door and carried the body to the trunk. His police were still leaving him alone. His police were still cooperating—he'd remembered everything—it was a miracle.

The last thing left to do was the most important—where to put the body? A river would be the best place, but was there one in L.A.? He drove away from Hollywood. Once he got rid of her he would take the first plane to New York. How could they trace him? Gordon Green didn't exist, his fingerprints didn't exist either. He drove down side streets looking for alleys or some kind of deserted area. He seemed to be looking for a long time but still his mind didn't panic. Then he thought he saw something and he pulled to a stop. He realized that he didn't even know where he was, but it was probably better that way. It was another miracle—there was no one around the alley wedged between two buildings. There was even a trashcan too. He backed into the alley, opened his trunk, put the socks on his hands again. Then he folded the body up and the cover even fit over it. He remembered staring in disbelief—it was like a perfect marriage of geometry and fate.

He was functioning impeccably. He was stronger and more competent than he realized. Now he would take the first plane to New York he could get at LAX. He still had a few thousand dollars in cash in his pockets. It was starting to get light out, he wanted to cry because he was so relieved, almost happy in a strange way, and for a second he wished Jordan was with him. But he couldn't let himself think of that, not with the way his mind had been functioning. He couldn't begin to open the door to regret when he'd worked so hard at keeping it closed.

More time passed and he continued to do what he was supposed to. He was playing life like Bobby Fischer played chess— daring but with no mistakes. It was only after he dropped off the car and he was already in line at the airport (when it was too late to do anything about it) that he realized he'd left the urn in the motel—his last direct link to his mother lost under the bed in that room. It was heartbreaking, he literally felt a break in his heart.

Then he realized (as he was now realizing again in New York, a month later) that her name was engraved where anyone could see it on the urn. If a detective was ambitious enough to follow up on it, it would inevitably lead to him. It was a permanent clue, a piece of evidence that would last forever. He felt his knees buckle then while he held his place in line. Then he dug his nails into his hands as hard as he could (just as he was doing now in his living room in New York) and shivered at the power of fate.

6

"So what do you think?" Barry asked, gesturing expansively with his arms. He was wearing a yellow silk shirt in striking contrast to his black hair that had only a few flecks of silver in it, as Roberta's did. By comparison, in his jeans and sweatshirt Elliot felt shabby and uninteresting.

"It's as good as advertised," Elliot said. "Actually it's better."

"You're talking about my apartment?"

"Yes."

"I meant New York. What do you think of the city?"

It was the middle of the second day of his visit.

"New York is New York—amazing and difficult. It's a lot easier to control an apartment than a city, though. You can't be responsible for New York."

"True, but what do you think about moving here now that you've visited me, that's what I meant," Barry said, suddenly standing up from his blue velvet chair and walking a few steps. "Why don't we sit on the sofa? You sit on the right side at the end and when you look out the window you'll see trees and a little slice of the East River."

Elliot got up, sat where Barry indicated, and looked out the window. "Again, better than advertised. There's no question this apartment is a knock-out. And living in New York would be enormously appealing on many levels."

"So, in what ways wouldn't it be appealing? Just be frank and tell me."

Elliot took an extra breath. "It's not so much New York . . . as other things."

"What things?" Barry said, raising his voice a little.

"My fear of change, my hatred of moving anywhere, in general. Not to mention my fear of unemployment if I left my school in Philadelphia."

"Can we take them in order?"

"You want to be logical about my fears?" Elliot said, laughing a little. Barry laughed too—it was like old times when he laughed, Elliot thought.

"It is kind of amusing," Barry said. "Let's do it as if we were a couple of Rationalists like Whitehead and Bertrand Russell. Number one, your fear of change. That's usually something that happens to people when they're older. Have you forgotten how young you are?"

"I guess I'm too old to remember."

"Very funny. But seriously, when Henry Miller was in his early forties he left his whole life behind in New York and moved to Paris without a penny in his pocket, and he was a lot older than you."

"But he was Henry Miller and he wasn't a lot older than me. I'm already. . ."

"I know how old you are," Barry said, cutting him off. "You're the same age as me."

"Anyway, speaking of Henry Miller, who is still one of the gods, right?" Elliot said, smiling broadly. "What's happening in the girl department these days?"

"You're trying to divert me. Let's stick to your fears before we get to mine," Barry said, laughing again. "Seriously, I'll just say this. I'm not in love with anyone, but I'm having a good time, capiche? Incidentally, what did you think of the women you've seen in my building so far?"

"A couple of them were pretty hot."

"And that was just one building. We'll be going to parties and clubs where there'll be women who'll make those wannabe writers look like street urchins. New York is the capital of women, real women, remember that. At least in the United States. But back to your fears, to fear number two, your hatred of moving. You can get professionals to do it. I'll be glad to pay for it."

"Don't be ridiculous. You're doing too much for me already."

"Don't you be ridiculous. Have you forgotten about the money I have?"

Elliot smiled and gestured at the apartment with both hands. "No, how could I?"

"My mother and I made some mistakes, but we did invest the money and grew it and you helped us get it."

"I wouldn't say that."

"You testified for us. You came through. I'm not sure I ever expressed my appreciation for that, but I'm grateful for it and for other things you did too."

"I guess I've become a little sensitive about money since our famous argument about the magazine."

Barry looked down at the floor. "I'm sorry about that, I regret it. I was in a very bad way then, or it wouldn't have happened. The whole trial experience made me extremely paranoid. I was looking at the world with dark eyes and it took me a longer time to recover than I thought it would," he said, finally raising his head and looking at Elliot.

"I'm sorry, too. My timing sucked. It was the wrong time to bring it up so bluntly right after the trial, I suppose, but it's made me extra sensitive to money issues with you. I can't deny it."

"Look, we can call it an interest free loan that you can pay back after you get your first full time New York job. I can print out a contract on the computer right now or else email it to you later. Would that be acceptable?"

"I guess. I can also do a lot of the moving myself. It's just packing things."

"Alright, so we've put fear number two to bed one way or another. On to fear number three, your fear of unemployment. But you know for a fact that in a year and a half you're going to be unemployed anyway, whether you move to New York or not."

"But a year and a half is a pretty long time and I do have to live it before I can get to the future, don't I?"

"Again I offer the solution of a loan."

"No," Elliot said, raising his right hand in a definitive gesture that seemed to startle Barry who once more sat down at his end of the sofa. "That is *really* out of the question."

"Alright, what about commuting? Why don't you commute?"

"Commute?" The word sounded strange to Elliot when he said it, as if it were an arcane scientific term.

"Live in New York with me in my mother's apartment as soon as Harvey and company move out of it, and take the metro liner to Philly, until you get something better in New York. Remember, your lease is up in a month anyway; it's the perfect time to move. The metro liner only takes an hour and you can get special rates. You could prepare for class on the way up on a laptop or whatever (I have a spare if you need one) and correct papers on the way back. It's such a simple and beautifully logical solution, I can't believe we didn't think of it before."

"We're not simple people."

"But really, think about it."

"I am."

"How many days a week do you teach?"

"Two."

"Well, do the math, Elliot, do the math. Subtract the money you'll spend on the train per month from your rent in Philly and you'll still come out way ahead and get to live in a much better place in a much better city. It really is just simple logic at this point."

"You're a convincing son of a bitch, I have to admit."

"That's because I'm right. In this case I'm right and when people are right of course they're convincing."

"OK, but am I the kind of guy who does the right thing?"

"That *is* the question."

"I think I'm more like the kind of guy who *thinks* about doing the right thing. But, still, I'll give it some serious thought."

"I'll take that as a 'yes,'" said Barry, who suddenly stood up from the sofa, looked directly at Elliot and extended his hand.

Elliot shook his hand reflexively then said, "I can't commit yet though, I really need to think about this."

"Oh," said Barry, with the same stricken expression on his face that he had when their eighth grade baseball coach announced the starting lineup that didn't include him.

"I live a little life but for me this is a big decision and big decisions need at least a little time to make."

"Of course. I understand. I'll try to be patient."

Barry smiled and the stricken look was replaced by what Elliot thought of as his Gatsbyish smile of infinite hopefulness.

"I guess that's one way I'm different from you. When an important decision is facing me I know what's right right away. I trust my instincts and just go for it. And in this case I know it will work, that it will more than work. The two of us together—with what we know now—we'll conquer New York."

Elliot laughed. Barry still had the gift of the spontaneous dramatic speech or gesture. What a good trial attorney he could have been.

"Seriously, why are you laughing? I live here. I know the world here, at least the literary world, and there's nothing to be intimidated about, not with our talent. I'm serious, Elliot, we're gonna conquer the world, and all you have to do is say yes."

7

"Don't you think you should let the police handle it?"

Susan dropped the cell phone on her bed. She should have picked it up right away, of course, but instead, for a few seconds she stared at it lying there like an oversized water bug. She could hear Megan asking her if she was there, which struck her as an ironic question. No, I'm *not* here, right now, she said to herself, that's the whole fucking point. She felt that if she tried to talk she'd scream at Megan so she picked up a pencil by the notepad on her bed table and snapped it in two. It made a quick, sharp sound like a gun which made her think of Gordon again.

Then the phone rang. Susan picked it up and said, "Hi, I guess I just lost the connection."

She hated to lie, even about something so small to Megan, her best friend, but didn't think she'd go to hell for it. Hell was where Gordon took her so she knew about Hell, much more than she and Megan had ever learned at Catholic High together.

"I don't want you to think I'm not being sympathetic," Megan said. "I've been crying my eyes out over this. You don't think that, do you? That I'm not being sympathetic enough?"

"No, of course not," she said.

"It's just that when you talk about wanting to make him suffer it scares me."

"You don't think he deserves to suffer?"

"Of course he does but that's what the police are for. I mean, to arrest him and bring him to trial. That's where you can testify against him."

"The police aren't going to do shit. Look, he was maniacally careful. He made me take a bath in front of him, where he hovered over me watching me the whole time a few inches away just to be sure there was none of his cum in me, just to be sure there was no DNA. Then he pulled a gun on me but never used it. He made me fall on my knees and took a picture of me praying to him but still he didn't touch me. Because of the gun, he could humiliate me without touching me. That's pretty clever, isn't it? And even if he hadn't of been careful about that, he still knew I didn't know his name, or his license plate, or where he lived. Does this sound like a case the police are gonna take very seriously?"

"It sounds like something nobody could solve, so why not . . ."

"Don't say 'let it go,' OK? Don't. Nobody ever remotely did the kind of things to me he did . . . ."

"I understand," Megan said, "but, I mean, what are you gonna do?"

"The first thing is I'm going to hire a detective."

"A detective? They're pretty expensive, aren't they."

She heard Megan talk more about how much money it would cost and how dangerous it was. It was just like in high school whenever she wanted to pull a prank Megan always put the brakes on it. She could feel her own mind drift, as if it were suddenly weightless—the way she sometimes felt following Gordon's orders. Then she began thinking about his gun, at first the image of it pointed at her in his bathroom, then about how many times she begged him not to shoot her, still bargaining with him and trying to please him right to the end. All her life she'd tried to please and flatter men, always hoping they'd say things they never said. She did it in high school and even to the gay men who taught her hair dressing before she quit, and, of course, to all the men she met through fixups or at bars.

She closed her eyes, suddenly feeling tired. How could she have made love with Gordon—someone with no human heart? And for that one terrible decision she nearly died. It was because she was lonely and loneliness made her panic and make bad decisions. Her job at Urban Outfitters was stupid—she'd be quitting soon—the men she met were stupid—she had no beauty in her life. Maybe she was searching for beauty and somehow didn't know it.

Megan had finally stopped talking so she had to say something back. She said she appreciated what she was doing. "It means a lot, really, just that you listen. I haven't told anyone but you, you know."

"And I'm really behind you a thousand percent," Megan said. "I want you to know that. I just worry about you when you talk about hiring a detective. I mean Gordon sounds like some twisted genius who left you nothing to go on . . ."

"Twisted definitely, but I'm not so sure he's any kind of genius 'cause lately I've been remembering some things and there were a couple of mistakes he made."

"What mistakes?"

"Like he should have taken my watch or else broken it before I got my blindfold off in the parking lot where he dumped me, 'cause the first thing I did was look at the time and lately I'm pretty sure I knew what time it was when I left his place."

"I don't get it."

"OK, he dropped me at the Paoli train stop and I know the ride there took about fifteen minutes, even though it seemed like forever.

Now, OK, granted I don't know what direction he came from, but there are still a limited number of towns within fifteen minutes of Paoli."

"Oh, I get it now. That's definitely a start."

"It's a start, plus I remember some things about where he lived. There were a lot of trees and it was very dark out and quiet. It was definitely in the country, which would eliminate some of the towns on the Philadelphia side of Paoli . . . . I've been studying some maps and things," she said in a lower, almost conspiratorial tone, "I've got the train schedules from 30th Street Station that show how many stops are within fifteen or twenty minutes of Paoli, and there're not many. It makes me think he probably has a place somewhere on the main line."

"You mean like Westchester?"

"Maybe, but I think that would be too close."

"Or Rosemont."

"Maybe Rosemont, maybe Exton, I really don't know those towns, but I'm going to get to know them and every other possible town. And I'll be looking for the kind of trees I saw and anything else I might remember until I find him."

Megan didn't say anything. She could feel Megan's silence solidifying and growing like it was alive.

"I know I haven't stuck with a lot of things in my life. I know you think of me as a quitter," Susan said.

"I don't think of you that way."

"Well, it's true, or it was. I know I dropped out of college and then the computer class and the hair dressing place, not to mention my history with men, which you've been kind enough not to bring up, but this time it's different. This time I'm not gonna punk out till I track him down and make him pay big time for what he did to me. Don't you believe me?"

8

Elliot kept his eye on the painting on the wall just behind Dr. Hodge (a fairly cheap reproduction of one of Franz Marc's expressionistic animals) waiting for the doctor to do something about his runny nose. It was a typical doctor's office painting, he supposed, but at least more soothing than one of Edvard Munch's screaming faces that adorned the wall of his internist. He'd been told once by Barry, when explaining why he'd never see one again, that there were three types of therapists: those who tried to be your friend and even hugged you at the beginning and/or end of each session (this type, of course, was more prevalent on the West Coast), those who said almost nothing and rarely if ever rendered a judgment (these were mostly neo-Freudians of one sort or another), and those who couldn't resist talking about and/or hyping themselves.

Dr. Hodge was of the latter group (though he probably also wanted to be a "friend" if he saw such an opening) and had already alerted Elliot at the start of the session to watch Eyewitness News that night because he was being interviewed for thirty seconds or so on the mindset of serial killers. (On another occasion he'd appeared on the same channel to "psychoanalyze" Britney Spears.) It was an annoying trait, at times infuriating, yet on balance he judged Hodge to be a kindhearted if narcissistically inclined soul. He'd been seeing Hodge, the first therapist he'd ever gone to, once a week for a few months while he licked his wounds about Linda, a young lawyer in the city he'd gone out with for nearly a year. Sometimes he second-guessed himself (especially when Hodge started talking about himself) for not going to one of his university's therapists for free, yet it had been comforting to talk with him last time about the death of Barry's mother.

Finally Hodge took a handkerchief and captured most of the material that had exited his nose before it became embedded in his thick, walrus-shaped mustache. "So you've reunited with your best friend, congratulations, that's great news."

"It does feel good, I have to admit."

"OK. So tell me about your visit. I'm all ears."

"It went very well. Actually, he offered to let me stay there in his apartment while I look for a job. He wants me to move to New York."

"Move to New York?"

Elliot nodded.

"But what will happen to your therapy with me? And what about your job?" Hodge added, almost as an afterthought.

Elliot chuckled to himself at Hodge's priorities. The truth is he hadn't given his future sessions with Hodge any thought at all.

"The plan would be for me to live there but commute to my job in Philly, so I could continue to see you. Obviously, the move is a very big decision and I have some misgivings, of course, though I'm definitely leaning towards doing it. That's what I wanted to talk with you about today."

"That's a lot of train riding, would be one of my misgivings," Hodge said.

Elliot shrugged. "It would only be two or three times a week. Lots of people do it."

"And does he have enough space in his apartment for you?"

"His apartment is pretty big and beautiful too, by the way, but I'd be staying alone in his mother's—or what used to be his mother's—apartment, which is almost identical to his only on the floor directly below it."

"Wow!" Hodge exclaimed, with an enveloping smile, "he really does have some serious bucks. How'd he get all that money?"

"It was his mother's money. There was a court case after her boyfriend died and the bottom line is she won it on the grounds of being his wife equivalent. And now, of course, that she's dead . . ."

"That was a real shocker, by the way, very sad," Hodge interjected. Elliot nodded, not wanting to revisit that pain that was still fresh.

"Now, of course, the money is Barry's," Elliot added.

"So you'd have your own place but one that he owns, and you'd still be seeing each other constantly. How do you feel about that? Have you ever lived together for any length of time before?"

"When we were about 23 and his mother was still working and supporting Barry while he tried to make it as a writer, I visited him in his apartment in Paris for a couple of weeks."

"Paris? I got a chance to lecture once in Paris. It was fabulous."

Elliot couldn't tell if Hodge was referring to the city or to his lecture and decided to ignore the comment.

"So he went to Paris to be a writer. He has expensive taste. Well, how did your visit go?" Hodge asked.

"It went really well. Of course it was tremendously exciting being in Paris at that age with my best friend. We did a lot of things but what I chiefly remember when I think about it now is the look on his face."

"What kind of look was it?"

"A kind of infinite hopefulness as he told me about his new life. We were walking in the Tuileries, or maybe it was really in his apartment as he told me, 'Elliot, I've increased my grasp of literature exponentially. The people that I've met here are incredible, the entire ambience—it's become my spiritual home, capiche? I only wish you could stay longer.'"

"You remember his exact words, don't you?" Hodge observed.

"Sometimes."

"Even though this was quite a while ago?"

"I don't remember all of them of course. But some of the things he said, I do remember."

"Do you know your voice changes when you're quoting him? I bet you could do a good impression of him if you wanted to."

Elliot shrugged again, hoping at the same time it didn't offend the doctor. "The other thing I remember from that visit is that's when I found out about Roberta's boyfriend, a wealthy Boston businessman she was now seriously involved with named Benjamin Walters. I think I told you Roberta was only eighteen when Barry was born, 26 when she was divorced. Since then she only dated a handful of colorless men. I always thought she was, you know, extremely youthful and attractive but I'd somehow never pictured her with anyone but Barry."

"I'm sure my sons feel the same way about their mother," said Dr. Hodge.

Elliot nodded. "Anyway, I pressed Barry for more details but he held up his hands to stop me."

"'I can only talk about it so much,' he said, forming a tiny space between his thumb and index finger. 'It could mean so much to her but I just don't want to say more until something definite happens.'"

"That revelation dwarfed whatever else I did in Paris. Within a week after returning to Boston Roberta took me into her confidence and told me about Benjamin, 'the special man' in her life, who'd invested prophetically in communication systems, and was very wealthy just like Barry said. Not only was he rich, but he was now investing in Broadway shows, radio stations, and independent movies, which put him in touch with people that Roberta, who'd never been out of Brookline, had previously only read about. Suddenly she was eating dinner with these stars and accompanying Benjamin for quick trips to Las Vegas and Hollywood. It was clearly the adventure of her life. Eventually I had dinner with them in the more expensive apartment she'd moved into, probably with Benjamin's help, near Copley Square, a pretty chi-chi section of Boston. Benjamin Walters, it turns out, was overweight, shy, and preoccupied with his work, but he did exude a certain gruff charm. At times he looked and acted a bit like a more tame, New England version of Tony Soprano."

Hodge laughed and Elliot waited for him to stop before resuming. "I remember getting a call from Roberta the morning after her dinner, asking me my impressions of him and how serious I thought he was about her. It was a question she'd ask me in many different ways over the next few years."

"How did you answer her?"

"I never gave her an absolute answer, I don't think, I was always slightly embarrassed, although also a little flattered when she asked for my opinion. Generally I tried to encourage her because when she felt encouraged she'd be happy and Roberta was wonderful to talk to when her basic optimism resurfaced.

"But finally, after four or five years, she began to get discouraged, then angry that Benjamin wouldn't marry her. One time at her apartment, where she'd invited me for lunch, she blurted, 'He says he's got a hangup about marriage, but I think he's just a cheapskate who doesn't want to part with any of his big bucks. I don't care for myself—it's Barry I'm worried about.'

"'Barry seems to be doing fine,' I said, 'he seems to be flourishing.'

"'Elliot, I still have to support him. I may always have to help him.'

"'Maybe you should give Benjamin, you know, an ultimatum of some kind,' I said."

"Good for you!" Hodge interjected. "Sometimes you really just have to give someone a little push. How did she react to your advice?"

"She ran her fingers through her hair, not saying anything at first."

"What kind of hair did she have?" Hodge said with a smile on his face. "I picture her as a blonde."

"She had black hair, raven black hair like Barry, only flecked with a few silver streaks. Her eyes were the same color green as his, too—she looked like a feminine version of Barry, only better looking.

"'I probably should give him an ultimatum,' she said, 'but the truth is I'm afraid he'd say no . . . . Anyway, he's promised to always take care of me.'

"Meanwhile Barry began publishing book reviews in *The New Republic* and then longer, more personal pieces in *The Village Voice*. It wasn't fiction, which is what he most wanted to publish, but I was enormously impressed, having only managed to publish a few short stories in literary magazines with circulations under a thousand. To capitalize on his literary successes and maybe also to help his mother with Benjamin, Barry finally left Paris and moved back to New York. He came to Boston a lot too, of course, where he stayed with his mother, but I didn't see him as much as I thought I would because by then I was already involved with Lianne, who I'd met at the junior college where we were teaching. Whenever I did see Barry for dinner or a drink, I couldn't seem to stop talking about her, as If my mouth took a compulsive delight in pronouncing her name."

"Paying him back for losing his virginity first, huh?" Hodge said, smiling.

"You remembered about that," Elliot said laughing. "But no, I don't really think so. I was just smitten with her and it was natural for Barry and me to always share our passions. Anyway, when I asked Barry if he was seeing anyone, he alluded to his usual list of brief affairs with glamorous writers or starlets (one was supposedly Ingmar Bergman's daughter, another was a French model whose name escapes me at the moment). I never really believed his stories and quickly changed the subject. Then, when he went back to New York, I felt guilty for not spending more time with him and a month later after I read a new review of his on Samuel Beckett in *The Village Voice* I wrote him a long congratulatory letter. Barry wrote me back immediately. Typically, his references ranged from Proust to Heidegger to grunge rock to performance artists. But it's the confessional part near the end that I still remember."

"You *remember* it? Word for word?"

"Pretty much—at least enough to paraphrase."

"Cause if you remember it word for word I'm gonna call up the producers of Eyewitness News where they're going to interview me tonight and tell them to put you on instead of me. Ha ha. Well, go ahead, I'm all ears."

"Barry wrote, 'You praise me for having so much to say about Beckett, but there is so much more I want to say, so much more inside me that I need to utter and I feel thwarted and ashamed that I still can't fashion it into decent prose. If only I could write better! Besides the desire to write something I'm not disgusted with, I want only three things in life: happiness for my mother who has sacrificed everything for me, happiness for my friends—most of all for you since you are my most treasured friend, and a little taste of the love you have found with Lianne. I realize now that I have not yet been able to fall in love.'

"Touching, huh?" Elliot said.

"Very touching and very impressive that you remember it. Now I know how much he means to you."

"I decided to never let too much time pass without seeing Barry. That summer he was in Boston a lot and I'd see him two or three times a week. Barry and I and Lianne would sometimes go to the movies together or walk around Harvard Square, but I was careful not to let him spend too much time alone with her. It wasn't exactly that I didn't trust them—it was just easier for me to deal with them separately, maybe because each required such an intense and different kind of attention. I also realized that I didn't understand Barry's sexuality—it was so ferocious yet detached, like a caged lion that was only temporarily calm. He was constantly evoking this or that starlet (usually European ones) as the apotheosis of beauty or sex appeal, but the only woman I'd ever seen him express any strong emotion for was his mother. It was Roberta who could provoke his temper as no one else could, Roberta who could still induce his screaming fits the same as when he was an 8th grader, and it was Roberta he would still unabashedly smother with kisses, even in my presence.

"One weekend in August, when Lianne had gone home to visit her parents, I went to Roberta's apartment to meet Barry. We were planning to go to a literary party of some kind. When I arrived Barry was still dressing, and I saw Benjamin Walters sitting on Roberta's sofa. Slow moving, almost obese, he was wrapped in his dark blue suit like a mummy. We exchanged five minutes of awkward small talk while Roberta, dressed in a tight-fitting pink gown that showed off her slim figure, fluttered around him like a cocktail waitress. That evening she was obviously going to cook him another dinner.

"'You know, I can't stand him,' Barry said to me in his car as we searched for the party in Cambridge. 'If it weren't for my mother I probably would have punched him out a couple of times by now.'

"'But he seems to make your mother happy,'" I said. "'I've never seen her so animated.'

"'Of course, and that's everything to me,' he said, as his voice softened. 'But it's ironic that the love of my mother's life should be such a bloated, petty, ignorant, self-involved, penurious nouveau riche . . . .' He searched for more adjectives and then started to laugh. 'I wish for two minutes I could be Marcel Proust just to once and for all do verbal justice to Benjamin. The point is, I could forgive him for being so culturally bankrupt, but he has the chutzpah to lecture my mother and me about how I should work for him in his business. The man is actually trying to parent me. Meanwhile, if he'd only marry her she could finally stop working for once in her life, but he's too goddamn cheap and he's been sleeping with her for five years now.'

"'Still, you know,' I said, 'he might marry her and you should try to be nice to him. It can only benefit you.'

"'Believe me he *will* marry her. And within one year after their marriage I'll launch the most important literary magazine in America since *Partisan Review*. Who knows, since he has millions, I may even start a small publishing company that will only publish books of real quality. Of course you'll leave that little college where they're mistreating you and be my partner.'"

"I didn't realize how Machiavellian he is," Hodge said.

"But don't you see how essentially innocent he is, too? He would never have done any of the things he bragged about. All his ruthlessness was in his imagination. Anyway, at the party there were a number of attractive women. I told Barry that I was being faithful to Lianne and that he should go after whoever he wanted, but Barry found something wrong with every one of them. One was a little too plump, another wore unattractive glasses, and a third, who was obviously pretty, he claimed had 'no hips or breasts. She might turn out to be a boy.'

"We ended up drinking a lot at the party and then walking along the Charles River afterward to sober up. 'If Benjamin ever double-crossed my mother I think I'd be justified in killing him, don't you?' he said as we walked past a series of couples making out on the benches or on the grass by the river.

"'What are you saying, are you serious?'

"'You don't agree, you think that's sick?'

"'I think you're too close to your mother. Can't you find a girlfriend, instead of all those one-night things?'

"'You're right. It's because I know she needs me; she's given everything to me.'

"'But she has someone. She has Benjamin and you're still alone . . .'

"'You're right, Elliot. As soon as I get back to New York I'm going to work it. I'll have a girlfriend within two weeks,' he said, as if he were telling his editor how long it would take to finish a book review.

"A few hours later, at two or three in the morning, I was asleep in my apartment when the phone rang. Barry's voice was saying words to me I could scarcely absorb.

"'Something unbelievable happened. Benjamin had a heart attack. I'm calling you from the hospital. My mother's in shock.'"

"Did he die?" Hodge's eyes were unusually open and intense.

Elliot nodded. "I remember at the funeral Barry was eerily quiet, his face rigid with a kind of heightened alertness while Roberta cried nearly the whole time."

"So that's how Barry eventually got his money?" Hodge said.

"Actually, it was a little more complicated. Benjamin hadn't left a will, then his brother claimed to have located one and tried to settle with Roberta. The whole thing dragged on in the courts for years. Almost from the start, Barry moved back to Boston to stay with his mother. I was a witness for Roberta, whose case was your basic palimony claim. She and Barry became obsessed with the trial and

Barry soon stopped writing completely. They spent their time either worrying over every detail of the case or else fantasizing about all the things they'd do when they finally got their money. When he was alone with me, Barry began talking about starting a literary magazine again, with me as his partner. 'We'll rule the literary world,' he used to say. Since I was worried about getting tenure at my school it was hard not to get caught up in all his grand plans. Anyway, when it was finally over, Roberta *was* awarded over a million dollars."

"Wow," Hodge exclaimed, "they weren't kidding around. Well, we don't have much time but I still have a few questions to ask you. If you do move into his building how would you feel about being in his debt? Can you handle it?"

"We've talked pretty frankly about that and any time I stay over a month I'll pay him back for. That's something I can control, so I'm not worried about it."

"What about how needy *he* may be since his mom died just a few months ago?"

"He seemed pretty together when I saw him. He seems to have accepted it."

"Of course you haven't seen him for so long, until your last visit. People change over time. At least some do."

Elliot shook his head. Had Hodge listened to anything he said? He knew Barry as well as he knew anyone on earth. "I'm not worried about that."

"Well, you also did say you had some misgivings. What are they?"

"Mostly about the fight we had over the magazine, which involved money, and now money is an issue again. But we did talk about that a little when I saw him. We both apologized to each other."

"You never told me about your fight. Can you tell me a shortened version? We can go a few minutes extra today."

"Thanks," Elliot said softly, surprised by Hodge's gesture. "About a month after they won their case, when Barry and his mother returned from a vacation in Europe, I invited him to dinner at a small French restaurant in Harvard Square to finally discuss the magazine which we both needed to revitalize our careers. Maybe because we hadn't talked about the magazine for a while, or because I wanted it so much, I led up to it gradually. I waited until we had our main course and were on our second bottle of wine before I mentioned how much I needed to publish to get tenure. Barry stared past me and gave me a rather perfunctorily sympathetic nod. I switched to another approach and began railing against those young critics in Barry's field who were publishing everywhere and whom we both knew were mediocrities. Again Barry didn't take the hint.

"'So when are we going to start working on our magazine?' I suddenly blurted.

"Barry's eyes focused on me darkly.

"'About the magazine you have to understand something, Elliot. It's not my money, it's my mother's. She deserves so many things and now that she has a chance to get some of them, she's going to decide how every penny is spent.'

"'Of course, I understand. But you could ask her. I mean, it's only ten or fifteen thousand we're talking about, initially.'

"'Maybe if we'd gotten the whole estate, but now? No, I won't even ask her.'

"'I don't understand. What have we been talking about all these years?'

"'I don't care about the past. My mother and I are starting a new life.'

"'But . . .'

"'No more *buts*,' he screamed, slamming his fist on the table and then standing up. The veins stood out in his thin forehead the way they did when he'd have a temper tantrum playing baseball as a kid, or else fighting with Roberta.

"'Is that why you testified at the trial? Is that why you've been my 'friend' all these years, because you want your cut? You want to rob me too, like Benjamin and his brother, and the courts, and my father. I'm nauseated. I never want to see you again!'

"Barry turned away from the table and left the restaurant. I waited a few minutes hoping he'd return, before going home, shaken. During that sleepless first night, I was sure he'd call and apologize. I'd seen him have these temporary rages before and then become profoundly apologetic an hour or two later. But the call didn't come. Then I thought he'd write me or that Roberta would contact me, but neither happened and soon a week passed, and then another one.

"I almost called him many times but my own pride and sense of justice stopped me. Finally I wrote Barry a long, conciliatory letter but he didn't answer me and when I phoned him a few days after that I learned that, incredibly, they'd already moved. And then the years started to go by so that was that. . . . But like I said, we did apologize to each other when I saw him and *I'm* certainly ready to let it go."

"Well," Hodge said, "I still think we should talk about this some more before you decide about moving, but now I'm afraid other people need me too and our time really is up."

"Of course," Elliot said. "What do I owe you for the extra time?"

"Don't worry about that. The extra time's on me. Just write me the usual check and don't forget to watch me on TV tonight."

Elliot nodded and made out the check. He felt his time thinking and talking about Barry was up too. First with Annette last week, now for the whole therapy session and much of the time in between. He was due for a break and doubted he would see Hodge again, certainly not next week when he had so many things to do to prepare for his move. He really couldn't spare the hour.

But once on the street walking back to his apartment he found that he was still thinking of Barry. He remembered how terribly he'd missed him and almost always when he least expected it, through an involuntary memory. He might be walking down a street and hear a basketball bouncing, look at a playground and remember a characteristic expression on Barry's face while they played basketball together. Or else he might be watching a kid who threw a baseball in an unorthodox way and think of Barry who was both strong and a pretty good athlete but who was never graceful, never used the correct form in sports and actually threw a ball in a kind of feminine way, though with generally effective results.

Holidays didn't do it, since neither of them was religious or sentimental about such things, nor birthdays either. But music might. It could be a phrase from a Bill Evans piano solo or a passage in an adagio of Mahler's or Prokofiev's that he might hear on the radio, or certain melodies of the Beatles or Stevie Wonder, and he'd be shuttled back in time to the carpet of Barry's Tappan Street apartment in Brookline or else, better yet, to his room in the castle where they used to listen to music together and simultaneously discover and argue about the merits of the piece they were hearing, never suspecting, of course, that they were creating a secret system of memory, or that in those wholly unselfconscious days that they were the composers of their relationship's immortality.

After six years he'd given up hope, or thought he had, but he still carried Barry around in his memory and still occasionally had dreams about him as well. He remembered his face and his voice, his expressions and his opinions, and while he blamed Roberta for much of what happened to Barry and for not intervening to save their relationship, he remembered her too.

He supposed Barry was the brother he'd never had and always wanted. He felt he had fallen in love with a few women yet never shared his soul in quite the way he had with Barry. He'd wanted to, but it just hadn't happened that way. And so he was still trying to understand the incomprehensible about him and those days when so many possibilities of life shimmered before them like their own private city of lights, even as he was preparing to move into his building, in a matter of days.

9

"You're here, it's unbelievable," Barry said. "We should celebrate—what do you want to do tonight?"

"Any good b-ball games on TV?"

"We watched basketball last night. I'm talking about going out, I'm talking about women, Elliot, pussy."

"I'd almost forgotten what they are."

"That's not good. It's not good for either of us to go too long without them. You used to tell me that all the time."

"True enough," he said, thinking of the conversation they had by the Charles River the night that Benjamin Walters died.

"When my mother got sick I went a long time without any because I had to take care of her or just be with her. I couldn't even think about women then, how could I?"

"No, of course not."

"But in normal life, under normal conditions, you've got to deal with them, you can't pretend they don't exist," he said with a strange little smile.

"It's more like they pretend I don't exist," Elliot said, making Barry laugh.

"Alright, let's make them notice you exist tonight. Let's make them notice big time."

Barry's eyes grew radiant as he revealed his plan. First they would go to KGB, where Barry was intrigued by their new female bartender. They could have a bite to eat and a few drinks and then they'd be ready for the evening to really begin, Barry said with one of his all enveloping smiles. Feeling it was his cue, Elliot asked what was next on the agenda.

"There's a party in Tribeca. It's in the loft of a guy who owns an art gallery in SoHo. But this is no ordinary gallery or loft and no ordinary party. Let me explain."

It was a pleasantly warm night for late November. A purplish light filled the sky.

"This is the same building where John Kennedy, Jr. used

to have his loft," Barry said, as the buzzer rang and they walked inside.

"Really?" said Elliot. "I'm glad I had a couple of drinks first to help me handle all this grandeur. Don't tell me you knew him too?"

Barry hesitated as they waited in front of the elevator. "No, but I used to see him and his wife all the time when I lived in Tribeca, just a block or two from here."

"When was this?"

"We lived here for a couple of years just before we moved to Beekman Place where my mother finally felt at home. If it were up to me I would have stayed in Tribeca."

They stepped into the elevator, which like so many loft elevators was both larger and slower than the ones in most apartment buildings.

"Who did you say was throwing this party?"

"Robert Fogel. It's to celebrate the opening of his gallery. It's kind of an 'after party' party. The actual reception was going on in his gallery while we were in KGB. But it's okay. I went to his old gallery all the time. I think he'll forgive me."

"I really hope I dressed OK for this."

"Don't worry, at these kinds of parties you can't go wrong in jeans or in black, and you managed to combine both. Here," Barry said, handing him some keys, "in case you get lucky, I better give you your keys now. Just keep them since you're going to need a set anyway."

The elevator opened and the enormous loft, already half filled with people, billowed out at them.

"Quite a place, n'est-ce pas," said Barry, his green eyes twinkling with pleasure.

"He must be selling a lot of art."

"He's got one of the hottest galleries downtown and guess what, hot places attract hot women."

"I'm noticing already," Elliot said, as he finally saw a bartender behind a table of drinks at the far end of the loft. Meanwhile Barry had walked ahead of him into the middle of the loft. Elliot asked for a vodka tonic and took a few swallows as he surveyed the scene in front of him. Barry was certainly right about the dress code at these affairs. It was a sea of black. Why its enduring popularity along with the ubiquitous pair of faded jeans? He imagined himself talking with Lianne about this and telling her (he had been embarrassingly fond of grand statements then) that it was about Americans' fear of being sentimental and their perennial quest to look tough and cool, which eventually became, of course, its own form of sentimentality. Lianne, looking bemused, would say something contrary like, "The black is about people wanting to look thin. The jeans is about looking casual and sexy for a low price."

He felt a little hit of pain thinking of her and quickly finished the rest of his drink. It was good vodka, expensive stuff, and he immediately wanted another. He turned, perhaps too abruptly, towards the table and brushed slightly against the shoulder of a young blonde woman who was wearing a pale yellow dress, of all things, making the top part of her drink spill.

"Jesus, I'm sorry," he said. The woman, who was quite pretty in a soft, almost indistinct way, and looked to be about thirty or so, seemed even more embarrassed than he was.

"Well, there's my first faux pas of the night," Elliot said. "Hopefully, the rest of them won't involve you."

"No, no, it's alright. It's really nothing," she said, blushing a little.

"My name's Elliot, Elliot Martin, but I understand if you don't want to risk shaking my hand."

She made a little sound somewhere between a laugh and a giggle.

"I'm Cheri," she said, shaking hands with him rather firmly as if to emphasize that she still trusted him.

"So, what's your connection to Robert Fogel?" he heard himself say. He thought of adding more to his question to make it less blunt but couldn't come up with an improvement and had to let the words stand.

"I'm writing about his new gallery for *The Voice*."

"You're an art critic then?"

"No, no. I'm writing more from the social angle about the reception and maybe a line or two about all this," she said indicating the loft with a brief gesture.

"Interesting," Elliot said.

"You think so? Anyway, this is probably the last piece I'm doing for them."

"Why's that? Is someone not treating you well there?"

"Oh no, everyone's very nice there, it's just not really the kind of writing I want to do. I only freelance for them anyway," she said, pushing a lock of hair behind her ear. He noticed then that she was wearing a hearing aid.

"What kind of writing do you want to do?" Elliot asked.

"Well, what I really want to do is some art of my own."

"That's admirable," he said, looking intently at her hazel-blue eyes.

"What about you? What kind of work do you do?"

"I'm a teacher and also a fiction writer. So, I'm kind of a permanent freelancer myself, always looking for someone to hire or publish me, I'm afraid."

"I admire that. I've always wanted to write fiction but don't have any talent for it."

"When can I read the article you're writing?" Elliot said.

Again she giggled slightly as if she'd brushed against some part of her childhood that stuck to her before she could detach herself and cross over the border to her current age.

"If they take it, I guess it will run in next week's *Voice*."

"I'll really look forward to reading it."

"So, do you have a story I could read?"

"I've published five or six stories in literary magazines, but nothing that's on sale now. Sometimes I think it's a fiction that I write fiction, that it's just a story I tell myself. Even when they're published I get such little feedback that it still seems unreal to me."

"I'd like to read your stories. I love to read short stories."

"That's very kind of you to say."

"Maybe I could find them in the library."

"Hmm. I hadn't thought of that. If you like, I could write down the names of a couple of the magazines that published me. I'm embarrassed to say I still know the names and dates of the issues."

"Could you? That would be neat."

"Or, I could just email or snail mail one to you if you felt like giving me an address. Where could I send it?"

"Oh, OK. I can do that," she said, placing her glass on the bar table and beginning to search through her pocketbook. "As you can see I have one of those endlessly confusing pocketbooks where I can never find anything I really need."

"Maybe I could . . ."

"Oh, here's something," she said, looking up from her bag and holding a pencil in one hand and a pad of post-its in the other. "Of course the pencil looks like a squirrel just had it for a snack but I think it will work."

He laughed and wrote down her information. She smiled again and he noticed that her teeth were little and extremely white.

"Thanks. Now I'll have something to look forward to reading," she said.

There were usually two reasons (he thought of them as forces) that sometimes kept him from talking effectively to people. One was because he was bored or uninterested and couldn't think of anything to say despite his wish to be polite, the other was that he was too interested and became acutely self-conscious or self-critical about the words leaving his mouth with the result that he couldn't release any. Despite Cheri's unpretentious eager to please manner, the second force was operating in him now at the worst possible time. He stood there shifting his weight (aware that he was perspiring), finishing his drink to camouflage his inability to speak, hoping for a miracle. Oddly, she seemed not to notice and was looking directly at him with her wide-open eyes.

Finally he went into his interview mode and found himself asking another series of questions about her work, which he actually was interested in. But when he asked her what kind of art she did, she looked away from him while rearranging various strands of hair.

"Well, I'm doing painting right now, so I guess painting is it."

"Is your work figurative or abstract? Never mind, that's the typical dumb question. It's the school teacher in me."

"No, I like the question. I paint objects and sometimes landscapes."

"Any people in the landscapes?"

"Not so much. Sometimes parts of them."

"*Parts* of them? That sounds mysterious. Why only parts?" he said, vaguely aware that he was talking too fast.

"I don't know. I don't think I know people well enough to paint them whole yet."

Elliot stared at her, thinking he'd found the first modest artist in New York or anywhere else for that matter. He looked out at the party to find Barry, as if to share the news with him but Barry appeared to be deeply engaged in conversation and Elliot only saw the back of his head. "I've never heard anyone put it that way. I've never heard anyone else say that."

"Really? I don't really know what I'm saying half the time or probably more than half," Cheri said with a smile.

"Half the time? That would be something I'd aspire to, to know what I'm saying half the time is more than I could probably hope for," Elliot said, with a little laugh. "But seriously, knowingly or not, you made a very astute observation. It's the same in writing. You can't really write fiction unless you know or think you know something about people. I think a lot of the indefiniteness and ambiguity, not to mention the overload of self-consciousness and irony that saturates so much of contemporary fiction is because the creators of it know so little about people and have even less to say about them. Anyway, I'm even more intrigued about your painting now that you've spoken about it. Do you have a studio where you work?"

"No, nothing that official. I can't really afford it, for one thing."

"Ah. So where . . ."

"Where do I do it? In my apartment. It makes it kind of tough to live there."

"It's not a big apartment?"

"It's almost a one bedroom," she said laughing. "But the good news is I answered an ad and I think I'm going to start sharing a small art studio with someone, so help is on the way."

"That *is* good news," he said. He shifted his weight again, then took a final swallow from his drink and saw that she too had picked this moment to swallow some of hers.

"You said you teach school," she said, looking at him hopefully.

"I teach creative writing and a couple of lit courses at a college in Philadelphia." He went on to explain that the job would be ending in a year and a half and used the line about having academic cancer again because he remembered it made Barry laugh. When she asked him how he liked living in Philadelphia (he hoped he'd detected a slightly disappointed look in her face as he said it) he told her about his plans to commute and a little about Barry who was making it all possible.

"He sounds amazing, that's such a generous thing to do. Will you be trying to get a teaching job in New York after your other one runs out?"

"That's a good question. Probably, but I'll also see if I can get some other kind of work too. I don't feel married to the profession," Elliot said, with another little laugh.

From the other side of the loft, where he'd just finished paying his respects to Robert Fogel, Barry was watching them. He watched for nearly a minute while he finished his new drink, then empty cup in hand, began to walk purposefully in their direction. But when he was about forty to fifty feet away he abruptly stopped and turned around so that his back was towards them for a full minute before rotating (mannequin-like) about 90 degrees. Now he could watch them if he wanted to and watch, or appear to watch, the rest of the party as well.

Intermittently he was aware that he might be cutting a strange figure—standing alone, a good ten feet from anyone else and not directly facing anyone either. Moreover, the only thing of consequence that he could be said to be looking at were some of the abstract expressionist paintings by Richard Darkfield who was the featured artist in Fogel's new gallery—though he was actually too far away to see them clearly. Besides, he was still holding his cup and finally decided to at least do something about that when the self-styled "avant garde polymathic artist," Darren Datz, approached him dressed theatrically in a black jump suit and triangular hat. Datz sidled up to him like a giant black cat. Immediately, Barry remembered that Datz had been trying to get him to write an article about his multimedia performance work called "The Datz Revolution" for *The Voice*, or failing there, at least for one of the literary quarterlies or online 'zines.

"I thought 'no man is an island,'" Datz said. Barry forced himself to laugh, remembering that Datz liked to embarrass people a little before asking them for favors—a peculiar and seemingly counterproductive habit, yet Datz had undeniably made a certain name for himself. Barry shook his hand.

"But you've decided to visit this island," Barry said.

Datz barely smiled. He was what Barry thought of as a first strike speaker and didn't enjoy repartee. Barry decided that he wanted to get rid of him as soon as possible.

"Did you see the article about me in *Night* magazine?"

"No, I didn't."

"I reprinted in on my blog. Don't you read my blog? Aren't you keeping up with my website? What's the matter, Auer, you're falling behind. *Literal Latte* is doing a piece on me too. They're mostly concentrating on my Language Poetry. It will be out in late December/early January."

"Congratulations," Barry said, as earnestly as possible.

"It's the third article that's appeared about me this year. Four, if you count the paragraph about my installation in *Time Out New York*. What do you think, should I count it as four or not? It was a short paragraph but it was still a paragraph and a good one too."

"Why not count it as four then? You can."

Datz appeared to check his face for traces of sarcasm so Barry quickly asked, "What did you think of the show?" having a pretty good idea what Datz's response would be.

"Darkfield's?"

"Yeah."

"Retrograde imitation Julian Schnabel, I'd say."

Barry laughed. "It still sells."

"Anything at Fogel's will sell with all the hype he's been getting. My work would sell at Fogel's too. But obviously there's a difference between work that sells and then disappears from human consciousness and work like mine that *changes* human consciousness. Speaking of my work, when are you going to write that article about me that we spoke about?"

"Sorry about that. I have a friend staying with me that I've been showing around town this week. He's from Philadelphia."

"Oh, a backwoodsman."

Barry forced himself to smile, "So I'll call you about it in a week or so."

"Is he a writer?" Datz said raising his eyebrows in interest because art or literary reviewers he didn't know were always of interest to him.

"A *fiction* writer. He doesn't do reviews. After he leaves, I'll get in touch with you about it."

"You still living in that Upper East Side ghetto among all the lawyers and dentists?"

"That's where I am."

"When are you going to move downtown where there's still some art being produced?"

"I'm really comfortable there," Barry said, looking at Elliot again and deciding he would leave Datz in no more than ten seconds. As if sensing his imminent departure, Datz extended his hand and said, "Adios for now, Auer. I see some so-called artists I have to mingle with."

Barry shook his hand, found the one rather minimalist looking black trash receptacle in the loft into which he finally deposited his clinging plastic cup and then looked up at Elliot, who was still talking with the blonde. Not only was she pretty, but there was something so innocently appealing about her body movements that he felt mesmerized. Why did Elliot always wind up with such women? This one seemed completely focused on Elliot as if no one else were in the room. In fact, their conversation seemed so intense it made Barry pause again. Maybe it would be better to wait. He could always ask about her later tonight, unless Elliot actually did end up going home with her. As sweet as she looked you never knew with women. He thought of the addiction to sexual humiliation that so many women had. His mother was a shining exception, but even she had succumbed once to Benjamin so what hope was there for other women? He thought of Jordan for a moment, too, then walked back to the table and ordered another drink.

10

Elliot looked out the window once more although he was aware that Cheri wasn't late and that on their first date in New York she'd been right on time. But so much more seemed to be involved once she made the surprising decision to meet him in Philadelphia so she could see the city for the first time—especially the famous Duchamp collection at the Fine Arts Museum. On the one hand it made him happy to see Philadelphia with her and think that he had something to do with her deciding to see it at all, but it also created additional anxiety—she could miss a train, or she could decide not to come.

Did he really like her so much already, that he should be feeling all this? He looked around Borders as if it might somehow provide the answer. Normally he avoided bookstores because he was so rarely represented in them (and then only with a story in a little magazine) but today felt it would be a good place to meet in case she was late so he could distract himself with newspapers or magazines. He'd already picked up a couple but hadn't made it through a paragraph. How naïve he'd been, to think he could concentrate on them, how little he understood himself. Barry knew that he liked her right away, saw it and told him so the night of the party. He had amazing insight that way. In one week he'd be completely moved in—he really was astonishingly lucky. It would be like a Lawrencian paradise to have his best friend upstairs and the woman he wanted a mere twenty minutes away. Yet he'd miss Philadelphia in a way he couldn't explain. Maybe it was because in places like Philadelphia which weren't burdened by the spectacular, as New York was, people resonated inside you more deeply if for no other reason than you concentrated on them more.

She was now ten minutes late. He thought he should call her on his cell phone to at least find out if she'd left. Why didn't he ask her if she had a cell phone and to take it with her if she did? He could have directed her to Borders the moment she reached 30th Street Station. He had been so careful, doing laundry, picking out an outfit and going to the cleaners, even in selecting the book on Max Beckman he was giving her as a present, and then he forgot something as elementary as asking her cell phone number, or her email address either for that matter.

Five more minutes passed. He was pacing from the door to the foreign newspaper section—the length of the picture window that he turned to look out every ten seconds—and then back. Fortunately there was no snow which could have delayed the train. It was an unusually mild day for early December—almost spring-like, and outside everything looked and smelled brisk and fresh—a perfect showcase for the city.

He looked out the window again as if to console himself about the weather then heard his name called. She was already inside the store (having magically passed through his "security system") moving towards him in a black coat that seemed to be shining. They hugged in front of the literary magazine section and she kissed him on the cheek.

"Sorry I'm late."

"You're not really late."

"I was at the other bookstore," she said, puzzling him for a moment until he remembered there was a Barnes and Noble close by on Walnut Street. Perhaps he'd forgotten to say the new Borders, after all. "Then someone told me about Borders."

"That was stupid of me to forget about Barnes and Noble, especially when the stores are practically Siamese twins."

He looked closely at her. She was even prettier than he'd remembered. She was wearing a black fur Russian hat but her blond bangs were clearly visible.

"You look great," he said, "really great."

She smiled more deeply. "It's too warm for this hat," she said, "but I thought you might like it so I kept it on."

"I do like it. It's beautiful."

"I don't think I need my coat either it's so warm out."

"Was it too warm on the train?"

"I'm sorry. I didn't hear you. You know about my ears," she said smiling.

He looked at her barely visible hearing aids and repeated his question.

"The train was fine and right on time. It was all very easy."

"So would you like some lunch now?"

"Sure, lunch sounds good."

"We could walk through Rittenhouse Square, through the park there, on the way. Would you like that?" he said, speaking a little slower and louder now.

She nodded vigorously, like a child but it was, like almost all her gestures, completely unpremeditated. They passed through the doors and he had to fight down the urge to put his arm around her waist. It was funny how normally you didn't think about your arm unless you were an athlete or a musician. It was almost dead to you until suddenly it burst into life with an untamed, urgent will of its own.

"Do you know the *Rocky* movies?" Elliot said. They were at the Philadelphia Art Museum where he'd taken her after lunch.

"Only by reputation."

Elliot looked at her carefully, thinking that may have been the first semi-sarcastic thing Cheri had ever said.

"Anyway, in *Rocky*, and I think in a couple of the sequels, the most famous shot takes place right here where we're standing, on top of the museum steps."

"I think I've seen that image."

"Almost everyone has. At least it's close to impossible to live in Philadelphia and not have seen it. Here it has a kind of religious significance for the city."

"He's a boxer, right? So why is he at the museum in the movie? Does he have a secret sensitive side?"

Elliot laughed. "Not exactly. I mean he does have a sensitive side but not a secret art-loving side. What happens with the museum is that he runs through the city every morning while training for his big fight and the culmination of his run is right where we're standing."

"You mean he runs up all the steps?"

"Every single one of them and then looks out at the city and lets out a primal scream and if you're a Philadelphian, especially a South Philadelphian, your chest is supposed to swell with civic pride and tears are supposed to come to your eyes."

"Did tears come to your eyes?"

Again he looked at her closely, but she seemed to be completely earnest.

"No, *Rocky* didn't affect me like that. Not that I never cry at movies, I have an embarrassing number of times, but not from old *Rocky*."

She looked him in the eyes. He wasn't sure if she'd heard him. "It's a very pretty view," she said.

"I think they tried to pattern it after the Champs d'Elysées."

"Yes, I see that. It really is a pretty city and a great museum. The whole day has been wonderful."

Elliot looked away for a moment at the cars below and then out at the fountains. "So now, I guess you have to go."

"I really should," she said softly, looking out at the view herself.

"When does your next train leave?"

"I still have almost an hour."

"Should I get you a cab now?" he askd, turning to face her, which he now realized made it easier to understand him, since she could read his lips.

"How far away is the train station?"

"I don't know. It's about a twenty-minute walk. I've done it a couple of times."

"Why don't we walk it then?"

"OK," he said, smiling. "Are you sure you really want to? A lot of it is just in a straight line without much to see."

"That doesn't bother me. Unless you're tired or . . ."

"No, no, not at all."

"It would be nice to walk with you."

"Yes, I'd really like that." He moved a half step closer to her, wanting to kiss her but not quite daring.

During the first part of the walk they talked a normal amount about the city as they passed by some of the smaller museums around the art museum and then some of the varied architecture near Cherry Street. It was like they were an old, relaxed couple which made Elliot regret even more that he'd not tried to kiss her when the moment had seemed so right. Then, to have this pedestrian conversation, seemed like a further fall from grace. (If he wasn't careful, he was afraid this would end up in another situation like he had with Annette.) He was surprised and angry at how banal he was acting, at how tepidly socialized he was turning out to be. It was odd, on the one hand the world pleaded for distinctive individuals while on the other it did everything in its power to keep you like everybody else. They did it with their writers and artists, pleading for more Kafkas or van Goghs while rewarding mainstream and politically correct artists at every step of the way. The same rule applied to human behavior in general and that invisible but all-powerful process of socialization (for want of a better word) had been what had shut him down today when he wanted to kiss her. If Barry could have seen him he'd have been disappointed and would've given him a stern lecture afterwards. Barry was probably the only person he knew who did act on impulse and emotion in his intellectual life and with women as well, although he had to remember he'd never really seen Barry with too many women (except Roberta) and that he'd always suspected that, at best, Barry exaggerated his dealings with them.

"How're you doing?" he said, as they crossed onto the long strip of sidewalk that led to the station.

"Fine, good."

"It's pretty much a straight line from here." There was barely room for the two of them to walk together on the sidewalk. To their left they saw part of a business section of Market Street. On the right there was a long chain link fence separating them from some construction.

"What are they building there?" Cheri asked.

"An excellent question. I think it's called perpetual construction.

You know, today we saw a lot of art for art's sake at the museum; this is a stellar example of construction for construction's sake."

She laughed, a high-pitched girlish laugh. He loved hearing it but it made it difficult to transition to a more serious level that he wanted to reach now that their day was coming to an end, especially since this street was so noisy. He made a couple of more jokes with her and then they fell silent. While he walked he stared straight ahead at the strong blue sky and at the massive station. Yes, it was good weather for walking. He was lucky that the weather had held. A lot of their day had been spent outdoors (although the centerpiece was probably the museum) and he was glad of that. It was always more memorable to be outside. There was their walk through Rittenhouse Park on their way to lunch at the Korean buffet on Chestnut Street. Then there was the walk past the science museum and the Rodin Museum on the Parkway that culminated at the art museum. He wished they'd been a little less goal oriented and had stopped to sit on one of the benches on the Parkway. Then he could have kissed her there. Now they were almost at the station and then there'd be no more outdoors for them today.

They walked inside the enormous, high-ceilinged station. "This station is right out of Kafka," Cheri said.

He laughed. "You should see the government buildings around City Hall. They're really Kafkaesque. Next time we'll go there," he said turning to look at her. He was glad he was at least aggressive enough to make that remark.

"Yes, I'd really like to see them."

"Let me get you a ticket," he said, turning to get in line.

"No, no, I got a round trip in New York."

"What? I didn't want you to do that. Let me reimburse you for it."

"No. I wanted to pay. It was worth every penny and much more."

"Can I mail you the tickets next time?" he said, moving a little closer to her.

"Yes," she said. "That would be lovely."

He put his arm around her, leading her a few feet further away from people. There was a bench twenty feet from them but he couldn't wait any more as he touched her face first and then kissed her.

"I wanted to do that for quite a while," Elliot said, touching her hair softly.

"Me too."

"Really? I didn't know. I never quite believe it when I like someone, those rare times that I do, and they also like me too."

"Maybe it will be different with me." She looked at him hopefully.

"It already is," he said.

11

He was in a rented car heading towards Philadelphia. Elliot had left for Philadelphia already and the next thing he knew he was in a car picturing the different bar options he had there—narrowing them down ultimately to two—one in Center City and one in West Philly, filled with college kids, near where he'd met Love Hunt at The White Dog. At any rate, he was sure he'd never met anyone in either place, that was the rule he had to follow. It really was dreamlike the way you met people in some places who would get in your car and didn't in others. The way you were in a room talking to your friend who was going to move into your apartment and then a few hours later he was gone. The way you had a mother one day and the next only a memory of a mother, and her ashes in an urn, and then the urn itself got lost. But he couldn't think about that, not while he was driving down a long highway at night. And he couldn't think anymore about his smitten friend who was probably writing a love letter that very moment to his new blonde, or calling to invite her to Philadelphia and disrupting all his plans again. Women were the great disrupters of plans, were the greatest disrupters of all.

He was in a bar now, the one in Center City. It was ornate. All the waiters and waitresses were dressed in black like vampires. There was gold on the tables and around the mirrors some form of gold that vampires liked. He was at the gold and black bar drinking then talking to a woman in a black dress who had gold hair too. It was like the ending of the movie *2001* where the astronaut views himself passing through different phases of his life in a matter of seconds. Why didn't Elliot see how great that scene was—the only realistic expression in movies of the dreamtime we all really lived in.

The next thing he knew he couldn't think anymore because the conversation with the woman required too much of his attention.

"Capiche, is that a foreign word? I don't know it," she said.

"It's Italian. It means 'do you understand,'" he said.

"Are you Italian?" she asked. She had long fingers, which were somewhat disturbing, but otherwise strangely appealing.

"No, but I lived in Europe for a couple of years in Paris, and I traveled a lot through Italy while I was there."

"My name is French, I think. It's Renee."

"Oh, oui, oui, C'est francaise vraiment."

"Jeez, you know French too. What'd you just say?"

"Yes, your name is truly French."

"What's yours?"

"Pardon," he said, with a French accent.

"What's your name?"

"Gordon," he said. "My name is Gordon."

"So are you really smart or something?"

"I do my best."

"Are you a lawyer or a psychiatrist or something like that?"

"Something like that," he said, touching the tip of her nose for a second as if it were a baby's and noticing that she smiled.

"I'm a writer. I write books but I don't work at a regular job of any kind."

"How come?"

"Because I'm in a financial position where I don't have to anymore."

"Oh," she said, quickly straightening her hair, and the next second, reaching into her purse and withdrawing a hand mirror and lipstick. "So how come a smart, successful good looking guy like you is alone?"

"I could ask you the same question," he said, resting his free hand just above her knee. She looked a little flustered, and he thought "shift the emphasis to *them*." It must have worked because she started talking while also letting his hand rest on her leg.

"This is the first time I've been out by myself in a long time," she said.

"Why's that?"

"I was with a guy for a couple of years. I thought we were gonna get married but it turned out he already was. You're not married, are you?"

"No, I'm definitely not married."

"But you like women, right?"

"I find they're a necessary evil," he said, laughing a little.

"I'm not evil."

"I hope not," he said, sliding his hand to her upper thigh and realizing then that he would score.

She laughed. He liked that she laughed a lot. It kept things light and entertaining.

He wished he'd drunk more. He was being overly careful, the very antithesis of his philosophy of living, of what he was always telling Elliot. When he got to Exton he could get high, he'd just have to hang on till then.

They were outside the bar walking towards his car in silence—just her heels against the cold sidewalk, making a weird kind of music until she said, "Do you really think it's a good idea for me to get in your car?"

"Why not?"

"I'm pretty high for one thing."

Pretty high and pretty tall, he thought, figuring that she was almost as tall as he was, and in her heels maybe an inch taller. "I was thinking we both should drink more."

"No, no," she said, gesturing haphazardly with one of her long, surprisingly muscular arms. "I had too much already."

"All right, we're almost to my car. Here it is," he said, leaning her against the side door and kissing her, with both hands on her face. He didn't like to do that, kiss someone by surprise—especially in public—but felt he had to. It was as if she were demanding it in order to get inside the car.

"Wow," she said. "Did you learn to kiss in France, too?"

He laughed and kissed her again. He liked her. He thought, *We will each have a blonde girlfriend*, although he was afraid Renee would not be as pretty in the cold light of day as Elliot's blonde. But if he continued to like her he could get beyond that. It was time for another kiss, he decided, time to press against her and feel her a little while she was against the car. When he kissed her she got hot quickly, actually moaning outside, where anyone could walk by and hear her.

He decided to open the car door. Had to fish and fumble inside his pants' pocket for a while to find the keys but then opened the door without asking her and helped her in. They continued making out immediately as if his opening the door and getting inside the car with her was merely a tiny interval between two kisses. She was moaning again, making even more noise. It was hard to tell in the half dark, but he thought her cheeks were turning red. Let Elliot have his sweet, shy girl, he'd take a truly hot woman every time.

She had her hands on his legs now creeping up towards his crotch. He didn't like women to touch him there until he was ready (which created a kind of Catch-22 situation at times, he realized) but to his surprise, in spite of all the alcohol, he was erect.

"Let's go in back," she said.

"Why?"

"More room," she said, breathing heavily.

"I have a better idea. Let's go to my place," he said, putting his tongue inside her mouth, as if to answer for her.

*   *   *

She'd said OK as long as it wasn't too far. He'd hoped that she'd pass out and not be aware of the long drive but she never quite made it to sleep.

"Where do you live?" she finally said.

"In Wonderland."

"Is that a town?"

"It's a state of mind."

"No, really, where do you live?"

"In the suburbs, in the country. You'll like it, it's …je ne sais quois, it's pretty."

"Can't we just pull over some place and continue what we were doing?"

"It won't be long. We'll be there soon. We can get a drink there, we can get high."

"I'm already high."

"Don't you like to smoke? We can do that there too."

"Seriously, how much longer do we need to drive?"

"Seriously?" he said, laughing a little, "I really like you, Renee."

"Then pull over some place and show me," she said.

It was like being cut by a knife, he could almost feel the blood being drawn, only he couldn't scream or even call attention to it. But he couldn't ignore it either, so he turned off the highway at the next exit, looked for and found a small parking lot near a tiny train station, then went to the far end, turned off the lights and parked.

"Come on," he said as he opened his door. But she waited till he came around the car and opened her door. "Let's get in back."

He couldn't see any parked cars, at least none with their lights on, which made him feel slightly better. He thought they would make out for a little while, ten or fifteen minutes, then she'd go to his place without complaining.

It was more cramped than he thought in the back seat because her body was so long. Still he managed to get most of her down and began kissing her neck, then her smaller-than-hoped-for breasts.

"Hey, slow down, will you?" she said.

"What?" he said. It was another cut—cut two.

"I need to get back into the mood. Can you just kiss me *slowly* for a while?"

He complied, thinking that was women in a nut shell, *acting* so passionate and impulsive while they demanded sex but then wanting it to be as slow as a Chinese Water Torture and making sure to criticize you as much as they could get away with in the process. But he went along with it, even closing his eyes while they kissed. It was an unearthly feeling, like seeing dark inside the dark as in a floating Chinese box. He suddenly got scared and stopped kissing her. At the same moment he thought he felt something strange, as if she had a tail where her bottom should be.

"Hey, why are you stopping? What's the matter?" she said.

"Jesus Christ!" he hissed. "Are you a man?"

"What? Are you nuts?"

"Get out of the car."

"Are you crazy, calling me a man?"

"Just get out."

"I'm not getting out in the middle of nowhere."

"You *are* in the middle of nowhere and you *are* a god-damned man. I felt it."

"You *wish* I had a dick cause yours sure isn't working."

"Get out! Get out," he screamed, throwing her against the seat, then swinging at her face with his free hand but hitting the metal part of the seat back instead.

It was like the first time he was stung by a bee when he was a kid, the pain shocked him and for a moment he saw orange and was silent before he began to scream. Renee was trying to get out but now he wanted to stop her, to make her pay for this. He put his left (and weaker) arm around her waist but she slithered away like a snake. He reached out to grab her waist again but she elbowed him in the groin and he doubled over.

He was still screaming as she ran out of the car leaving the door open. Then he stopped. He could feel the cool air as the world returned to black. His pain was manageable now. All his senses felt heightened. He could even hear the same kind of music she made again while running in her heels across the parking lot. He went into the front seat and opened the glove compartment where his gun was. He fumbled a little but finally loaded it with three shells thinking that she wouldn't get far in her heels. He turned his lights on, so he could see better, see something at all, then started to run after her, not even talking any more but just running after her as if any kind of speech, any kind of sound except the one his feet were making would slow him down. It was like the world had been reduced to speed alone, yet it wasn't that simple either. It wasn't pure speed, it was more like hunting an animal that ran in a jagged pattern. It was like chasing the dark in the dark, so he couldn't shoot because he couldn't risk hitting someone else or attracting attention from someone else who might be there—some sleeping vampire he didn't want to awaken or some stray zombie dreaming of a meal of dead flesh.

Then there was a flash—it might have been a pocket of orange exploding again, it might have been lightning, but he saw Renee running.

"Stop, stop running," he hissed as if he were a snake talking. He raised his gun and fired into the dark but the sound continued. He thought it was her running so he fired again. Then he stopped and listened hard. He could smell the bullets he'd fired in the air around him. A few seconds later he thought he heard the sound again in the distance like an echo of the music he'd heard earlier—heels against cement. And he was relieved now, as if the world had reversed itself yet again. "Jesus Christ," he muttered, though he couldn't be sure if what he heard was Renee running, couldn't tell if she was alive or dead any more than he could now be certain that Renee was really a man.

He was still sitting in The End of Night on 12th Street in Philadelphia almost as far from Exton as he was from New York. And he was still sitting on a bar stool too, though sometimes when he closed his eyes to stop seeing the "videotape" he felt dizzy.

People were watching him, smiling at him probably because of how much he'd drunk and because he was white, but he was no longer worrying. He loved black people so why should he be worried? He was in the heart of Philly's hooker district and wanted to buy a woman to take home with him to Exton but now thought, given how much he'd drunk, he'd have to spend the night with her in a nearby hotel.

Two or three had come in since he'd been here that he wouldn't have minded taking but somehow he couldn't ask them. How could he buy a black women in front of the black men in the bar? He thought he'd go out instead and get one on the street as soon as he finished his last drink. It was a much sounder plan.

He found one within a block of where he'd parked and she hustled into his car.

"What're you doin'?"

Barry turned on the light in the car and stared at her.

"Why you checkin' me out? You already looked at me on the street. You already bought me, mister—don't be changing your mind now."

"You wouldn't believe what happened to me tonight," he said, wondering if he would make sense when he spoke.

"Start the car, mister, then tell me 'bout it. This ain't a good spot right here."

He shut off the light and drove slowly, for a few blocks. There were three or four hookers walking near his car, nearly colliding with his windshield like low flying bats. He turned up a lightless alley and stopped, then turned the light on and looked at her again.

"Why you still lookin' me over? You already done that. You already made up your mind and bought me."

"Earlier tonight I was with a woman, or so I thought, and after we started fooling around I found out she was a man."

"So? What that got to do with me? You see my titties, they half out of my dress, ain't they? These ain't no man's titties," she said, cupping a hand under each of her breasts. "These are a woman's, see?" she said, finally taking them completely out of her bra and wiggling them in the air.

Barry laughed. "OK. You convinced me."

"You sure now?" she said, raising her eyebrows and looking at him seriously or mock seriously, he couldn't be sure which. "I don't want you tellin' me later I'm a man. I ain't no man but it gonna cost you to know that fo' sure. What you wanna do with me, mister?"

He saw a chipped front tooth now when he looked at her and then shut the light off.

"I want you for the night. I want to spend what's left of the night with you."

"That gonna cost you five hundred," she said, her voice wavering a little.

"Come on, don't bullshit me. You don't charge that much."

"You heard what I said."

"Anyway, that's way more than I can pay."

"What you got to pay?"

"Two hundred. There's only three or four hours of night left, so you'll still be making fifty an hour," he said, feeling strangely proud of his logic and convinced now that he wasn't drunk at all.

"What you wanna do during those four hours?"

"Sleep mostly. Just sleep next to you."

"You wanna sleep next to mama?"

"I'm tired, really tired."

"OK. I hear you. But after you wake up and see how nice I been, I hope you give me a little more 'fore you leave."

"I will," he said. "What's your name? Mine's Barry."

"Name's July."

"July?"

"Yah, you like it?"

"I love it."

"OK, Barry. There's a place a couple blocks from here."

"Is it safe?"

"Sure it's safe. You worry a lot, don't you?"

"How do I know it's safe?"

"I lay my ass there every night, so it must be pretty safe."

"So, it's your place?"

"Evidently," she said.

It was on a side street, a dark walk up without a doorman but at least you needed a key to open the doors. July lived in one room with a queen-sized bed in the center, and not much else that he could see, not even a refrigerator or a desk. It was as if the bed was the whole purpose of the room. Certainly it received most of her attention with its red satin sheets and black pillows and its coverlet with a red heart in the middle. Facing the bed on a little stand of some kind was a small TV.

"I'm glad you've got a nice bed," he said, taking off his shoes.

"I got a toilet, but if you wanna wash yourself you got to use the bathroom out in the hall."

"That's OK."

"Hey, Barry, 'fore you lie down and get comfortable, you wanna take care of me?"

"Sure, I was just going to," he said, reaching in his pants and withdrawing four fifties from his money clip. She took them, looking at them quickly but closely in the half dark of the room (the only light coming from a red light bulb in a black floor lamp) then unzipped her boots and put them there in a kind of secret purse he hadn't noticed before.

"OK, you lie down now if that's what you wanna do."

"What are you doing?"

"I'm gonna smoke me a number 'fore I try to sleep. Wan' some?"

She turned her back to him and stood by the window while she smoked. She had a big bottom, semi-transparent in her short skirt, and heavy thighs. She was probably the fattest prostitute he'd ever been with, but she had a nice smile, and there was something soothing about her that made him feel it would be safe to fall asleep with her.

It was like a sneak attack the way fear suddenly seized him like a Zombie with its hand around his throat. Maybe he shouldn't have smoked with July. Maybe what she gave him was cut with Angel Dust. He went out on the floor—it was like the bottom of a lake with strange fish and water snakes lying in wait—trying to find the lamp. Light was the first step, he tried to concentrate on it and forget about the water snakes on the lake floor.

When he finally found it and turned it on, the lake evaporated. The lamp was like a red god, silent but powerful enough to bring back the room in an instant. He stood up (not even aware that he'd been on his hands and knees while he was looking for the lamp) and saw her big bottom sticking up in the air. She was wearing only a thong and her enormous breasts (too flabby to be artificial) fanned out on either side of her. She was snoring, too, every ten seconds or so. It was a mysterious sight, a mysterious presence and for what seemed like a long time he stared at and listened to her, wondering how her life allowed her to sleep like that.

Then he lay next to her, eventually closing his eyes. But as soon as he closed them he saw an image of Renee's face when he first kissed her—saw her purple streaked eyes just before they closed and just as her moaning started when they were outdoors. Then he remembered the way she slithered out of his car like a water moccasin, and the sound of her heels running on the parking lot like rattlesnake music.

He opened his eyes and began shaking July and when that did no good punched her (though not too hard) on her shoulder.

"What, what?" she said, turning on her side away from him.

"Get up, will you? Talk to me."

"What's the matter? Shit, I was sleeping."

"What's in the pot? Is it Angel Dust or just poison?"

"The weed? Shit, I didn't make you smoke it."

"I was seeing snakes and fish."

"Ain't none of either in this place, mister."

"Give me something to drink."

"You been drinking too much. That's why you're seein' things."

"No, no, I need to pass out. I haven't been to sleep yet."

"You wanna grind for awhile, that'll calm you down. See my titties, honey. Least you know I ain't no man."

"They're enormous," he said, glad to divert himself by staring at them. "Can I touch them?"

"You bought 'em, didn't you? You can do pull ups with 'em if you want to."

He put his hands on them—they felt warm and comforting like putting on a pair of gloves in winter. She made a few soft moaning sounds though he wasn't trying to stimulate her. It was like a jukebox responding to a quarter.

"Why don't you grind with me for a while?"

He thought about it, but he couldn't feel himself, as if his dick had flown away like a bird to a distant island.

"I can't. I drank too much."

She laughed a little. "You got all kinds of problems, don't you. Shit."

"Just get me something to drink, I got some really bad stuff in my mind, and I need to pass out, OK? I'll pay you for it in the morning."

"Shit," she muttered as she stood up from the bed. "I got some whiskey. Ain't the best stuff in the world, but it'll knock you down. You gotta drink it warm though. I ain't goin' out to the hall, Barry. That's the only place where there's water, but I ain't goin' out there."

"Sure, anything," he said. "I'll drink it straight."

"One more thing," she said, holding the bottle as she returned to him from across the room. "You feel like you're gonna heave, go do it in the toilet over there," she said, pointing in the dark. He pretended to look but even that pretend effort made him dizzy.

"Don't be puking on my bed, all right?"

Everything speeded up like the dam of his being could no longer hold back his words. It was as if he could hear it break and the waterfall of words rushed forward no longer caring, simply needing to say themselves the way zombies simply need to move if only to feel themselves moving before they eat.

"That man/woman I told you about, remember?"

"Sure I do."

"Something terrible happened."

"You sure you want to tell me this?"

He tried to think about what she was saying but the waterfall words kept on rushing through. "I might have killed her."

"Shit."

"She was running and I was chasing her in the dark and I shot a number of times. I don't know why I did it. I felt tricked but I shouldn't have shot at her."

"Where was you?"

"In a parking lot in the dark, as dark as this room so I couldn't be sure. I ordered her out of my car once I found out she was a man and at first he wouldn't leave and then he wanted to and I didn't want him to and that's when the chase began. But I couldn't see, could only see the actual body for a few seconds, maybe less. I was running and he was running, you listening?"

"Yeah, I'm listening."

"I was trying to see in the dark, but I couldn't. I'm not a bat, I'm not batman, capiche? I could only go by the sound of his high heels on the ground. So I shot at a sound target, not even at an image. And then I didn't hear the heels any more and I thought I'd hit him, that it was over but then I did hear something again. Not exactly the same sound but like the sound coming from a distance. It could have been Renee, it could have been someone else. I don't know. I'll never know. You understand? You listening? I've never shot anyone, I don't want to have killed him."

"You probably didn't. You heard the heels again, right?"

"Yah, but it sounded different."

"Course it did, cause it was farther away. Who else would it be? If someone else was there you woulda got your ass arrested."

"It was a miracle that no one else was there. A miracle." He started to shake.

"Where the gun now, Barry?"

"I got rid of it before I saw you. I got rid of it a long time ago."

"You ain't got no other, do you?"

"Not with me, no."

"You ain't mad at me neither, right? I been nice to you, haven't I?"

"Yah, don't worry. I like you fine," he said with a little laugh. Then he thought of something else.

"You're not gonna tell anyone what I told you, are you?"

"Course not. I ain't dumb. I may be a 'ho but I ain't dumb. I wouldn't do that."

"You sure?"

"Sure I'm sure. I don't blame you for what you did. You didn't want to have sex with no man. Shit—you didn't ask to be tricked that way. You just relax about that. You want me to suck your dick now?"

"No, no. I'm too out of it. Just let me lie down on you, OK?"

"On my titties."

"Yes, they're warm," he said. "You don't think I killed anyone?"

"Course not. You would have heard it or seen it. You would've heard the body fall. You wouldn't have heard no heels neither."

"So I didn't kill anyone, right?"

"No, just yourself with all your worryin'."

He laughed—she had a point. Finally he closed his eyes and was relieved that the snake and fish images were gone. At first, there was nothing but darkness with little pulsing specks of light, then gradually he saw an image of Elliot's blonde, Cheri, like a creature in a fairy tale—infinitely alluring. It was both disturbing but ultimately calming. Then he lay down on July's chest as if between two soft basketballs and felt he could sleep soon. That was the thing about basketball, you always knew if you made a basket. What kind of world was the rest of it when you couldn't even tell if you'd killed someone or not?

12

He was sitting on Barry's living room sofa, the same sofa where Barry had first pitched the idea of moving to New York.

"You see, it didn't take that long," Barry said from the kitchen where he was fixing them drinks.

"What didn't?"

"The move. It was less than four hours, I think. I told you that company was good. And there were no problems, right? Everything went smoothly."

"You were right. You've been right a lot lately. Plus I wound up putting most of my stuff in storage—it really can't compete with your furniture."

Barry was smiling as he walked into the living room carrying their drinks on a tray. He was wearing his favorite "wine drinking shirt," as he called it—the silver, silk shirt he'd bought in Rome. He put the tray down on a glass table but remained standing. Elliot stood up to take his vodka tonic, vaguely aware that a ritual of some kind was imminent.

"Salud," Barry said, clinking his glass against Elliot's. "To your New York life, to new beginnings."

They sat down, Elliot on the sofa in front of the windows, Barry in his blue velvet chair. He was looking at Elliot somewhat carefully but smiling at the corner of his lips at the same time. "So," Barry said, "are you happy now?"

"Yes, strangely enough, I am."

"Is it what Sartre would call a 'privileged moment'?"

"Yes, it is a privileged moment and I owe it all to you, of course."

"You owe me nothing," Barry said, making a disparaging gesture with his free hand.

"We'll have to agree to disagree about that. But I do insist on taking you to dinner. Have you thought about where you'd like to go?"

"I don't know about eating out."

"No, no. I really mean it. You have to."

"I think I might be better off just drinking a bit and eating cold cuts and ice cream right here. Here isn't bad, n'est-ce pas?" Barry said, indicating the living room with a brief gesture like a conductor paying homage on stage to the orchestra behind him.

"Here is great, I just wanted to buy you dinner."

"You can do that another time. The truth is, I'm a little tired. I've been going out a lot lately so I'm just a little stressed out. Stressed out from going out, capiche?"

Elliot laughed. "In other words, women."

"Something like that," Barry said, taking a long swallow of his drink. "The 'eternal feminine' is getting to be a daily grind. What about your eternal feminine, your Cheri? Have you called her yet to tell her you're all moved in?"

"I'll call her later."

"Why don't you try to see her tonight?"

"I'll see her tomorrow. Tonight is our night."

"Well, sorry to poop out on you," Barry said, smiling cryptically.

"So, what's going on? Anything you care to talk about?"

"Just tail chasing at different bars. Nothing that's going to lead to anything."

Barry finished his drink and poured himself another. "You look disappointed," Barry said.

"I'm not if you're not."

"I know I'm not going to meet the love of my life in those places. But I need *some* excitement, right?"

"Of course."

"Of course there's good excitement and bad excitement, isn't there?"

"That's also true."

"I guess I've been having too much bad excitement lately."

"By bad excitement you mean bad sex, or . . . ?"

"That the woman I pick up turns out to be a witch, or even worse and we never even have sex because I just can't stand her."

"Hmm, that *is* a drag. I remember that happening to me sometimes when I first came to Philadelphia and started answering the singles' ads. The horror of having to make conversation for an hour with someone you wish would just evaporate."

"The horror, the horror, as our friend Kurtz would put it," Barry said, returning to his drink.

"On the other hand," Elliot said, leaning forward as he spoke, "I did meet some interesting women through dating ads so maybe that's something you might try. I mean they even have personals in *The New York Review of Books*, don't they? Not to mention the internet, of course. Have you ever done Match.com or Yahoo?"

"No, Elliot. Those kinds of manipulations of reality aren't for me," he said, as he finished his second drink.

"But what *isn't* a manipulation of reality? When you drink isn't that a manipulation of reality, too?"

Barry laughed. "You may have a joint, I mean point," Barry said, laughing again.

"Speaking of which," Elliot said, "it's quite amazing how much you do drink and eat and yet you're in better shape than me. What's your secret?"

"I walk a lot. That's why New York is important for me—I can walk everywhere here. I only use a car when I leave the city."

"Hmm, maybe I'll eventually lose a little weight then, too."

"There are fewer fat people here, percentage-wise than anyplace in America. Haven't you noticed? You'll lose weight, too," Barry said. "Just walk everywhere, and sometimes run."

It was nine o'clock; they'd been talking for over three hours.

"Want some more cold cuts?"

"No, I'm stuffed," Elliot said.

"I can't resist a little more roast beef," Barry said. They were eating from paper plates on the glass table. A big box of chocolate ice cream was on the table as well as a bottle of coke, tonic water and vodka. From the right corner wall a TV was showing a basketball game without the sound on which Barry and Elliot looked at intermittently.

Barry fingered the bottle of vodka for a moment, saw a look of consternation pass briefly over Elliot's face, then switched to the long spoon sticking out of the ice cream box and scooped out a large chunk which he placed where the just devoured roast beef had been.

"I want to meet her," Barry said.

"Cheri?"

"Yes. She's obviously had a major impact on you, you've spent half the night talking about her."

"Sorry."

"I'm not criticizing you. I completely understand, but naturally I want to meet someone who's so important to you."

"OK," Elliot said, running his fingers across his forehead. "I'll set something up. What would work better for you, lunch or dinner?"

"Let's make it a dinner—it's more of an occasion that way."

"Fine, terrific. Would you like me to try to fix you up with one of her friends?"

Barry didn't answer right away, signaling that there was ice cream in his mouth.

"Does she have any cute friends?"

"I don't know. I assume she has friends . . . I guess I could try to find out if any of them are cute."

"Maybe it's simpler for it to just be the three of us the first time."

"No, no, don't worry about it. I'll ask, and I'll report back to you what the situation is right away so you can make your decision."

"I really just want to meet Cheri. I don't expect a fix up. It doesn't have to be a big deal."

"It's no big deal at all, for anyone. I know Cheri will want to meet you—I've told her all about you."

Barry raised his eyebrows and looked inquiringly at Elliot.

"Well, not all, don't worry. You're much too complicated to be summed up by anyone."

"Did you tell her about my mother?"

"No, not much. Just that she died and how close you were."

"What about my father?"

Elliot seemed surprised by the question. "Just that your parents divorced and you didn't see him much."

Barry nodded as if to show his approval. "There's something I've been wanting to ask you," Barry said. "Do you remember my father? I know you met him at least once."

"Yes, once, years ago before we were really close friends. I think I was in the sixth or seventh grade coming home from the playground carrying my basketball and you were riding in a car with your father and you called out my name and your father pulled over to the curb. I remember he had a nice smile and stuck out his hand to shake hands and said, 'Hi, my name is Manny. Want to hear a joke?' I nodded and he said, 'You know why your basketball's so dead? Because it's been shot so many times.' I laughed and you two laughed. That's about all I remember."

"He had a smile that could charm the world, or more likely con it," Barry said, with a strangely proud look in his eyes. "The smile of a king."

"Anyway, did you tell Cheri I'm a writer?"

"I told her you're a writer and a true Renaissance man. Believe me, she's really eager to meet you."

"I guess we'll have to do this on a day when you're not teaching. Otherwise the commute'll take too much out of you."

"Not necessarily. Like you said, the commute isn't that bad, and I've already learned to work on the train. It's all just a question of attitude or concentration. I can make it work to my advantage if I concentrate right."

"I told you you could do it."

"So I'll just get a couple of different possible nights from her and we'll do it on the one you want, whether I teach that day or not. OK?"

Barry shrugged and smiled slightly.

"So she's smart, too, your Cheri amour?"

Elliot smiled. "Yuh, she's smart. She's no ostentatious intellectual but she's very smart."

"Thank God."

"She's probably not an intellectual with a capital 'I' is all."

"How lucky for you. I've never been able to fuck an 'intellectual,' well, except for years ago with you know who."

Elliot assumed Barry was alluding to Susan Sontag, but since he'd never given that story any credence he didn't comment.

"Fucking an intellectual is almost a contradiction in terms, don't you think?"

Elliot laughed.

"No, really, I'm serious. It would be like fucking a woman body-builder or a wrestler."

"That might be fun."

"My point is it's getting harder and harder to find a woman who's really feminine, don't you think? Who really *is* a woman, capiche?"

13

Deux Amis was a French bistro on the East Side that managed to be both glamorous and a relaxing neighborhood restaurant. It had been a long time since Elliot had been on anything resembling a double date with Barry and he felt, if not exactly nervous, peculiarly hyper-conscious. As a result he hadn't been saying much but so far didn't think anyone had noticed. Barry seemed to be enjoying himself though he wasn't paying much attention to Gretchen, Cheri's friend, who was a little sharp featured, perhaps, but attractive—the kind of woman other women would say is pretty, Elliot thought, but definitely not Barry's type. He wasn't sure if she were an artist or a critic which made her (like Barry, now that he thought about it) representative of their times in which the boundary between the two was becoming increasingly blurred. Fortunately conversation thus far had stayed away from the arts, though that was bound to change sooner or later. Instead, they were discussing favorite vacation spots which Barry quickly turned into a game of "where would you live if money were no object?"

"Live, or just take a vacation?" Gretchen asked. She was wearing a red sweater and matching lipstick that emphasized the darkness of her hair.

"Good point," said Barry, already close to finishing his second drink. "How about both."

"All right. Money no object I'd live in Paris but I'd take my summers in Santa Barbara."

"Good choice, but why not in the South of France for your summer?"

"All right," Gretchen said, apparently warming to the task. "Number one, I wouldn't want to lose all contact with America and Santa Barbara is my favorite place in the States, especially with its climate in the summer. You know, it's pretty cool, has low humidity and good air, and the combination of mountains and ocean is hard to beat."

Elliot snuck a look at Cheri wondering if he would ever get to go to California with her, or more immediately get to go to bed. That was on his mind more than he cared to admit, even to himself, though he'd said nothing about it to her yet.

"What about you, Cheri?" Barry said, gesturing towards her with his now empty glass. "Where would you live?"

"Hmm . . . I haven't gotten to travel much yet in my life. I want to, but right now I wouldn't feel equipped to say."

"Well from what you've heard then?"

"I don't know, I like it here. New York is pretty much all I can handle right now."

Barry smiled, "Fair enough," he said. "How long have you been in the city?"

"Four, no, almost five years, I think."

"How about four and a half?" Barry said with a laugh, his voice changing almost as if he were talking to a child. Cheri laughed too and blushed slightly while Elliot finished his drink.

"Elliot tells me you're an art critic and, more importantly, a painter."

"An aspiring painter, I haven't really had any shows yet—at least not in New York. And I'm definitely not an art critic—that's what Gretchen does. I just write about the social side of the art world and . . ."

"Oh really?"

"Gretchen's the real art critic. She's really excellent. She writes for *Art Forum* a lot and does freelance movie reviews too."

Barry nodded, but kept his eyes focused on Cheri. "I'd like to see your work sometime. Elliot speaks very highly of it."

"Oh sure," Cheri said, "that would be great."

"Yes, it's really strong," Elliot said, realizing that "strong" wasn't the right word at all to describe her hazy, sensitive painting. "Neo-impressionist" might have been better but would have sounded absurd coming out of his mouth especially at a table of art critics. He remembered how attracted he felt towards her during the twenty minutes he spent in her tiny apartment looking at her work. He remembered the tense elevator ride up with her (she'd surprised him by meeting him in the lobby) then once in her room how he'd tried to avoid looking at her bed, wondering if she was feeling awkward too and more importantly if she were feeling any kind of attraction towards him. Since they'd first kissed at the end of their day in Philadelphia he'd been able to feel somewhat reassured but two weeks had passed since then and that reassurance had faded, been reduced now to something like a wild hope.

He thought of Lianne, and the times the two of them and Barry would sit in Cambridge cafés talking about favorite authors or movies. Now, as then, he'd felt a curious mix of exhilaration and anxiety, and the uncomfortable feeling that Barry was letting himself get attracted to his girlfriend in the wrong way. Meanwhile, both Barry and he were almost completely ignoring Gretchen.

"Who do you write your movie reviews for?" Elliot said to Gretchen.

"Let's see. I've done a few for *The Voice* and a couple for *The New York Observer*. I do longer pieces for *Film Comment* and sometimes for literary magazines."

"I'm planning to start a literary magazine," Barry said. "That will also include the other arts. So maybe I'll be soliciting some work from you."

"Great, just let me know," said Gretchen.

Elliot stared hard at Barry.

"You look surprised, Elliot. I was planning to tell you very soon. I just made my decision about it today."

"Really?"

"Of course. Needless to say I want to do it with you. We'll talk about it later. Why don't we drink a toast to it now?"

Elliot raised his glass, surprised that this hand was trembling slightly. Everyone else raised their glasses too, waiting for Barry who had a big, if slightly cryptic smile on his face.

"To old times and old friends and to new magazines and new friends."

Everyone's glass clinked with distinct clarity as if the steady hum of talk and laughter around them had suddenly ceased.

"Now wait," Barry said, suddenly producing a small disposable camera. "I'm going to get a waiter to take a picture of us all. This moment should be commemorated, don't you think? The moment when literature and friendship triumph."

He was sitting next to Cheri in the cab, wondering what she thought of the dinner. They'd all been talking animatedly, mostly about the magazine, until Gretchen got out of the cab at Lexington and 88th (Barry had already walked home after kissing the women goodnight in front of the restaurant and giving him a big bear hug). The bear hug surprised him and made him realize Barry had gotten pretty high. Now he suddenly couldn't think of anything to say. Cheri was looking out the window—there were lots of lights out, it was a pretty drive. Finally, she turned towards him and asked if he was all right.

"I'm good . . . I was wondering about you."

"I'm fine. I had a terrific time. Barry is really…amazing, just like you said…you must be excited about the magazine."

"I am . . ."

"So, did you like Gretchen?"

"Oh sure, she's very bright, very nice."

He looked out the window himself; they were getting closer to The Village where she lived on Grove Street.

"Maybe you're a little tired," she said, half to herself, as she removed her hand from his. "Or maybe you're a little disappointed in me?"

"Why do you say that?" he said, turning to face her.

"I'm not exactly a sparkling conversationalist—especially at dinners like that, and tonight it was kind of noisy and with all the background noise I couldn't always hear everything," she said, pointing to her hearing aids.

"You were perfect. I'm not disappointed at all in you. How could I be?" he said, rubbing his hand slowly against her forehead and feeling her hair. "I'm only disappointed that I have to leave you. That makes me kind of sad."

"Would you like to come up for a while?"

"Of course I would. That . . ."

"My place is a mess but . . ."

He moved closer to her. She touched his face in response and then they kissed slowly two or three times.

He overpaid the driver, leaving without his change, and held her hand as they crossed the street, then kept holding it as they went up the elevator. He wanted to kiss her in the elevator but didn't want to risk acting like he assumed her invitation to her apartment meant they'd make love. He wasn't a child, he reminded himself, and shouldn't act disappointed if she wasn't ready.

"Sorry that things look the way they do," she said gesturing towards her apartment.

"It's quite neat compared to the places I've lived."

"You want anything to eat or drink?" she said, walking into the kitchen area.

Just you, he thought, walking behind her, though the idea of having a drink with her did suddenly seem appealing. "Something to drink would be nice."

"OK, OK," she said, opening the door to her small refrigerator. "Let's see what I have." For the first time she sounded nervous and he felt a little sorry for her and even more attracted. "Oops, I'm afraid I don't have anything alcoholic I can give you."

"Oh. You don't drink then?"

"Sometimes. I did tonight at the restaurant, but no, it's not really part of my life. I usually have a bottle of wine around, though, in case a friend is over. Sorry I don't have that for you."

"It doesn't matter," he said. He was battling a flash of jealousy imagining her giving wine to other men. Then he remembered her describing Barry as "amazing," a remark he now thought would live in his mind forever.

"I'm afraid I just have apple juice or Coke or else some good old American water."

"Apple juice sounds nice," he said, to be polite. She poured him a glass, finally turning towards him so he could take it from her.

"I'm sorry about this. It's pretty embarrassing. I need to do some shopping."

He drank the apple juice quickly, putting the glass on the counter.

"Tell me what you like to drink so when I go shopping I can get it for you."

"You," he said, taking her face in his hands and kissing her several times.

"I'm crazy about you," he said. "I love you already, I think. I do."

"Oh," she said. He saw little tears in her eyes. "Would you like to stay over tonight?"

"Yes, I'd love to. I accept."

"I really wasn't expecting this."

"Neither was I," he said, putting his right arm around her. "I can't believe someone like you exists. Everything you say is so fresh, so new, do you know what I mean?"

"I feel the same about you and your writing, too, by the way. It's tremendous."

"Thanks," he said, trying not to focus on her compliment that he'd been yearning for. "I've just never met anyone even remotely like you. I wish there were a new dictionary filled with different words that would be better at describing you."

She laughed and kissed him on the forehead. "Want to lie down now?" she half whispered in his ear.

He hadn't thought about what she'd be like in bed, as if it were off limits to his imagination. Many people of course, had a bedroom persona almost the opposite of the one they showed the world. It was so common; in fact, it was almost the norm and made speculations about what someone would be like to make love to completely futile.

But even before they undressed he realized Cheri was no "sexual schizophrenic." She was passionate, but also modest, oddly innocent in a way and seemingly totally unedited. "I can't tell whether to take my hearing aids out or not," she said. "It's a little more comfortable with them out, but if you're going to talk to me while we make love I want to be sure to hear you. Do you think you will?"

"Probably."

"OK, I'll keep them in then."

Afterwards, they held hands with the covers up close to their necks. He could hear and feel the heat hissing from her radiator, and smell traces of her paintings in the air. He decided he would look more closely at her work that was all around them in the morning but for now didn't want to move.

"That was magical," she said.

"I know, it's almost scary for it to be so good the first time when it's usually so awkward and disappointing, like some kind of vaudeville act that doesn't quite work, you know, some unintended comedy."

She turned towards him and kissed him. "I'm so glad I know you, that we know each other. Just think if we hadn't met . . ."

"You mean if I hadn't literally bumped into you at that party. Talk about vaudeville acts . . . at last my lifelong clumsiness finally paid off."

She laughed. "You weren't clumsy in bed. You were a magician, *my* magician."

He squeezed her hand and kissed the side of her head, then lay back and closed his eyes. He heard the radiator again and felt her hand relax, and suddenly wondered what Barry was doing. For as long as he could remember Barry typically went to sleep very late. Since he'd never had a regular job he could get away with sleeping till ten thirty or eleven the next morning. Then he thought about the magazine, and remembered how he felt his heart beat when Barry made his surprise announcement. Why had Barry done it that way—when he thought about it he was angry (or perhaps "hurt" would be closer to it) that Barry had kept his plans a secret and told him at the same time as he told Cheri and Gretchen.

Barry was probably watching Sports Center or an old movie on the American Movie Channel now or maybe listening to a radio talk show while he ate his chocolate chip ice cream. He could see him so clearly in his apartment in his underpants and undershirt sitting in the blue velvet chair as he had sat in his Lazy Boy in less prosperous days—looking relaxed and contented but nowhere near sleep.

He tightened his grip on her hand. He could feel himself getting erect again. It surprised him that it was happening so quickly and he wondered if he shouldn't simply leave well enough alone, since things had worked out so well the first time. He gave her a tentative, investigative kiss on the forehead and she surprised him by kissing him back on the lips and then touching him. The next thing he knew their tongues were in each others' mouths and their legs entwined.

14

Barry was writing on yellow notebook paper. His penmanship was small, slanted, cramped and close to illegible for most people but Elliot would be able to read it. First he drew a line down the middle of the page with some semblance of a ruler he managed to find. On top of the left hand side he wrote "Expenses," on the right "Income." Under expenses he wrote the estimates he'd received for printing 5,000 copies of a two hundred page magazine and then the estimates for typesetting, author's payments, mailing and website maintenance, and the salary for one paid helper he'd call managing editor. In the income column he wrote estimates for various potential grants from the New York State Council of the Arts, the National Endowment for the Arts, to the Coordinating Council of Literary Magazine "seed grants" as well as estimated income from subscriptions, and sales (figuring in the distributor's fifty percent cut from an eight dollar cover price) and charitable contributions *if* he decided to make the magazine a nonprofit organization, which was the route most literary magazines took.

On the second page he wrote a list of potential titles: *Minotaur, Cold Ocean, The International Review, No Exit, The Aleph, The Beekman Place Review*, etc. He knew Elliot would want to contribute some titles of his own. It would be fun to talk about it over some beers at his place or in a café or bar. He decided to leave the pages out on the living room table in front of the sofa where Elliot liked to sit so he couldn't miss it. He could picture him coming home from work, having just ridden the train to Grand Central then switching to an uptown line or perhaps walking home as he sometimes did now that he had Cheri and a real incentive to get in shape. He'd probably been blissed out last night, having finally nailed her, but even so, much of that would be faded by another pedestrian day at his school and then the numbing commute, where he was not quite able to read or sleep and where he would have to face his anonymity again which is what New York did to people of course, reduced your ego to the size of a peanut keeping you hopeless but addicted to the hope of success simultaneously.

Then Elliot would walk into the apartment, sit down to

narcoticize himself with more TV again and there in front of him on the coffee table would be the figures and names for the magazine like a blue print to a different world. He was glad he'd handwritten them instead of using the computer. It was more dramatic this way. He could almost feel the new life that would suddenly suffuse Elliot. In the grand scope of things, to bring someone life made up for making someone else lose theirs, didn't it?

If Elliot took his usual train, the earliest one which he always took unless he had a meeting or something else he had to do at school, he should be walking in the building any minute, then calling or better still using his key and just walking into Barry's apartment, although Elliot usually called first. Actually, he was glad that Elliot was so deferential. He had a perpetual fear of being a buttinsky, which was a welcome trait, especially in New York.

Of course he might not come directly home. He didn't know any of the details from last night but if things had gotten really hot he might go straight to Cheri's place and do her again.

Barry wrote one last title, then got up from his blue velvet chair and went into the kitchen. He was suddenly feeling hungry and opened his refrigerator scanning the contents excitedly. But there was nothing exciting there, or even appealing. He was going to go to a deli or else to Azure, the huge Korean take out buffet, when he decided on a couple of carrots which he started slicing rapidly by the sink.

Yes, Elliot had struck gold with Cheri. She was pretty and probably had a better body than one might imagine because she dressed down all the time. She was a little shy, too, maybe because of her hearing aids, but sometimes the quiet, modest ones were the hottest once you got them in bed. Physically she actually looked a bit like Love Hunt, only Love Hunt was thinner and had better legs, but Cheri's face was more refined. Though he complained and felt sorry for himself all the time, Elliot was really very lucky when it came to women. First there was Lianne and now Cheri. Even Elliot's mother was still alive and showed no signs of slowing down. By comparison what had he had? A slut like Love Hunt, his mother's ashes in the urn lost somewhere in the world . . . he thought of Jordan for a second, saw her shocked face, then looked at the sink and saw blood. He'd just cut himself. He dropped the knife in the sink and ran to the bathroom to get a Band-Aid.

It was hard to say what happened to Elliot, who didn't call him until half past six.

"I missed my usual train," Elliot said, so he supposed that's what happened. With complicated people like Elliot he'd long ago decided to take what they said at face value—difficult though that often was to do. Why was it so difficult, he asked himself, while pacing around the living room and intermittently squeezing his bandaged finger. Because people like Elliot had multiple motivations behind almost everything they did and to start delving into *that* was an invitation to madness.

Barry had just finished his second glass of wine when Elliot walked into his apartment. One look at him and he could tell what happened at Cheri Amour's. It was that same dazed, little boy awestruck expression that Elliot had when he once scored 23 points in a high school basketball game.

"Vidi, vici, veni?" Barry said, barely looking up at him. Elliot smiled sheepishly.

"It was very nice."

"*Nice?*" Barry said, irritated by Elliot's typical understatement with all the multiple reasons that lay behind it.

"It was more than nice."

"How much more?"

"It was extraordinary."

"In your top ten?"

"Come on, Barry. I don't want to think of it that way."

"Mon Dieu! This is really serious then."

Elliot smiled again. "Yes, I guess it is."

"Guess or know?"

"Jesus, can't we have a conversation instead of a quiz show."

Barry laughed, then finally looked at Elliot. "You're right. I'm being silly." He suddenly extended his hand. "Congratulations, seriously, congratulations for having Cheri in your life. She's great. She's a great person."

Elliot shook his hand. "Thank you," he said softly. "I don't deserve her."

"Yes you do. You're one of the nicest men in New York, maybe in the world—accept it. So, are you gonna see her tonight?"

"No, no plans to."

"Any other special plans?"

"No other special plans."

"Well, that's about to change. I thought we might talk a bit about the magazine tonight."

"Oh yes, I was wondering about that."

"Sit down, look at what's on the table in front of you."

"Ah," said Elliot, picking up a page and holding it close to his face like a mask. "You must have spent a lot of time on this, I can actually read it."

Barry laughed. "What do you think?" he said, pacing off a few steps before stopping just in front of his chair.

"Did you research these figures? Are they accurate?"

"Yes, they're accurate."

"Looks good. Very impressive. You've done a lot of work on this I wasn't aware of."

"Sorry I was so secretive about it. After all these years I wanted to get something down on paper before I showed it to you."

"Well, like I say, I'm impressed."

"Look at the other page. They're potential titles for the magazine."

"*Cold Ocean*, huh?"

"Not all of them are equally serious contenders. What do you think? Naturally I'm hoping you'll contribute some title ideas."

"Some of these are interesting. *The Beekman Place Review* sounds nice, or maybe just *Beekman Place*. That might be my favorite from the list."

"It's my favorite, too. See, we're agreeing already."

Elliot smiled for a second. "So how can I help? What role, if any, do you want me to play in all of this?"

Barry sat down and looked carefully at Elliot. "I want you to edit it with me, of course. Just like we always planned."

"OK. But from a practical point of view, how's that gonna work?"

"We'll split it up. I thought you'd edit fiction, I'd edit the essays and book reviews, and we'd divide up the poetry since it's not exactly our forte."

"True. And where exactly will the magazine be located?"

"Here of course. That's the beauty of it. No money wasted on office space. The world will come to us."

"So let me understand . . ."

"There's nothing to understand. We each have two bedroom apartments. We can each have our own office. This magazine will really be *The Beekman Place Review* because it will be located on two floors at Beekman Place. Not a bad address for a literary magazine, n'est-ce pas? Unless, of course, you don't want to have an office, if you'd feel too cramped."

"No, no, it's the least I could do. You should be listed as Editor-in-Chief, though."

"No, we'll be co-editors, Elliot, editorial equals, I insist."

"At least be listed as publisher then. I mean, it is your money."

"Let me think about that. I'm not sure I'll want to especially since I'll probably want to run my own stuff, at least in the beginning and it wouldn't look right to be listed as publisher. Let's see about that."

"You have something to drink?" Elliot said.

"Of course."

"This is all getting a little too exciting for me."

"Red wine all right?"

"Sure."

"It's from Chile, cheap but good," Barry said, pouring a glass for Elliot from a bottle he hadn't noticed before.

Elliot took a good-sized swallow, set his glass on the table and looked closely at Barry. "So, how does this all get started? How do we become a magazine?"

"My lawyer will help us there. We'll have to get incorporated. He'll probably advise us to get nonprofit status so people can make tax deductible contributions to us."

"But how do people even become aware that we exist?"

"We tell them," Barry said, with unusual intensity. "We send emails to writers and to key literary blogs, we send to agents and the media and get business cards to give out and we advertise in lit mags and on the net. It doesn't take long in New York for something to get known. There are lots of writers here and they're always on the lookout to pounce on new markets. As long as we do things in a first class way, there'll be an instant buzz about us. That's why the first thing we have to do, besides talk with my lawyer, is to get a good designer so our stationery and business cards will look first class and, of course, our website too. I have a couple of potential webmasters in mind—naturally I'd like you to meet them or at least see their work before we decide anything."

"Sure," Elliot said, drinking more of his wine. "But how do we get the material for the first issue, and how do we physically get that first issue into stores and get people to buy it?"

"Those are all good, understandable questions. As I said, we place ads with a call for manuscripts in *Poets and Writers* and we write letters or send emails to writers we admire asking them for material. I think we need at least three stars in the first issue to give people an incentive to buy us. Then we take the first issue to a distributor who'll probably give us a trial run in New York while we make sure it sells. We throw a party for the first issue inviting the press and if we have to, we buy the issue ourselves to make sure the distributor keeps us, and gives us national distribution. Then it's up to us. We have to keep it first class. It has to rise above all the others, be something people will instantly start talking about, capiche?"

Elliot finished his wine and smiled. "So it looks like this is really happening."

"It's definitely happening."

"And it looks like it's really gonna be a pretty big deal."

"I only do big deals, Elliot. You should know that by now."

"It's gonna take a lot of work."

"I realize that."

"And you're ready to start now?"

"Absolument. No time like the present, am I right?"

"So how should we divvy up the work?"

"I can do most of the preliminary stuff, that's only fair, right? Since you have to teach and ride that train three days a week."

"I can help, if you want me to."

"Of course I do and you will. But for right now, I'll call my lawyer and set up bank accounts and work with our getting incorporated and make appointments with the designer about the website. Obviously we have to have a very strong internet presence."

"I thought you wanted me to help with the designer?"

"I do want you to weigh in on it. I said that. Believe me, I want you to help me with everything. You're my partner, Elliot, and you'll soon be complaining about there being too much work."

Elliot laughed and pushed back some hair that was hanging over his eyes.

"So you don't feel any ambivalence about this at all?"

"Anxiety yes, ambivalence no. It is possible to live without ambivalence; I discovered that with my mother, Elliot. I only wish she were here now to witness this meeting and then the birth of our magazine."

"Yes, of course."

"No, there's no ambivalence. Why should there be? You don't feel any ambivalence about Cheri, do you?"

Elliot paused a moment. "No, incredibly, I don't think so."

"You see," said Barry. "You're probably a lot less ambivalent than you realize. In fact, you're probably well on your way to becoming the Unambivalent Man."

"Love is never having to be ambivalent, huh?" Elliot said, with a little laugh.

"Well, I wouldn't go that far. Of course you'll be ambivalent about lots of little things but you'll never be ambivalent about wanting her as your lover, am I right? Does that seem like a good definition of love?"

"Not bad on a first hearing. I'll have to think about it a bit," Elliot said, smiling, until he noticed that Barry's hopeful smile had faded and was replaced with the same look of disappointment he had all those years ago when he found out he wouldn't be starting at shortstop. "It is a pretty ingenious definition though, the more I think about it, it's pretty wise."

A little of Barry's smile returned, not as much as was there before but at least the expression on his face had normalized.

"So you're not ambivalent about the magazine," Elliot said, "and I'm not ambivalent about my girlfriend and soon I won't be ambivalent about the magazine either, in fact, I think I'm already less ambivalent about it which would put me ahead of you unambivalence-wise two to one, and frankly, being ahead of you in something like that makes me ambivalent."

Barry laughed deeply, no doubt nursed along by the wine. "All of which means that we need to find you a woman you feel less ambivalent about, too," Elliot said.

"I won't argue with you there," Barry said, with a sudden seriousness that took Elliot by surprise. "I keep looking but I don't find."

"Maybe you're not looking in the right places. Maybe bars aren't the best place to look."

"I think the magazine will help me there, too. I think I'll meet her through the magazine, don't you?"

15

"You sound surprised to hear from me. Are you?" Barry said.

"No…well, yes, maybe a little."

There was a short silence and Cheri scratched her neck. Fortunately she got the phone back to her ear just in time to hear his next question.

"I hope I'm not calling at a bad time."

"No, not at all. It's good to hear from you. How've you been?" she said in an upbeat voice.

"Well enough, well enough…I've been busy with the magazine lately."

"Oh, of course. Elliot told me."

"That's one of the reasons I called. I'm very eager to see your work because we're going to be featuring art in the magazine…"

"Yuh, I remember you said that at the restaurant…"

"What would be a good time then…to see your work?"

"Oh, anytime would be good."

"How about now?"

"Now? You mean right now?"

Barry laughed. "I happen to be in the Village near your neck of the woods. I just finished seeing the work of a prospective designer."

"Oh."

"So I left his studio, looked up and saw Grove Street and thought I'd give you a call on my cell just in case you were in…Elliot gave me your number."

"Oh sure. Great. How close are you?"

"Less than a block. You sound hesitant. Is something the matter?"

"Well, my place is a mess. I didn't know you were coming, so…"

"Please, my whole life is a mess, not to mention my apartment. I promise not to look at your place, or if I do, to forget what I see. I promise to only look at your paintings."

Strange how people felt when they were surprised the way she was surprised now, he thought, with no expectation of your coming and so no preparation for it either. The odd mix of pleasure that someone thought of you, coupled with anxiety for what they would see without their having prepared.

He was staring right now at her refrigerator—at the little notes and photographs on the door. It all looked like a marriage of the bourgeois and the bohemian. Typical, sentimental, kitschy possessions adrift in a mess of clothes and papers. Finally he looked back at the canvas in front of him with its fragile lines and delicate colors.

"I like this one a lot."

"Thank you," she said, looking down at the floor while he looked quickly at her slightly bent body. She was wearing a gray jersey she'd put on quickly after his call—she'd barely had time to comb her hair and wasn't wearing any lipstick.

"I like the way people are hinted at, suggested by very faint lines as if they're ghosts half-submerged in the background. I like the others too, of course."

He looked at her as if for approval.

"Thank you . . . you speak about painting better than I write about it. I guess that's why I'll never be a critic."

"Believe me, I'd far rather be able to paint like you than to write like Meyer Shapiro, or Harold Rosenberg, or any other art critic."

"Well, thank you again, you've really made my day."

"Now about the magazine . . . I'm not sure . . ."

"Oh no," she said, raising a hand and half waving it at him. "I wasn't thinking about that. Just that you liked some of my work made my day . . . that's what I meant."

"But I do want to use it in the magazine and the other one, the one in the corner. You interrupted me before I could say it."

"Oh, sorry about that," she said, slapping the side of her thigh in mock punishment.

"I'm not sure either would be right for the cover, though."

"Oh sure, I can see that."

"But they could work well inside, I think."

"Thank you a lot, that's wonderful news."

He stared at her, nodding his head slowly. "So," he said, "here we are."

"Here we are," she repeated. "It's not much of a *here* though, I'm afraid."

He laughed a little. "I think your place is charming, it's adorable."

She blushed for a moment and he wondered what it was like to be a woman and blush, to feel that exact sensation in your mind and body.

"Can we sit down and talk for a few minutes?"

"My only chairs are by the table in the kitchen. Is that all right?"

"That's fine," he said. "The table is adorable, too."

She supposed it was magical thinking but it worked for her, so what did it matter if it was magic—the world needed more magic anyway, not less. All she knew was that since she stopped analyzing things and just started accepting them the way she had before she moved to New York, things began to get better. It wasn't like she had gone to church or to a therapist and had a revelation or something like that, it was just an internal decision she'd made gradually after her first year in New York when things hadn't gone so well. Fortunately she'd already changed before she met Elliot. She could have doubted him any number of times in the beginning but she just stuck with her basic good feeling about him and accepted everything he said at face value and it all worked out better than she could have imagined. People responded well to being trusted, she knew she did. In fact, (and this was probably more "magical thinking") she thought if you trusted people, it actually made them more honest.

She was sitting opposite Barry now and feeling nervous. She knew he was Elliot's best friend, which should be all she needed to know to trust him, but she couldn't get rid of the uncomfortable feeling she had, like walking into a test unprepared.

"I get the feeling something is upsetting you, am I right?" Barry said.

He moved a little closer to her at the table and looked at her closely, like a policeman studying a suspect.

"Oh no. What would I be upset about?"

"Maybe 'upset' is too strong a word. Something seems to be on your mind."

She shrugged and felt her face reddening.

"You have a very open face, probably because you're a very honest person and it's not that hard to read, am I right?"

"My mother used to tell me that. She could always tell when I ate a cookie I wasn't supposed to or stole a quarter from her purse, so after a while there didn't seem to be any point in doing either. I guess I became honest by default."

He laughed and she said, "Speaking of cookies, would you like to have one?"

"Would I like to have one?"

"Yes, to eat . . . as a snack."

He continued laughing and she, herself, laughed a little and thought of the wine in the refrigerator and that she could offer him that (and would like to have a glass herself) but probably shouldn't.

"Thank you, I'd love to have one of your cookies," he said, looking closely at her again. "It would hit the spot."

She got up from the table and opened a cabinet door. She felt he was looking at her while her back was to him.

"I just have store cookies, Oreos and some Vanilla Chessmen."

"An Oreo would be fine. Chessmen sound too intellectual to eat."

"Oh, wait, I do have a few sugar cookies I made a couple of nights ago. I don't know how well they turned out," she said, turning to face him.

He looked at her, eyes moving up and down her body as if on rapid escalators.

"I'm sure they turned out great. I'd love to try your sugar cookies."

She turned away quickly and opened the refrigerator. "I can only offer you some water or pineapple juice to drink."

"Pineapple sounds good. Let me have your pineapple juice."

She took it out and poured it into a glass. She would have to ignore what he was saying that seemed to be all double entendres though at the same time said with just enough sincerity or ambiguity that she couldn't accuse him of anything. She put two cookies on a plate for him—the last two—and gave herself an Oreo. He bit into the cookie.

"Hmm, this is excellent. You can paint *and* cook. Elliot's very lucky to have you . . . *really* lucky."

"Thank you. I'm lucky to have him, too, don't you think?"

"Of course. And I'm lucky to have Elliot, too, as my neighbor and best friend in all the world. I guess Elliot is the kind of person a lot of people are lucky to have—in their lives."

"I'll drink to that," she said, raising her glass. He raised his glass, making it clink against hers.

"He's lucky to have you, too," she added quickly after the toast. "You've been so generous to him."

He nodded once, and then looked away. "You know in many ways I am lucky, I know that, and this is an exciting time in my life with the start of the magazine and being reunited with my best friend but two things are haunting me, one is my mother...I still really miss her."

"Of course. I can't imagine what I'd feel if I lost mine."

"It changes everything, believe me. Especially in my case when I don't have any relationship with my father...anyway that's not going to change, not with my mother or with my father. I've learned to live with that. In the first months after she died I didn't know if I could live with it and I thought about ending it sometimes but, here I am, n'est-ce pas? Here I am, with my best friend and his wonderful girlfriend in the greatest city in the world about to start what will become, I hope, the greatest literary magazine in the world. I just wish I had someone to share it with, a woman to love like Elliot has, capiche?"

"What did you think of Gretchen,? Or maybe I shouldn't put you on the spot."

"She's a very bright, nice woman and I'd like to involve her in the magazine. But no, she isn't my type, romantically."

"Well . . . if I think of someone else . . ."

"Oh no, I didn't mean to have you do that, although if it happens I do seem to be eternally available."

"You never know. I meet women from time to time…you'd be surprised how many of them are alone and searching like you."

"I wouldn't say that I'm searching exactly. If I was *searching* with a capital 'S' I would have found someone by now."

"Oh of course, I'm sure you would have."

"My problem is I can't get sufficiently motivated and now that I'm so busy with the magazine on top of my own writing it makes it even harder and then I begin to get discouraged."

"Sure. Anyone would."

"Believe me, I *have* tried and I've had some horrendous dating experiences."

Cheri laughed inadvertently, slapping her thigh again, as if to discipline herself.

"Sorry, I didn't mean to laugh."

"Believe me, I see the humor in it."

"It was just something in the way you said it that made me think of some of my own horrible dates."

"Mine were a lot worse than ordinary horrible dates. They were living nightmares."

"Really? What happened?"

Barry shook his head from side to side slowly but said nothing. Then he looked up and smiled cryptically. "It's not something I can talk about very easily."

"And it's none of my business either, of course. I just hope there's *someone* you can talk to about it. I just believe that does some good."

"Really?"

"Yes, I do."

"Unfortunately, these aren't the kind of experiences you can tell anyone. They're a little beyond the pale. But if I ever were going to tell anyone, you'd be the kind of person I'd tell."

"Thank you, that's . . ."

"Because you're so kind and sensitive, and very understanding too."

"Well, gee, thank you," she said softly. She could feel her face reddening while her mind cast about quickly for something else to say but all she could think of was to ask what kind of woman he was looking for.

"Someone kind and sensitive and understanding . . . like I was saying," he said, looking directly at her, "and someone—how should I put this—who doesn't necessarily have to be beautiful but who's feminine. Believe me, that's not as easy as it sounds. Not these days. You'd be surprised how many borderline types there are out there. How many women—at least they dress like women—are out there who really want to be men. It's frightening."

Cheri stared at him, unable to say anything.

"Of course I don't mean you. You're at the opposite end of the spectrum. You're extremely feminine in everything you do. Elliot's incredibly lucky to have you."

"Why don't we call him now and ask him over?" Cheri said, backing up in her seat and beginning to stand up. "It would be a nice surprise, don't you think?"

"It would, but he's teaching today. He won't be home for another three hours."

"Oh yuh, that's right," she said, standing behind her chair now.

"It would have been a nice surprise though. Years ago, when we both lived in Boston, in Brookline to be precise, Elliot and his girlfriend and me used to go everywhere together—the movies, restaurants, parties, cafés. We were like the three musketeers."

"Sounds like fun."

"It was. It was great fun."

"How'd you feel about taking a walk now?" she suddenly blurted.

"A walk?"

"That's not much of an adventure for a Musketeer, but I was hoping to get a little exercise in before I go back to work."

"Sure, I can walk. Where do you want to go?"

"How about the park?"

"Washington Square?"

"Yuh. I go there a lot. Do you too?"

Barry smiled. "All too often, I'm afraid."

"We could go somewhere else then, it doesn't matter."

"No, no. I don't mind going there. What I meant was, well the truth is I often go there to buy pot."

"Really? Isn't that dangerous?"

"Hasn't been so far."

"Don't the police kind of camp out there to try to catch people?"

"Oh well, one can't start worrying about the police. Come on, let's walk. It'll be fine."

"OK," she said, turning towards the door—stopping only to put on her coat and to pick up her keys from a small circular table near her sofa.

"Let's walk downstairs," she said, "do you mind?"

"Très bien," Barry said, following behind her.

Outside it was cold and blue. The sun seemed to be shining directly on her face. She forced herself not to walk ahead of him. She was afraid her face was turning red from the sun and cold and because of the situation itself that embarrassed her. Women's faces were always turning red, she thought, whether from sex, lying, compliments or insults.

She was walking beside him now. The sidewalks were narrow and crowded—Christmas shopping was dominating the Village, which was now essentially an extended shopping center. Just before the curb a teenage boy bumped her shoulder and probably said he was sorry though she couldn't hear him.

"What did he say?" Barry said, stopping in his tracks and making her look at him for the first time since they'd been outside. He looked genuinely angry, as if he were ready to start a fight with the boy.

"It was an accident. It was nothing."

"He bumped into you. I don't think that's nothing. What did he say?"

"He said he was sorry."

"He better have," Barry said sternly, before resuming his walk.

She tried to walk next to him but lagged a step behind the way she used to lag behind her older brother who was a great one for starting fights too. She wanted to disappear now, or at least to be alone, anything but this walk in the crowded cold that seemed to have been going on for a century, or at least for most of her life.

When they reached the park, and the arch first came into sight, she caught a brief glimpse of Barry without his noticing. The sun was shining directly above him and in the glare his face looked distorted, almost preternatural. It was strange how two people, like Barry and Elliot, could be the same age and size but if one of them took a step too near the sun, as Barry had now, he could deviate so sharply from the other, as if grotesquely lighted from within. Cheri moved a step closer to look at Barry's face again and realized he was smiling. It was one of the strangest smiles she'd ever seen.

16

Cheri was looking at herself in the mirror of her tiny bathroom. She wanted to see how Elliot had seen her this morning and she wasn't pleased with what she saw. She should have checked her eyebrows *before* he came over, and possibly done something about that vengeful zit that had set up residence on her chin. Why couldn't she be like other women and be proactive about her appearance? Why, instead, did she always seem to be reacting to ambushes she could have prevented if she'd just remembered to check in time?

The evening hadn't been a success. Elliot was as sweet as ever but she knew he wasn't as happy as he usually was, though he'd never admit it. How could he be, tense and strange as she was acting because of Barry's visit, though she tried to cover it up and had decided to not even tell Elliot about it. And then this morning when she couldn't come again—that was the cherry on a very poor sundae. What was the matter with her—was it this Barry business again, along with the memories it stirred up?

She felt herself give way to a kind of panicky feeling and left the bathroom looking out the window of her studio at New Yorkers on their way to work. Still, Elliot couldn't have been nicer about it and she supposed it was good that they didn't dodge the issue or obsess about it either. She tried to reconstruct their conversation of just a half hour ago. Elliot had turned on his side and reached for his underpants that were still sitting there like a white cap on the wave of her bed.

"I'm sorry," she'd said, or something like that.

"Don't be ridiculous," he said, putting them on with his back to her. "There's nothing to be sorry for."

"Yes there is."

"What are you talking about?" he said, turning to face her with a look of mock exasperation, she thought.

"We're both happier when I'm able to, right?"

"Nobody does it every time. There'll be a time probably when I won't be able to and it won't have anything to do with you either."

"I think I missed your voice."

"You wanted me to talk more to you?" he'd said, as if he'd just discovered a terrible mistake he'd made.

"No, what you said and what you did were great, I just didn't hear you as well because I took my hearing aids out—didn't you notice?"

"No, but I'm not exactly the world's most observant person."

"Well I did," she said, reaching for them on her dressing table and saying "see?" as she put them in her ears.

"Why did you take them out then?"

She'd told him she wanted to feel his face against her ears for once without the hearing aids making all that noise when he brushed against them. And that part of it was very nice. But she'd missed hearing his voice. What she was saying was true but she knew it wasn't the real reason she didn't have an orgasm.

"It's fine, it's not a big deal," he'd finally said, running his finger softly across her cheek. "I'm crazy about you. I love you."

"I love you too," she said, a few seconds later. He smiled and continued getting dressed. Then for a few seconds he looked at her as if trying to divine her thoughts, but she walked towards him and gave a peremptory kiss and he said nothing. Then they made their plans about lunch on Tuesday and a movie the next night. How could he have handled it any better? How lucky she was to have him but how long would her luck last the way she was acting? She went to the phone and called Gretchen.

"Hi, it's me. Did I wake you?"

"No way. How are you? How was last night with Elliot?"

"I didn't tell him about Barry."

"Why not?"

"I don't know. Things are so fragile—they're good but they're fragile too and I just didn't want to upset him. So I chickened out."

"Hmm. Of course, Barry may tell *him*."

"I don't know, I suppose he will, or might. I guess there's a good chance that can happen."

"Won't Elliot wonder why you didn't mention it then? What will you say, that it was so unimportant it skipped your mind?"

"Sometimes when I go over it all, I do think it's unimportant."

"Cheri, the guy said 'I'd love to try your sugar cookies' and 'let me have your pineapple juice' while he was staring at your body, come on."

"I guess that's not the normal way someone says they'd like to eat some food, is it?"

"No, of course it isn't."

"The way he looked at me when he said it was even worse. I hate to say it, but it reminded me of the way that Jeff looked at me the night I was raped."

"Christ."

"It really did."

"Does Elliot know about *that*?"

"No, I haven't told him. I just don't see the point in saying, 'Oh, by the way, one night about five years ago, the week before I moved to New York I got raped by a guy I met at a party who also smashed my hearing aids. Just wanted to share that with you. I mean, what's the point?"

"You're probably right. Men are really weird about rape anyway; they're kind of all over the place about it. Especially so-called 'date rape.' I think a lot of them really think it's not such a big deal on the one hand, but if it should happen to their girlfriend then it's a horrible stain on her permanent record they can't ever get out of their minds. It's like they're out of focus about it and can never see it for what it is."

"How can they understand? They're just socialized differently."

"They have so much fantasy around it."

"They have so much fantasy about women in general."

"True," Gretchen said. "Though I have to say, based on my meeting with him and all the things you've told me, Elliot might be one of the few men who could understand."

"No," Cheri said, waving her hand dismissively, "I'm not gonna drag that into our relationship. Things are so good now…for the first time since…then."

"The rape?"

"Yes, and even longer than that, so why should I jeopardize it? Why take a chance?"

"Exactly."

"You know, when I was a teenager, I used to think love was infinite communication; now I think it's selective communication, you edit out what will hurt the other for the sake of your relationship. Don't you agree?"

"Reluctantly, but yes, I agree there too."

"So, about Barry, I'll just have to wait and see and try to minimize the times I see him….He was telling me how years ago he and Elliot and Elliot's girlfriend used to go everywhere together when they all lived in Boston."

"Oh, oh."

"Yes. Oh, oh is right."

After her call to Gretchen she remembered feeling an odd sense of something portentous about to happen, and yet it was the most ordinary of days. She painted—not quite two hours (her usual limit) and made some progress on what she was temporarily calling "Landscape with Person." As she put the brushes away she remembered that Elliot had asked her about the genderlessness of her painted figures and she'd laughed or giggled and hadn't known what to say. She wondered if this time she would make the figure a woman and was somewhat frustrated that she couldn't decide.

What else had she done? A laundry, a little shopping at the corner grocery. She fixed herself a small supper (she was trying again, without announcing it to anyone, to lose a little weight) while she watched MacNeil Lehrer. Later that night she read Gretchen's review in *ArtForum* and then spent most of the rest of her night reading *The Unbearable Lightness of Being*. It wasn't a great novel but she felt it made a great point about life not being a dress rehearsal, and about the horror of always having only one chance to do things. What pressure to choose wisely and yet one only learned, if at all, from one's mistakes!

Shortly, after finally falling asleep, she had a dream that was unusually clear. She was a child riding her tricycle beside her older brother who was on a bright blue bike. Another boy joined them who was riding nearest the street to her left. She wasn't sure who he was but he seemed to be sneaking furtive looks at her. The road soon came to a fork. The new boy went to the left down a dark rocky path covered by thick irregular trees. Her brother went to the right down a path of smooth sand. A lake sparkled in front of them.

Pointing to the lake he turned towards her and said, "This is what we've been driving for," but by then it was no longer her brother who was speaking—it was Elliot.

She woke up feeling strangely exhilarated (the lake had been so beautiful) and saw again the ineffable expression in Elliot's eyes when he said goodbye to her that morning. Then she wondered why she'd had a dream in which they both turned out to be children and realized that having children with Elliot was something she'd been thinking about lately and wanted to talk to him about at some point. She smiled and thought about the dream again which continued to fill her like a fully satisfying meal to which nothing needed to be added. Perhaps, she thought, in its own modest way the day had been portentous, after all.

17

He was on the subway coming back from Cheri's feeling something very odd. He was happy in a way he couldn't remember since he was fifteen or sixteen when he'd be walking home from Barry's apartment on Tappan Street having one of their typical marathon discussions about music, sports, literature and girls. Sometimes he'd also had that feeling with Barry in the early years of their friendship after playing basketball on the playground when they'd stop for an ice cream then walk home slowly, barely talking at all. It was literally almost half a lifetime ago since he'd last felt that. He'd never trusted Lianne enough (with good reason as it turned out) to feel quite the same thing. But now with Cheri he *had* felt it only with the added, poignant awareness of how rare a thing it was to feel. The other thing that was different now at his age was the vague feeling of anxiety that accompanied his ecstasy. He remembered a line from a story he'd read years ago. "Nothing threatens identity like a flight into ecstasy no matter how brief." He didn't remember the name of the story or who wrote it or even what it was about but the line had stayed with him and now perhaps he knew why. Looking at the other seven or eight passengers in his uptown train, he saw the typical distracted, bored or anxious expressions, the faces of discontent. He saw, in other words, how *he* would appear normally in a subway if someone were looking at him. That's what the line he remembered was talking about—the oddness of happiness and how it isolated you by violating your concept of self—based as it was on your connection to others—in his case the passengers on the train.

Strange, too, now that he thought about it, how rarely literature described people honestly, or completely. People were generally depicted as good or evil and the ambivalence that inhabited almost every decision and feeling in life was all but ignored. Besides, his own failure at it, what surprised Elliot the most about literature so far was this lack of honesty. He had talked about some of this to Cheri the night they'd met at the loft party, but he hadn't really explained it right. It was a hard thing to talk about because writers, and their readers too, were in such denial about it and you can't admit publicly or even articulate privately what you haven't admitted to yourself, much less *do* something about it in your own writing.

It was only after a hundred years passed that people could look back and say the literature of the 19th Century was so romantic and exaggerated on the one hand while, of course, they had to be so polite and dishonest about sex on the other. But the literature of the 20th Century, even the second half of the 20th Century, despite all its four letter words and graphic descriptions of sex was far more dishonest. It was as if there were an all-pervasive, unspoken conspiracy emanating perhaps in the network of MFA writing programs and fanning out from them across the country (and eventually through literary magazines to the world) to not make honesty about human life a top priority in fiction or perhaps any kind of priority at all. Instead of devoting their art to describing how people really thought and behaved, the goal was to represent people according to what publishers thought the literary marketplace could sell. No wonder biographies were more popular than fiction and that documentaries were so popular now at the movie theater and even "reality TV" was such a big thing—not that any of them provided much reality either. But people were starved for truth, even if they couldn't articulate it, and they knew on some level they weren't getting it in their fiction.

Of course the advent of Political Correctness which now held almost all of literature in its noxious grip made a serious quest for truth all but impossible. Certain ethnic writers sold books while other ethnic writers didn't (but *all* writers were "ethnic," weren't they?) and therefore certain ethnic groups could only be depicted in noble ways or so thought the publishing conglomerates—who feared their constituencies would otherwise be offended. Could a play like *Othello* even be produced today, Elliot thought? Of course not, it would be condemned as racist and sexist, it would never even be written because the writer would censor him or herself first before the industry did it, and so there could be no new Shakespeare now either.

He stood up to get off the train, thinking that he had the chance to pursue truth in his writing but doubted he'd written more than an honest paragraph or two himself. He had the will to do it, but the question that haunted him was did he have the talent?

Well, he'd have to refocus his mind and think of other things now, he thought, as he walked through the subway station. He had a meeting with Barry about the magazine to discuss the new designer. Barry also said he had a surprise for him, concerning the magazine, he supposed. Had he ever known anyone who loved surprises as much as Barry? He was probably addicted to them on some cellular level. Just in the last half year there was, of course, his surprise phone call after all those years, followed by the invitation to live in his apartment, followed by the surprise announcement in the restaurant about the magazine.

Elliot was almost there now and couldn't resist looking behind himself at the flags by the United Nations building—a landmark he was always surprised to realize he lived near. Then he looked at his watch and started to walk faster, although he would be, at most, one or two minutes late for his meeting. He smiled, thinking that he loved punctuality the same way Barry loved surprises—it was one of the many differences between them. Yet he sensed there was a secret core inside them that they alone shared, that not even Roberta or his own mother ever completely reached.

He passed by the food stores and restaurants on the way to the apartment. So, now that he'd had his mandatory dark thoughts about literature and life perhaps he should start focusing on the magazine meeting ahead.

...Barry was in the living room wearing a tee shirt and black jeans. It was funny the way things worked out—he'd converted the extra bedroom into an office for *Beekman Place* but they still talked in the living room whether it was about the magazine or not. Barry was in his blue velvet chair, Elliot on the same side of the sofa where Barry had asked him to sit and assess the view when he first came to visit. On the long wooden table in front of the sofa where Barry generally ate while watching TV were some samples from the designer and some manuscripts that had already been submitted.

"Can you believe it?" Barry said, picking up a clump of manuscripts and shaking them in the air. "We're already getting inundated and we don't even come out for three and a half months."

"You predicted it."

"Christ, they're coming out of the woodwork."

"A lot of people want to be writers."

"Or think they already are," Barry added with a smile.

"What's in that pile?" Elliot asked.

"Those are sample logos that Paul came up with."

"For the cover?"

"The ones on top are for the cover, and underneath are some samples for our stationery."

Elliot picked them up, surprised at how intensely he was concentrating. "I like them—especially the first one, it's a nice, clean look. Distinctive and unpretentious."

"I thought you'd like it."

"The stationery is really elegant," Elliot said, "very classy."

"I told you Paul was good. You'll have to meet him—he's a first rate guy."

"Yah, I'd like to—well, I guess this is all really happening."

"Oh, yes, it's happening," Barry said. "And something else, you'll be pleased to discover. Look under Paul's portfolio and tell me what you see."

Elliot fumbled for a while but then pulled out two slides.

"Look at them," Barry said, "hold them up to the light. What do you see?"

"They're Cheri's."

"That's right. They're good, aren't they? They're really good, and we're going to run both of them in our inaugural issue."

"How'd that happen?"

"Didn't she tell you? I got them from her the other day at her apartment."

Elliot turned his head away and looked out the window. "Oh, so what'd you think?"

"They're very good. Her art doesn't really look like anyone else's."

"I meant about her place, and . . . what'd you think?"

"Oh, Cheri's great," Barry said, watching Elliot closely. "You have a real winner there, no question."

"Thanks," Elliot said softly, "I guess I do. Hey, I gotta pee, Barry, I'll be right back."

Barry saluted him as Elliot left the living room and walked into the bathroom. He shut the door, turned on the light, and stood before the mirror while he assessed the situation. Barry was acting normal enough but why hadn't Cheri told him? He'd have to ask some questions, while keeping his cool, of course. It was just like when he was with Lianne, he thought, as he flushed the toilet that he hadn't used, then splashed some water over his face. He dried off, breathed deeply a couple of times and reentered the living room.

"So when did all this happen?" Elliot said.

"What?"

"Your seeing Cheri."

"Yesterday, in the afternoon."

Elliot moved a couple steps to the side and looked down at the floor.

"I'd just come from Paul's apartment, he lives in the Village, too, and thought I'd give her a call since I was in the neighborhood. You'd told me where she lived so it was easy enough to get her number."

"Sure. I'm glad you did. I'm sure she was thrilled that you'll be running her work."

"She was happy. I already knew you liked her stuff so I didn't think I had to show you the specific pieces before I accepted them."

"No, that's fine. You know much more about art than me anyway. I thought we already agreed that would be your domain."

"Still I would and will normally consult with you about any art because I want you to like everything in the magazine and also because of your sensibility, of course. That's why I showed you Paul's work, too."

"Yes, sure, I appreciate that."

Barry had an expression somewhere between puzzlement and concern. "So you do understand about why I accepted Cheri's work on the spot?"

"Yes, I do."

"Maybe I shouldn't have set a precedent like that, because I do remember telling you I'd always consult you but in this case…"

"It's all right, it really is."

"And you like them, the ones I chose?"

"Yes, let me see them again," he said, picking the slides up from the long table. "Yuh, I like them, they're some of her best."

"Très bien," Barry said, "we're still on the same page then, still meshuga after all these years, n'est-ce pas?"

Elliot laughed and felt a little tension break inside him. "So how long were you over there, at Cheri's place?"

"Less than an hour, less than a half hour probably."

"What did you talk about besides the magazine?"

"A little of this, a little of that. We talked about you, of course."

"Oh?"

"Don't worry," Barry said, smiling. "She's crazy about you, as you know."

"That's good."

"I didn't realize she wears hearing aids."

"Really? I'm sure I told you."

"Maybe I didn't hear you. Maybe *I* need them. Anyway, it's barely noticeable, in fact, I didn't notice when we all met for dinner in the restaurant but she had her hair up when I was over. Anyway she hears everything it seems, you could never tell."

"She reads lips too. I could have sworn I told you that."

"I would've remembered, but anyway, what does any of that matter? She's just great in every way. Really great. You're very lucky, don't you think?"

"Thanks, yes, I do feel lucky."

A half hour later he left Barry's apartment with eight or nine manuscripts and walked downstairs to his own apartment. "His" apartment was a little smaller than Barry's but still almost a twin. When he looked at it and realized where he was living in New York it was sometimes hard to believe, and when he considered that he was living for free and could do so for the next six months or so (Barry had told him he could *always* stay) it really was incredible. What had Barry said to him a half hour ago? "You're very lucky, don't you think?" How could he think otherwise when he looked at his apartment and realized Cheri was only half an hour away.

He thought he'd work on a story he was writing for an hour

or so, listen to some music and then read some of the unsolicited stories for the magazine that Barry had given him. He had a desk in his office that he'd brought from his Philadelphia apartment but usually wrote on the living room table, where he also ate a lot of his meals, accompanied by his TV. It was a bigger space and he liked to spread out his various drafts and look at them from a standing position while he wrote. Meanwhile, he barely used his computer, which was back on his office table beside his phone.

He poured himself a glass of ginger ale, walked to the living room window and looked out at the street, trying to focus on his story but couldn't think of what should happen next. The key thing when neither ideas nor any phrases were coming to him was not to panic, of course, to realize that eventually words would come in the same way they always had and would end up on the page in front of him. (Unlike Barry, he wrote longhand in a notebook first and only then would copy it on his computer.)

But he soon realized it was not just a case of an absence of ideas this time. The problem was he couldn't stop thinking about Barry's meeting with Cheri and why she hadn't told him. It was Sunday afternoon, he had to take the train to school tomorrow to teach and wasn't supposed to see her till Tuesday for lunch. He could call her—but was that really a good idea? While it would offer an immediate answer of some kind and thus give him some relief, it was unlikely to be fully satisfactory. Without seeing her face, observing her body language, and looking her in the eye, he wouldn't be able to tell if there were anything she was hiding.

The best thing would be to see her but he'd just come from her apartment scarcely two hours ago. He might be able to arrange a short dinner with her and even more but wouldn't he then have to dissemble himself? Wouldn't she sense that something was troubling him and was that what he wanted her to feel on the same day they discussed her recent inability to have an orgasm? He could simply lie, of course—it wouldn't be a lie really—and say he just needed to see her because he missed her so much and then ask her about Barry halfway through the conversation, but he didn't want to scare her so soon with such needy behavior, not when she'd told him how much work she had to do—and he, too, had work as well. Besides it was rarely a good idea to tell a lie, even a half one, as a means of trying to obtain the truth. She might well spot it too. She had proven herself to be extraordinarily sensitive to him so far, so there was no reason to assume she wouldn't spot the intent behind his question no matter how well he camouflaged it with his timing and tone of voice. In a way, he'd be disappointed if she didn't.

The only option, then, was to carry on as if nothing out of the ordinary had happened. That meant, at most, a short phone call tonight, *after* he'd given her a chance to do her work and better yet, no phone call at all. And if she called him, the self discipline not to ask her about it on the phone. In short, it meant waiting till their Tuesday lunch and asking her only after she'd had a few bites of food and they'd both had a chance to relax a little. It wouldn't be easy to wait like that but there was no other way.

18

They ate lunch at Fameli's, not his favorite place by any means but an important or identity-confirming one for young artists like Cheri. Already it was noisy and filled as usual with artists in their de rigeur "uniforms" of faded blue jeans and tee shirts, or for those more sensitive to the cold, black shirts and/or sweaters.

"I missed you," he said, squeezing her hand just above the table. It was a cold clear day and she was wearing an anomalous white knit sweater and a red beret. After lunch they were planning to do some Christmas shopping, which once again he'd put off.

"I missed you, too."

"It seems like a long time, though I guess it's just been two and a half days."

"I know. Even though we talk on the phone, it's so distant by comparison it's like it takes place in a parallel, invisible universe where everything is much weaker and…"

"Invisible," he said with a little laugh.

"Yuh, invisible."

"So what's been happening? Any news?" he said, trying not to look at her too intensely.

"You're happening," she said.

He laughed. She certainly knew how to talk to him. He could already feel himself starting to erect. "So, congratulations," he said.

"For what?"

"Barry told me he accepted two of your paintings for *Beekman Place*, that's great news."

She looked at him for a few seconds before speaking. "Thank you," she finally managed.

"I was surprised you didn't tell me about it when I was over, actually."

Her cheeks reddened slightly.

"I know, I should have. When I see you I just go into a different world and I forget about other things from my world apart from you, or they just don't seem so important. And then, I didn't think to tell you on the phone cause that's like a parallel world, like I said, it just takes me to another place where I just think differently.…Besides, I knew he'd tell you anyway."

It was an odd answer—both reassuring and upsetting—and seemed to also be both spontaneous and rehearsed. He looked down as he finished his spoonful of soup, reminding himself to control his voice though the restaurant was getting increasingly noisy.

"So how was his visit, apart from taking your painting?"

She looked away for a second.

"That was the main thing for me. The art, of course. Outside of that, we talked a little, he wasn't there very long."

"Oh."

"It was a little awkward, I guess."

"Why was it awkward?"

"I'm not exactly the world's most socially sophisticated person."

"And you think Barry is?"

"Well, you told me he lived in Europe and I know he's very smart and knows a lot of famous people."

"He doesn't *know* a lot of famous people, he *talks about* a lot of famous people, but…"

"Well, I don't know. He called out of the blue, my place was a mess, I didn't have time to prepare anything. He just called and came over and so it felt kind of awkward in that way. That's what I meant."

"Oh."

"Naturally he said nothing but good things about you and us."

"What good things did he say to you, besides complimenting your art?"

"That you were lucky to have me, that kind of thing."

"Well, that's certainly true."

"And I told him I was lucky to have you," she said, smiling, though he thought she was forcing her smile a bit.

"What other good things did he say to you?"

"I'm not sure I remember anything else, oh wait, he ate some cookies . . ."

"Some cookies?"

"Yes, I offered him some cookies, that's a fairly standard thing to do, isn't it?"

Elliot nodded, forcing his own smile.

"And he said he liked them, he complimented the cookies or whatever."

"So it sounds like a good visit. I'm glad."

"He wasn't over very long, you know. And then he left with my slides. I don't know why I didn't tell you. I wish I had."

"It's no big deal. I'm glad everything worked out well and I think it's great about the magazine. I was wondering about the best way to approach Barry about it . . ."

"About what?"

"About getting your work in the magazine. I didn't want to be too pushy and I didn't want to just drop a subtle hint. Sometimes Barry's a bit of a contrarian, and sometimes subtle things go past him, but even there he's unpredictable. At times he's excruciatingly sensitive to hints and details you yourself aren't even aware of and other times his head's in the clouds or he's thinking in grand, abstract terms and hints go right by him. Anyway, I don't have to think about that anymore because he took care of it on his own."

"You never had to think about it," Cheri said with some emphasis, "and I never expected it or ever really gave it any thought."

"Well you should have thought about it. You should think about obvious things that could help your career. Everyone else does. And you deserve it too—your work is very, very good."

She smiled and he felt they were over the tense conversational moment. But even as he returned to cutting the lettuce in his chef's salad he was remembering her averted eyes and reddening cheeks as if sensing that they were now permanent installations in his interior museum of doubt. He couldn't challenge her any more than he did, couldn't convey any more doubt and so he had really not found out anything except the first sign, however small, of a kind of fissure between them.

19

"But you have to go. It's far too important to even consider not going," Barry said.

Elliot shifted the receiver until it felt more comfortable against his ear. It was strange to be talking with him on the phone when Barry was only one floor above him, but they'd begun doing it increasingly the last month or so.

"Do you realize what an incredible opportunity this is for the magazine?"

"Yes, I see that. I believe you. I just don't see why you can't represent it yourself. You're the publisher and editor, after all."

"Not a good argument, Elliot. First, there will be more important people there than I can possibly talk to. Second, it makes us twice as impressive to be represented by two people instead of one, and you are, don't forget, the co-editor."

"But let's face it, you're far more socially adept than I am."

"Bullshit."

"Bullshit?"

"Remember the last big party I took you to?"

"At that gallery owner's loft?"

"Yes, that's right. Isn't that where you, the inept and reclusive one, met Cheri and seemed to be quite adept at getting to know her."

He laughed and told Barry he had a point. So this would be another time when the three of them would be together. Since Barry still hadn't found anyone he would consider taking to "an A List event like this," it meant the three of them would probably leave together. It seemed that once a week or more during the last month, Barry would announce a meeting or party that required the three of them to attend.

This new party was being thrown by Lillian Davis, a well-known New York socialite and patron of the arts. Since becoming a widow eleven years ago, she'd tripled the time and financial support she devoted to the arts (adding literary magazines to her charitable interests) and had become not only a fixture on the New York social pages but something of a national figure as well. Even Elliot, who didn't follow such things, had heard of her and couldn't pretend not to be impressed. Barry had gotten the invitation through Darren Datz, some of whose multimedia projects had been sponsored by her. "I don't know how that son of a bitch does it," Barry had said, laughing contemptuously when he first told Elliot about the party.

"OK, you've worn me down, I'll go, unless Cheri strenuously objects to it," he finally said.

"She can't object, she won't. Just explain to her how important this is. Many key editors will be there, big-time agents will be there, patrons of the arts, celebrities from show business. She's famous for bringing people together from all walks of life—the media will be there, too, in force."

"I'll do my best but Cheri's a bit on the reclusive side," he'd said, not without a trace of pride.

"She went to Fogel's party, didn't she?"

"That was different, that was part of her job."

"But this is five times more important than Fogel's, ten times. The place will be crawling with millionaires, and millionaires buy art, especially these millionaires, because they all want to be Lillian Davis. They're all looking for painters to support and magazines to sponsor like childless parents shopping for kids, capiche?"

Now having auditioned his shirts and finally deciding on one, he was putting on a navy blue sports jacket for the first time in New York, shining his black shoes and applying deodorant and/or cologne to all the key places. He wasn't late but for some reason he was rushing. He couldn't deny that as Barry was asking him to do more and more things for the magazine, especially things involving his being with him and Cheri, he felt less and less comfortable in his apartment (which was really Barry's, of course) and more comfortable at Cheri's, small and cramped though it was. He had to start looking for a New York job in earnest, the commutes to Philadelphia were also more exhausting than he'd imagined, and he had to, sooner rather than later, find a place of his own or perhaps one with Cheri.

His cell phone began ringing.

"I'm here," Cheri said.

"Stay in the cab. I'll call Barry and we'll be right there," he said, relieved that they would not meet in the lobby or worse still at Barry's where he felt especially uninhibited about dispensing hugs and kisses.

"You look great," Barry said to Cheri in the taxi. "Foxy and classy at the same time."

"Thanks," she said softly, as Elliot squeezed her hand.

The conversation in the cab was pleasant enough but the last few blocks Barry became quiet, and then Elliot, as if taking his cue in a fugue, stopped talking as well. It was as if the reality of going to a Lillian Davis party, of setting foot in her storied Fifth Avenue apartment across the street from Central Park had suddenly hit them full force. It was far more than just the chance of meeting someone who might help their magazine or career, Elliot realized. It was the sense of participating in history in a way, certainly in the social history not only of New York but of the country. That's why there were any number of people in the arts or show business, or simply moneyed people who heard about them and yearned to be invited to Lillian's parties—people for whom such an invitation would be the crowning touch of their social life. Just the chance to talk to Lillian Davis, who had simultaneously lived a life both fascinatingly public and private and who knew everyone, it seemed, was in itself something one might never experience again.

The doorman greeted them and pointed out the elevator. The lobby was elegant but restrained in much the way Elliot imagined it would be. A butler let them into the enormous penthouse but Lillian herself, wearing a full-length purple dress and an elegant emerald necklace was soon there to greet them personally. She had the gift of focusing on each person she talked to so completely that even the twenty seconds or so of sweet nothings she uttered upon greeting one of them had the effect of a powerfully intimate experience.

Elliot kept Cheri's hand in his and after Lillian moved on to shake other hands or hug other people they looked at the paintings, sculptures and especially the signed photographs that adorned the walls. Here was Picasso, there was Judy Garland, Elizabeth Taylor, Barbara Streisand and Tennessee Williams, and in the room Elliot already recognized E. L. Doctorow and Woody Allen in the flesh.

"Pretty incredible, huh?" he said to Cheri. She shrugged and smiled.

"I feel like I'm in a museum," she said softly in his ear.

"You are. The museum of unnatural history."

They both laughed and he squeezed her hand again. "I need a drink. You want me to get you something?"

"Any kind of white wine would be good," she said in what he could only describe to himself as an unnatural voice. He looked at her realizing she was nervous, too, when someone tapped him on the shoulder.

"Darren Datz here," the man said, extending his hand.

"Elliot Martin," he said, shaking his hand while trying not to react to the extreme pressure of Datz's grip. Datz was tall, oddly muscular, with a fairly thick black beard. He was wearing a purple shirt almost the color of Lillian's dress, a white necktie in the shape of a triangle, a flowing black sports coat, blue jeans and boots. The whole outfit not only screamed for attention, Elliot thought, but also proclaimed, "don't think I'm intimidated for one second by this event. I *am* the event."

"I saw you come in with Barry Auer. Are you his roommate?"

"No, I'm not his roommate, actually, I…"

"But you live in one of his apartments. You're his friend, aren't you?"

"That's right."

"You're also working on his magazine, correct?"

"Yes, that's true."

"You see how much I already know about you? I'm the person who arranged for you to come here."

"Well thank you very much for that."

Datz barely smiled in response. "Are you familiar with my work?"

"Oh sure, with some of it."

"You're a writer, I understand."

"Yes, a fiction writer."

"So you don't do reviews."

"Not very often."

"You're probably familiar with my literary writings, as opposed to my work in the other arts."

"I've read and admired some of your critical pieces."

"What about my fiction and poetry? Have you seen my performance art, or gone to any of my concerts?"

"I'm sorry, I haven't had a chance to."

"Well the first thing you should do is go to my website: www. DatzRevolution.com. Also, there's a kind of mini-retrospective of my mixed media work at the Urdang Gallery. You should check that out too."

"I will, thanks for telling me about it."

"Maybe you could consider reviewing it or else my new collection of language/collage poems for either *The Voice* or *The New York Observer*, or for one of the quarterlies."

Elliot nodded.

"So who's the lovely lady standing next to you? Aren't you going to introduce me?"

"Of course, this is my friend Cheri. Cheri, this is Darren Datz."

Datz shook hands, keeping her reluctant hand between both of his for a few seconds before finally releasing it.

"Cheri is an artist, too, a painter."

Datz raised an eyebrow. "Painting, huh? That's a quaint thing to still be doing."

"What kind of art do you do?" Cheri said.

"I'm a polymathic artist—I do performance art, earth art,

conceptual, internet interactive art, and even a few constructions. I've pretty much touched all the bases though it never occurred to me to paint. Maybe I should try it? What do you think?"

Cheri shrugged, blushing slightly. It occurred to Elliot that in her relatively short time in the city she might never have encountered a true New York egomaniac or at least not one in full press release as Datz was now. Come to think of it, Elliot wasn't sure he'd encountered that either.

"So are your paintings as beautiful as you are?" Datz said, smiling at Cheri as if he'd just uttered an impeccable witticism. Cheri continued to look confused.

"Yes they are," Elliot said.

"Then I'd like to see them."

"When she has her first show, we'll invite you."

"He's exaggerating, of course," Cheri finally managed.

"I rarely go to painting galleries," Datz announced, "though I'd certainly go to see yours."

"*Painting* galleries?" Elliot said.

"Galleries that only feature painters. They've been almost uniformly hostile to my work. They're really the leaders in an ill-hidden conspiracy to keep my art as suppressed as possible, but of course they'll never succeed."

"A conspiracy?" Elliot said. "Why would they do that?"

Datz sighed briefly as if he were explaining something elementary to a child. "Because it's not in their interest to change or even to challenge consciousness and that's what my work is about. You see, you can't put a frame around my work and sell it, because my work occurs *in* human consciousness, it's an event, an experience and you can't hang it on a wall. It has no decorative function and so the ultra capitalist gallery owners are threatened by it. Some of them won't let me in their doors, much less show my work."

"Really?" Elliot said.

"That's awful," Cheri added.

"There are actually a few uptown galleries that have barred me from their premises. Believe me, I wear it as a badge of honor. If you want to know who they are and why they've literally locked me out just go to DatzRevolution.com and scroll down to 'Plots against the Datz Revolution.'"

"Yuh, I will," said Elliot, "thanks for letting me know."

"Now tell me how you're liking the big city?" Datz said, with a smile Elliot tried not to consider condescending.

"I'm enjoying it a lot," he said, giving Cheri's hand another inadvertent squeeze.

"Quite a change from Philadelphia, huh?"

"Quite a change from anywhere."

"You were from Philadelphia, correct?"

"Originally from Boston, Brookline to be exact. Barry and I grew up there together. I moved to Philadelphia seven or eight years ago. And now New York."

"Congratulations. You've made it here at last."

Before Elliot could answer, Datz said, "I see someone from the *Times*. I love to push their buttons—they just don't know what to make of me. Adios," he said, then turning slightly he bowed to Cheri and said, "I'll be looking for your show."

"Thanks," she said, but Datz had already turned and walked away.

They looked at each other and shook their heads.

"What was that about?" Cheri said.

"I'm not sure. The only thing I do know is that I really want a drink."

"Me too," she said, as he took her hand and led her towards a long white clothed table where the bar was set up.

From the other side of the room where Barry had meandered, he intermittently watched them, then heard the bell ring again. So far, except for the greetings he'd exchanged with Lillian, he hadn't spoken to anyone, preferring instead to watch the procession of famous guests enter the party by himself. This time he saw Eric West, the director, who only a few years ago had won an Academy Award. He had a silver goatee and long silver hair and wore a tie and sports jacket but also his trademark blue jeans and black cowboy hat to enhance his western image. Though he'd grown up in New Jersey and lived mainly in New York and Malibu for the last thirty years, West was born in Arizona, or so his bio claimed, and he continued to promote himself as a cowboy director. With him, sporting a huge diamond ring he'd given her before they married last year, was Louise Leloch, the young actress. She was West's fifth wife, by Barry's count, and one of his youngest. As Barry recalled, she'd appeared in supporting roles in West's last two movies.

Barry had just had time to finish his vodka tonic when Lillian took his arm and said, "Barry, I'd like you to meet some people."

He was surprised that she'd still remembered his name much less that she was apparently going to introduce him to Eric West. He supposed it was one of the traits that made her such a legendary hostess. First, however, he had to shake hands with Alex Hornstein, the renowned divorce attorney who was probably fifteen years older than him but with a full head of convincingly black hair and an impeccably deep, confident voice that he modulated with supreme skill during his frequent TV talk show appearances. Next to him was his wife Kathy, blonde and outrageously attractive, who was much younger, of course, and looked like a model. He shook hands with her too, until finally Lillian introduced him to Eric West. Barry thought to himself quickly, "at last this is where I belong, this is my world." And to remain a member in good standing in this newly minted world he forced himself not to stare at the ample cleavage of West's wife, the actress Louise Leloch. When he shook hands with her he merely smiled then turned towards West. He just had time to tell him how much he admired his films when they both saw the revered novelist Margo Garret with her good friend, the art gallery owner Maurice Germand.

"Oh, the Great Garret," West exclaimed, turning away from Barry to kiss her on the lips. Immediately Barry remembered that West had directed at least two movies based on Garret's novels, and that she had co-written the last screenplay with him. The movies had done well at the box office, too.

"Eric!" she said, taking his hands, her cheeks coloring slightly after he kissed her.

"This is Louise, fire in my loins, my sin, my soul, Louise—the Great Garret, who deserves to win next year's Nobel Prize and every year's, for that matter."

He was impressed that West knew Nabokov as well as Fitzgerald but he had said it with such grandiloquence that Barry cringed. (He certainly hadn't sounded very much like a cowboy.) Neither Louise nor Margo seemed the least bit embarrassed, however, as they exchanged kisses on each other's cheeks, and talked about how absurd it was that this was their first face-to-face meeting. Lillian and Margo kissed and exchanged enthusiasms, followed by a similar exchange with Maurice. But true to her training, Lillian remembered to introduce Barry to Margo Garret, an occasion that he thought he handled fairly well. After Garret resumed talking to West and company, Barry sneaked a look at Elliot and Cheri standing by the bar then, for one horrible second, saw an image of Jordan before he was able to banish it.

Without any discernable announcement the guests suddenly began moving further into the middle of the living room with its enormous crystal chandelier in the center of the ceiling and its mirrors reflecting the paintings and photographs from the wall. Soon caterers began to carry in a large table from the smaller dining room and then a second table that attached to it so the fifty or so people could be accommodated. Barry hadn't even realized there'd be a dinner. Had Datz told him? He quickly looked at Datz across the room, who smiled and gave him a thumbs up sign. Datz never lost his cool if Datz could be described as cool. At any rate, whatever he had, Datz never lost it.

Lillian never lost hers either, of course, which allowed her to risk things few other hosts would. She had, for example, quite original ideas about seating. Most hostesses split up couples and sat the most celebrated people next to each other, or at the same table. Thus a powerful editor or literary agent was seated next to a famous author so that (potentially) deals could be made. Lillian, however, often seated unknowns next to the powerful.

At this dinner, Barry was seated next to Kathy Hornstein on one side and Louise Leloch on the other. The food—chicken, fish and pasta, a delicate tomato salad, and two kinds of wine—lived up to its reputation, the conversation less so. At least at first. No one topic dominated the table for any length of time, instead everything seemed skittish and a little forced. It reminded Barry of an acting troupe improvising from audience suggestions in fitful one or two minute spurts before moving on to the next suggested topic. Finally, the guests found something to talk about that interested them all—the recent much publicized wedding of the singer/actress Deanna Russell.

The Hornsteins asked most of the questions about it and Lillian and West, who were at the wedding, gave most of the answers. Barry, making a mental note to not entirely recede into the conversational background, asked some questions too.

The wedding and reception, which about a thousand people attended, had been filmed for a future television show and was covered by much of the nation's (and a good deal of the world's) media. When one movie star found out that a television show was involved she apparently changed her mind and decided to go at the last minute, but demanded and apparently received two hundred thousand dollars to attend. She arrived, looking in the words of West, "pale, bloated and horribly depressed." Margo opined that the actress did have "the worst taste in the western world. What a paradox to have all that beauty always clothed in such glaring trash."

There were stories and jokes told about Michael Jackson and Elizabeth Taylor and there was the anecdote about two actresses who'd had a fight thirty years ago. One approached the other at the reception to make up only to have the latter turn her head and walk away. All the stars were referred to by their first names and Barry wasn't always certain who was being discussed, though he'd immersed himself fairly well in show business lore over the years. Tuesday and Liza he knew, of course, but which Janet were they referring to, which Gary?

Then the discussion turned more to the celebrities at the reception who were ill and to speculation about who might not live long. The brief moments of hilarity were replaced by a somber mood, which got considerably darker when they somehow began discussing what they were doing when 9/11 happened.

"I was writing," said Margo. "I didn't find out for a long time. And then I worried about my friends who worked near there and started calling frantically but by then, it was impossible to get through."

"Was anyone you know hurt?" Barry asked.

"A friend of mine who worked at the World Trade Center..."

"Yes, Paul," said Maurice quickly. "He unfortunately didn't make it."

"I'm sorry," Barry said, "that's awful."

Margo bit her lip and said, "It was very sad, very cruel."

"Margo wrote a beautiful poem about it that *The Atlantic* published," Maurice said.

"No dear," Margo said, "it was actually published in *The New Yorker*."

More condolences and testimonies followed until they led to an uncomfortable silence. Then West began describing a Hollywood birthday party he'd been to that was thrown by a famous director.

"I heard that was an enormous party," Lillian said. "I couldn't go, I think I was in New York."

"Yes, lots of people, in lots of rooms. His house is really extraordinary."

"Does he still supply cocaine to anyone who wants it?"

"I didn't notice any coke, but I'll tell you what I did notice," West said, with a twinkle in his eyes. "I walked into one of the guest rooms to use the john and there was no less a movie star than Brian Kove doing something very strange to some model or other, I think, and damned if he didn't go right on with it. I think he was giving her an enema while dicking her from behind at the same time."

A couple of the guests laughed uncertainly.

"I mean he didn't even stop when I walked in. Just turned his head and looked right at me and continued till I left."

"Darling, you probably made his day," said Lillian.

"You probably made him come—which I understand isn't that easy for Brian," said Maurice. "I mean, there is a not so secret gay part to him, too, isn't there?"

"I've heard of Hollywood decadence," said West, "but this was ridiculous."

"I know an actress who had an affair with Brian sometime last summer," said Louise. "You know who I mean, Eric, and she told me that all he ever wanted to do, besides watch his own movies, was play games with enemas. Enema love he called it."

A few more guests laughed.

"Well there you have it," said Lillian to West, "the idea for your next movie."

"Yes," said Eric. "Adultery and drugs are old hat. Everything has to be anal these days to be up to date."

"It's the new intimacy," said Hornstein, clutching his wife's shoulder.

Everyone laughed again, including Barry who managed to force a laugh as well, as he tried to see what Elliot and Cheri were doing next to Woody Allen at the table's end.

It was just after the waiters had cleared away the dessert and brought the after dinner drinks that Louise Leloch started talking to Barry. (Throughout dinner he had mostly talked to Kathy Hornstein, made a few contributions to the group discussion and listened a lot.) In her tight, low cut yellow dress, she was showing to maximum advantage her perfectly positioned breasts and ample honey blonde hair, neither of which was probably real.

"Are you in the business?" she said.

"If you mean the film business then no, not yet. I'm in literary publishing. I'm the publisher and editor of a new literary magazine called *Beekman Place* and I'm also a writer."

"No kidding. Do you write novels?"

"Yes, I've published a couple of novels and a book on aesthetics and philosophy in France where I lived for a number of years," he said, correctly guessing that she wouldn't know French and ask for the titles.

"Wow," she said, parting her collagen-enhanced lips, "that's really impressive. You guys who write these serious, important novels, you may miss out on the big bucks that Hollywood writers get but you get something much better, cause your books will make you immortal."

"Thank you, that's nice of you to say but I really don't think so."

"Really? Why not?"

"I don't think anybody's writing will make them immortal. I know a lot of writers think so, but it's just an illusion. I think everyone's art and movies and novels will simply, eventually, be forgotten."

Did he really believe that, he wondered? Hadn't he lived and fantasized his whole life based on just the opposite assumption? Even in Madrid he remembered feeling differently, wasn't that why he started the magazine? Yet this opposite point of view had just spewed out of him. He thought of Jordan in the Motel 6 room for a moment and began blinking his eyes rapidly to get rid of it.

"You know, I had an editor friend," Barry continued (for a moment imagining he really had such a friend), "an editor, you see, not a writer, who once said to me, 'art is the last illusion,' and I think he was right."

"Art is the last illusion," Louise repeated, "I like that."

"If these artists are so hung up on immortality, I think having children is a much more direct route, a much better solution."

"I sure wish Eric felt that way," she said, moving a little closer to Barry and lowering her voice. "I've been trying to convince him to get me pregnant for a year now. Course he's had so many children already but couldn't he give me just one more?" she said laughing. "Do you have any children, Barry?"

His face reddened.

"No, I'm sorry to say I don't. You see that young guy in the blue jacket sitting next to the blonde in the yellow dress beside E. L. Doctorow? He works for my magazine. He's my best friend in the world and he and that woman, who's a very good painter by the way, they'll have children because she's the kind of woman who could really love children. Believe me, I had a mother like that, and I know."

"What are their names?" Louise said in a hushed voice just this side of Marilyn Monroe.

"His name is Elliot and she's Cheri."

"Are they writers, too?"

"He's a writer, she writes some articles about art, but is mostly a painter. They're both talented but will probably never become famous cause they just don't have that...murderous drive you need to succeed, capiche? They're just good, normal people who will probably find their 'immortality' through having children one day. I know Cheri will; Elliot, I'm not as sure of. But it would be a crime if Cheri didn't have children cause I know she'll be a great mother."

"So they're a strong couple?"

"Right now they are, yes. You never know how long these things will last. I'm not sure Elliot is really the right man for her, immensely fond of him though I am. But whether they stay together or not I think they'll both eventually have children, and I know she will."

"That's really neat, it's beautiful really, the way you talk about them."

"I care about both of them deeply."

"How did they meet?"

"At a party, just by chance. He'd come with me actually and later they met just because he literally bumped into her. It could just as easily have been me who bumped into her, or someone else. But it was him, and, of course, he fell for her right away."

"That's really romantic. That's the way it was with Eric and me, too. I was just a bit player in one of his movies, I think I said ten words in the picture, but one day during rehearsal our eyes just met in a special way and he invited me to dinner that night and then boom, we just clicked. So, yuh, I was crazy about him right from the start but I also had a lot of hang-ups and insecurities about dating a man who was so world famous and, you know, older—a man who knew so much more about the world than I did."

"But they all went away, obviously. The hang-ups."

"Not completely," she said, laughing, as she finished her drink. "I mean, you see the nice breasts," she said, pointing to them for a second, "but behind them beats the heart of a hick."

Barry laughed and spilled some of his drink, and Louise laughed too, holding his wrist for a few seconds as if to steady him.

Back in his room at quarter to three in the morning, Barry remembered that laughter, the touch of her hand around his wrist and the sight of her breasts, when he looked down briefly at them as if staring too closely at something forbidden like the sun. But far more than that image of Louise, he was thinking of Cheri, especially the sight of her seated at the long white table with her blank, slightly frightened expression. She wasn't wearing anything revealing, she never did. He'd never seen any of her cleavage, not even a quarter inch, and could only imagine what her tits looked like because he knew she had them. He had met Woody Allen, John Ashbery, Eric West. He'd met Margo Garret. He'd been touched and complimented and seen half the breasts of Louise Leloch, one of the hottest looking actresses in Hollywood, who even gave him her and Eric's phone number for a potential interview, and still he was thinking almost completely of Cheri. He thought of her when he lay still waiting for sleep, seeing himself like a restless vampire in a casket, and when he got up to pace, as he was doing now, like a lion in the dark den of his living room.

Even when he got another image attack of Motel 6, which no longer necessarily included Jordan or Jordan's face, but just the half darkness and a bit of the room, he still thought of Cheri and used her image to stop thinking of M6 as he now labeled it in his mind. This was something remarkable—the one hope he had, really—that it was easier, far easier the last week or so, to stop thinking of M6 than it was to stop thinking of Cheri. Actually, it had been this way for weeks now, perhaps even two months. He'd tried to ignore it, dismiss it, deny it, argue against it (because of Elliot), but he couldn't anymore. His police wouldn't believe it, he would lose his argument with them if he didn't admit it to himself first.

What could he do? He would have to see her, speak to her. She would have to get to know him better—right now she didn't know him at all. And Elliot? Elliot would have to eventually understand. Elliot had always gotten everything, but now he would have to understand that no one got everything. He'd already given Elliot a home, a magazine, a woman. He'd saved his life, really, which made up for the one he'd accidentally ended, didn't it, just as he planned.

Elliot wasn't really the right man for Cheri anyway. He'd blurted that to Louise but it was true. He didn't have the kind of imagination Cheri needed to really discover herself and so go forward in her life or art. Elliot was very nice but ultimately too limited for a soul as rich as Cheri's.

He was in his Lazy Boy with his eyes closed. Within an hour he had an unusually long dream about Jordan. He was swimming underwater. It was dark but there was light above the water. He wasn't sure for a moment how he got in the water but he kept going forward anyway as fast as he could. He was an adolescent, a child, and she was the same age as him, maybe a little younger. Then he remembered how he and Jordan jumped off the raft together. He stood too close to her when he jumped and his leg brushed against her hip, making her fall clumsily into the water. Worse still, when he jumped, he'd inadvertently kicked her in the forehead while they were both in the air.

He remembered this now while he was swimming. He looked back underwater and couldn't see her. It was a shock—like a shark had bitten him—and he reversed himself as if he were a fish himself and swam underwater in the opposite direction looking for her. He'd realized many things while he swam but none of them could be put into words except maybe that he was much more like a fish, a shark even, than he realized.

There was nothing to see but clear water slightly illuminated by the light above. Then, finally, he saw something like an oddly positioned coral reef. He swam toward it, trying to remain calm and therefore swimming at a normal speed. Even though he knew what it was, he pretended to himself that he didn't. When he got a few feet away from the body, however, he couldn't pretend any longer. It was Jordan, sitting at the bottom of the lake like part of a lifeless tree. He knew she was dead but he swam closer to touch her skin, as if to prove to himself that he'd done everything he was supposed to do to revive her. She was dead, but it was an accident. He was next to her pushing her in her shoulder to test her and to prove to himself that he wanted her to live.

He opened his eyes, blinked, and shook himself. He tried to think of Cheri, but Jordan stayed with him. Then he began to pace. He remembered Louise Leloch, Lillian Davis. "It was a hell of a party," he said to himself as he walked into the kitchen. "I don't think Elliot or Cheri were disappointed."

He quickly poured himself a glass of wine, which he drank almost immediately. Finally, he saw Cheri's face—the way she shyly smiled in the cab while he complimented her. Then Jordan went away—back to her home underwater, perhaps, back to her life as a phantom. He stayed awake with Cheri till the light came up.

20

There was something in the light, especially around the trees, that gave her hope and made her drive more slowly. This had happened before in other towns but not as strongly as now. Of course it had been fall light then, and it was winter light now. It had also been dark then—the darkest place she'd ever seen—in part because it was night, in part because of the thick trees. She remembered it was November then and many trees would be bare. That meant there were a lot of evergreens where Gordon took her, and also no traffic lights like what she was seeing on some of the side streets now.

But besides the trees, what else should she look for? Trees weren't enough. If that was all she looked at she'd be like the girl in *Blair Witch Project* and get hopelessly lost.

What had happened, what had she seen when she'd stepped out of the car that night? They'd been in a parking lot, a fairly good sized one as she recalled, that had to service his whole building, which was low—two stories at most. Probably there was a law about how high you could build—country people loved their trees and sky and didn't want their buildings to block them. She'd definitely remembered that she'd stepped out onto a good sized parking lot and been immediately struck by how dark it was and how quiet. She'd seen a lot of stars, though not much of a moon and no street lamps she could recall, which wasn't to say one wasn't on someplace—there almost certainly had to be one on the nearest road, didn't there?

She remembered looking at them for a second, but there was also some other light coming from the ground. Maybe she saw it just before they left the road or maybe while she was walking into Gordon's apartment. It was in the distance, perhaps across the street, and she'd tried to remember it for a hundred nights, thinking now, as she drove down Plum Point Drive, that it might have been the lights from a swimming pool lit from the bottom, although that was only one possibility, and wouldn't it be odd to have a pool area be lit when it was too cold to swim?

Still, she began driving more slowly now, looking for pools, as well as evergreen trees that were near parking lots. She felt her eyes twitch, something that had begun once she started looking for

Gordon's place. Of course he'd said he didn't live in the apartment, that he didn't even live in the state. He'd said he didn't own the car he was driving and that Gordon wasn't his name. He'd said a lot of things.

She stopped the car and let a boy walking his bike cross in front of her. He was wearing an Eagles football cap pulled down over his orange hair. One thing was almost certain—there were no motels of any kind around here so Gordon had to have his own place, unless he had the keys to someone else's, some fellow pervert he shared the place with, or some unsuspecting roommate who was out that night. She felt herself shudder and watched the boy pedaling uphill as fast as he could.

She started driving again. Gordon lived here, she knew it. Maybe not all the time, but he had a place here. It gave her a nervous feeling in her stomach, but it was true. And as long as she knew that, she knew he was still doing what he did to her to other girls or maybe worse. She saw an image of him, the look on his face when he first sat on her and she trembled again, closed her eyes for a second and shook her head, then looking up to the left of the road saw a fairly large illuminated swimming pool.

21

Was he a scarecrow that he could stand so still, half shielded by a lamp post that he sometimes leaned against? Strange, the different roles one played without even realizing it. He was now a private detective waiting for a woman to appear. When he'd finally see her he would have to become something else again. But until then he was a scarecrow, a city scarecrow or more accurately a scared crow, and his job was to stand still, keep people away from him and watch for her.

He remembered a few days ago, when he was a different kind of detective, more like a spy. He was also waiting and watching for Cheri then. But that time when he saw her, after a mere fifteen—or twenty—minute wait, he didn't walk up to her and start talking as he planned to do now. Instead, he crouched low like a monkey behind a dumpster and continued to follow her on foot, hiding behind parked cars and the occasional sycamore trees or else the corner of buildings as she went towards St. Mark's bookstore.

He remembered that that time he was tempted to run ahead of her and then when she passed in front of him to suddenly appear from behind the parked car, or dumpster and scare her by "accidentally" bumping into her. Had anyone ever invented a better game than Hide and Seek? The pity was people weren't allowed to play it past a certain age unless they had kids, which he'd never wanted, but with Cheri he'd been thinking of it lately.

Yes, the old games were the best games and the older the games got, the more he cherished them. But "Scarecrow" was a new one. Nor had he ever played it with anyone else. Maybe that's why he was simultaneously bored and alert, because beneath the monotony, or else blended in with it, was a sense of danger.

He knew which window was hers. By now, he'd figured it out. She'd kept her blinds up, too. Typical of her. If he stayed and watched her long enough he'd eventually see her naked, perhaps. But was that what he really wanted? He was well aware that it was a strange question to ask himself while he was standing still on the sidewalk behind a lamp post and a skinny tree with one eye cocked on her window. Of course he wanted to see her naked, simply from an objective, aesthetic point of view he was curious, but that wasn't the way he wanted it the first time. The first time he wanted her underneath him, kissing him, and moaning with her hand on his neck or back. He wanted her wearing a blouse with buttons so he could undo them rapidly one after another like going down a flight of stairs. Then, at last, he could free her chest with one definitive motion as he unhooked her bra. She wouldn't be wearing one of those Victoria's Secret Wonder bras or whatever they called them these days, and he'd be glad. It made him love her more that she ignored or possibly didn't know about that stuff. She would have a plain old white, girl-next-door bra and that was more than fine with him. In fact, now that he thought about it more closely, he didn't want to rip off her buttons in a burst of passion either. It might be preferable to unbutton them slowly and watch the expression on her face as he proceeded, or better still, to tell her to unbutton them and see the slightly nervous but ultimately compliant look on her face as she undressed for him beneath his body then shyly gave him his first view of her—her cheeks red pink from emotion.

It would be the same with her skirt and panties. Did she perhaps just wear simple white underpants as well? Probably not, she wasn't a character from *Northern Exposure*, after all, but if she *did* that could be very charming too. It was much more likely that she wore thin pale yellow or pink panties, something quintessentially feminine though nothing elaborate or haute couture.

He doubted that her smell would be complicated either. Certainly she would be clean, immaculately clean in all likelihood, in a soapy, baby powder kind of way. That was what he'd smelled from her so far and there was no reason to think it would change when he'd know her better. If there ever was perfume involved or body cologne it would be just a drop. Her own smell would be sweet enough, he knew.

More mysterious would be whether she'd shaved or not, or possibly just trimmed it. He knew he would prefer it shaved, but he wanted to be the first person she shaved for and actually wanted to cut her hair himself.

He thought of Louise Leloch. There was no question that she'd shaved, that she was as bald as a baby there and undoubtedly had an "Eric" tattooed just above her clit. It's probably what he did instead of a pre-nup, or more likely what he got in addition to one.

A kid walked by wearing a Yankees baseball jacket and gave him a funny look. He gave him a hard look back and the kid immediately stopped staring and moved away quickly. He was and always would be a Red Sox fan. He hated the Yankees and cursed all their bought pennants (something else Elliot and he had in common) so didn't feel bad about scaring the kid.

He thought about the party again. He had one eye on the

window, one eye on the door to her building but he was thinking about the party. He went over his conversation with Eric West. It had been short—he wished it had been longer but it was very short. He had actually memorized it but he went over it anyway. Even when he was still at the party five to ten minutes after talking to him, he'd gone over it. Even while he was staring at Louise's tits he went over it too. No wonder Louise felt overwhelmed by him, no wonder she carried around his tattoo. In New York, fame trumped beauty every time. At least he hadn't made any mistakes with Eric, though he hadn't made any impression either—on Louise, perhaps, but who knows if she ever told Eric about him or how that would all translate. Anyway, he did have her number and would call her and ask to interview her. It would be a real coup for the magazine just because it would be so outrageously different. It would definitely create buzz.

He did better with Margo Garrett—the Great Garrett. He'd even solicited work from her after exaggerating the contents and financial strength of the magazine and she gave him the name and address of her agent. Of course he couldn't expect her to whip out a short story or poem from her pocketbook—he was, after all, a flea in her universe. Nor would she give him her private address either (though he'd hoped she would), and telling someone to contact their agent was often a standard way of dismissing people. Still he would make the effort—he had nothing to lose. He needed two more good pieces and at least one more big name and Elliot was too shy to contact anyone famous—useless as far as that went—so he'd have to do it himself.

Still, nothing in the window, not even a ripple. Not that he could be really surprised, not that he even knew if she were home or not. What am I doing, he thought for a second, I should be writing, what am I doing on the street? His eye went to the street then as if to verify that he was there and he thought he saw someone. An older woman with a nice body looking at him. He thought she looked like Marianne, the woman on the beach in Chicago whose money he eventually took, but she was wearing sunglasses so he couldn't be sure. There were so many people in New York that eventually you saw people who resembled almost everyone of consequence in your life. Everyone had a double, it seemed, and in New York you saw them all and realized that while people might be unique, they were hanging on to their uniqueness by a thread, just like he was.

22

When you woke up like that you were never really sure if you screamed or only thought you had in your dream. In that sense, everyone was deaf. The only way to tell would be if the person next to you in bed heard it but she'd been alone last night, had been the night before too. There were two possibilities, she thought, while brushing her teeth. Either she screamed in her dream but not in the waking world, or the scream did carry over for a moment into the world but without her hearing aids she didn't hear it.

It was odd. The dream was so powerful yet she could remember very little of it and less now than when she first woke up. It was as if her preoccupation with her scream distracted her from recalling the dream that produced it and now it was lost forever.

She looked at herself in the mirror. There were lines under her eyes and her eyes, themselves, were slightly red. She was glad, in a way, to be alone when she looked so awful. It was only after her breakfast of a hard-boiled egg and pineapple juice that she realized how late it was—she hadn't been able to fall asleep until well past midnight. But on the plus side it was late enough to call Gretchen, though she hated to disturb her when she knew she was working on a piece for *ArtForum*.

"Hey," Gretchen said. "What's up?"

"You're working, right?"

"Beginning to, but I've got some time."

"Well, don't let me talk for more than five minutes, OK?"

"You sound upset, what happened?"

"I just woke up from a nightmare. I think I actually woke up screaming. Then yesterday I think Barry was following me."

"Shit. That would give me a nightmare."

"Maybe it was a coincidence, but it definitely felt like he was following me."

"Where was this?"

"In the Village, near my neighborhood. I was walking when I got that feeling and then when I looked I saw him but pretended I didn't."

"Jesus."

"I know. I mean, if he were going to pretend that he wasn't following me, then I could pretend I didn't see him. So I tried to maintain my regular pace and not act flustered. I was near St. Mark's bookstore and almost went in there but thought it would be too easy for him, you know as an editor, to justify going in there too, and then I'd be trapped. So instead I walked another block and a half, did my slight head turn and saw him again. Then I suddenly turned a corner knowing he wouldn't be able to see me for ten or fifteen seconds and went into a Rite Aid to the back of the store and waited about ten minutes."

"Don't tell me he followed you in there, too?"

"No. When I went outside he was gone—at least I didn't see him, but once you know someone is following you, you continue to feel followed—at least I did—for the rest of the day."

"How much about this does Elliot know?"

"Almost nothing. He knows that Barry came over to see my work, of course, but he doesn't know about Barry's creepy double entendres or his following me. A lot of times Barry arranges to be with us, usually for things having to do with the magazine, meetings for the three of us, or parties that we go to together. I'm supposed to see Elliot for lunch in a couple of hours, you think I should say something?"

"I really think you probably should."

"Really?"

"Yes, I mean you're not sleeping well and..."

"It will make him upset and things haven't been so great lately, you know, with my sex life, not that I can exactly blame Barry for that."

"Who knows? He's certainly making you nervous, and nervous doesn't go well with coming."

"He's reminding me of Jeff again, that's what he's doing, but I never told Elliot about Jeff either."

"Maybe you need to do that too. I mean you feel close to the guy, why not give him a chance. He might surprise you."

It was Gretchen's last line on the subject that she kept replaying in her mind as she recombed her hair. Of course, if Barry persisted, as it appeared he was, she'd have no choice but to tell Elliot. Besides, Elliot might notice it on his own anyway. Why was she so reticent then, so afraid to bring anything up? Because she didn't want to be the person who caused trouble between two lifelong best friends. Even with the six year hiatus, and the horrible fight that preceded it, Elliot loved Barry like a brother, and in a way idolized him. If she caused trouble between them he might side with Barry and she could well be cut out from his life. That's what happened to women who caused trouble—she knew that. Wasn't she trouble enough already—poor, not fully employed and burdened with hearing aids that made sounds in bed and other times actually kept her from understanding him (especially on the phone) half the time, though she usually covered it up. Not to mention watching TV with him with closed captioning (which never worked right anyway) or not understanding songs without the words printed out in front of her and now, as an added bonus, she suddenly wasn't coming either. She was definitely not dealing from a position of strength, though she supposed she could bring up something about Barry—in an offhand way—she could move towards telling Elliot, give him a nudge and see what happened.

As for telling him about Jeff and her rape—she knew she wouldn't do it. Gretchen herself had said it would be a bad idea a while ago, so why was she changing now? The way she, Cheri, saw it there were two kinds of male reactions to such a confession. One was not wanting to hear anything about it with the subsequent anger that one was forced to hear anything in the first place. The other, more enlightened one, that would probably be Elliot's reaction, was to express concern and sympathy that covered up an inner pain and possible devaluation of the woman, something the enlightened man would always feel but never mention, like a covert infection.

The bell rang. It was Elliot, and for a moment she felt a tingling kind of pleasure. Just before he opened the door she wondered where they would have lunch, but from the way he immediately kissed her, realized he had other ideas. He was also wearing her favorite blue sweater and the French cologne she loved.

"I thought you were hungry," she said between kisses.

"I have many kinds of hunger but the strongest is for you."

She giggled, then reaching around, put a hand on his bottom.

"But for now," he said, kissing her once more, "I have to postpone that hunger cause we got company."

"I don't understand."

"Barry's downstairs. I invited him to have lunch with us."

She looked away at her recently raised Venetian blinds.

"Oh. That's a surprise."

"I know, I probably should have called you but it was a spontaneous thing. He bumped into me in the lobby and asked me where I was going so I invited him to join us. It's OK, isn't it?"

"Of course," she said.

She disengaged from him and checked on her hearing aids, then on her hair in the bathroom mirror, wondering if Elliot's meeting had been an accident or if Barry were following him to arrange just such a coincidence and create yet another opportunity to be with her.

As soon as she saw him on the sidewalk in front of her building staring straight at her, she knew what he'd do.

"Cheri," he said, opening his arms as he gave her a hug in front of Elliot, then kissed her on the cheek. She tried not to bristle as she mumbled his name.

"Where are we off to?" Elliot said. "I'm hungry as hell."

"Where would you like to go?" Barry said, turning to her. "I think we should go where Cheri wants."

"It doesn't matter," she said, avoiding his eyes. "I don't feel much like eating." She caught a quick look of genuine disappointment from Barry.

"Should we go east and eat Polish?" Elliot said, walking beside her but still not taking her hand. "Pirogues sound pretty good to me right now."

"We could do that. Would that be OK with you?" Barry said, squeezing her arm a little. She was walking between them which allowed him to touch her. Why had she wound up in the middle? Probably Barry had planned it that way when they first started walking. She should have paid more attention.

"Sounds good to me," she said, trying to inject some enthusiasm into her voice.

"Or we could eat at an Indian place, or Greek," Elliot said, "they're each within a block or so."

"How about Japanese?" Barry said.

"I didn't know there was a Japanese place near here," Elliot said.

"Yes, it's actually in the West Village. I used to go there a lot with a friend of mine named Harvey who manages Three Leaves bookstore. You remember, Elliot, he was in my mother's apartment the first weekend you visited."

"I kind of remember."

"He's a friend, but of course not a friend like you and Cheri are . . . . He was someone I turned to after my mother died, not because I like his personal qualities so much but just that he was . . ."

"Sympathetic," Elliot said.

"Yes, sympathetic to me, to what I was feeling because his own mother had died. In that sense he kind of helped me through my crisis," Barry said, turning to look at Cheri as he added, "but now he's not that important to me, really, and I hardly think of him at all."

"OK, let's go there," Elliot said. "All right with you, Cheri?"

"Sure, of course," she said, thinking why can't he ever call me "sweetheart" in front of Barry, why can't he ever hold my hand or put his arm around me?

Barry had aptly described the restaurant as quiet and refined.

She only wished it were better heated, or perhaps it was sitting next to Barry that was making her feel cold and intermittently shiver.

"So, what do you think?" Barry said. "Has the restaurant lived up to my advance notice?"

"Definitely. It's a cool place and the food is good—a little slight but good," said Elliot.

"That's the Japanese way, capiche?"

She nodded as if he'd said something witty. She wasn't hungry and had barely touched her sushi or miso soup.

"So what's happening at the 'zine," Elliot said. "Any new interesting pieces I should know about?"

Barry told him that he'd just gotten some work from two pretty big name poets whose names she didn't fully hear, as well as a story from a well published fiction writer. Through much of the lunch she was observing the way Elliot interacted with Barry. She was struck by how much he tried to please Barry, how careful (even when he was joking) his responses or the topics he selected were, as if he'd thoroughly vetted them before speaking.

"I think we can feel very good about our progress so far," Barry said. "We're ahead of my projections, significantly ahead in some areas. I think the ad in *Poets and Writers* paid off, I think our website is first rate and will pay off, and I think the high profile parties I've been dragging you both to have been paying off, too. Pretty soon, we'll be planning our own inaugural party for *Beekman Place*," he said, smiling broadly. She thought of it as the big Gatsbyish smile Elliot had first described to her, too spontaneous a gesture to be contrived. So there was that part of him, too, she thought, but that part was emerging less and less the last two months and for long periods of time it seemed to be in eclipse.

She snuck a direct look at him again. The "Gatsbyish smile" was already gone, replaced by a colder yet fiercely concentrated expression that looked to her like pure, rapacious ambition as he began describing what he imagined, or rather, thought he *knew* would happen the night of his party.

"I'll invite Margo Garret and Woody Allen."

Elliot laughed. "You really think they'll come?"

"It's possible. OK, maybe not likely, but Eric West will be there and so will Louise Leloch."

"That would be quite a coup," Elliot said.

"Yes, it would," Barry said. "I got pretty friendly with Louise at Lillian's party and got their phone numbers. I'm going to call and ask to get an interview with Eric. Anyway, beyond them Roger Fogel will be there too. You know the gallery owner at whose loft you two met?" he said, turning towards her again with that strange little smile like the one she'd seen the day of his first visit when they'd walked together to Washington Park.

"Can you find a way not to include Darren Datz?" Elliot said, with a smile.

Barry laughed. "Unfortunately that won't be possible. I owe him for too many parties already. Remember he's the one who got us invited to Lillian Davis, speaking of which, I'm going to invite her too, and I think she'll come, I really do. We spent quite a bit of time talking at her party and she asked a lot of questions about *Beekman Place*. I'm going to invite *The Paris Review* crowd, too, and her crowd. I networked my ass off and now I need a way for that to pay off."

"So you see this as a kind of fundraiser?" Cheri said, thinking she'd been too quiet and needed to say something.

"No, that would be a sign of weakness and we need to create an image of strength—at least at first. Strength creates buzz in this town and we need buzz. For the fundraiser we have to exist a year then throw a first anniversary party replete with big name readers like Margo and, say, John Ashbery. People on that level. But don't be surprised if Lillian or Eric West sends us a check on their own. That's the way the rich operate. They give when you don't ask. You'll see."

"Yuh, I have to admit that part of your plan puzzles me," Elliot said.

"Why's that?" Barry said.

"I don't know, it seems like a contradiction. I mean, if you're trying to project an image of strength—that you're rich and don't need money—then why would anyone think of giving you any?"

Barry's face reddened slightly as he finished his beer. "No, no, what I meant was I'd never directly ask any of *the stars* for money—after all, their contribution is creating buzz just by attending. They'll get us press and they'll make everyone else there feel like we're the next big literary happening. Plimpton did that kind of thing for years with *Paris Review*. But, of course, we can discreetly mention on the invitation that tax deductible donations are appreciated. That way we ask without asking. It's different from a formal fundraiser where we have Ashbery or DeLillo reading and we charge money that goes to the magazine in the form of a minimal donation to attend, capiche?"

"Yuh, I think I get it," Elliot said.

I get it now, too, Cheri said to herself as she made an effort to avoid Barry's searching-for-approval stare. Elliot had pointed out the contradiction in Barry's thinking but Barry couldn't admit it. Instead, he had to continue to project an aura of infallibility with his gobbledygook about discreetly asking for money on the invitations—which was essentially Elliot's point all along. And Elliot, ever in the supportive role, went along with it, always trying to pad and cushion Barry's ego in even the most trivial matters. But why? Was he so afraid of losing Barry again? Was it the magazine and the free apartment? She didn't really think those latter reasons were it. He'd recaptured the past with Barry, or a big part of it, and couldn't bear to let it go. She knew what that felt like—not wanting to let something go. She felt that way towards Elliot, and during this ridiculous lunch that soon would be ending (with Elliot going back to Barry's for a meeting) she wanted all of Elliot to herself in her room, wanted to feel his weight on her, wanted to feel penetrated by him, wanted to hear his voice as he came. Why weren't they doing that? What were they doing instead? What?

23

They were eating takeout from Azure in Barry's living room. A basketball game was on TV but the volume was barely audible and neither of them was fully watching. Elliot was beginning to yawn—it had been a teaching day in Philadelphia and he felt tired. Then Barry said something and Elliot thought he hadn't heard it right, that the TV or his yawning caused him to hear incorrectly.

"What did you say?" Elliot said, leaning forward in his green Lazy Boy.

"I said when are you gonna ask Cheri to marry you?" Barry said, from his blue velvet chair, twisting his head a little to catch Elliot's eye.

"Don't you think it's a little premature for that?" Elliot said, forcing an incredulous laugh.

"No, not really. How long have you two been together?"

"We met in November, so four months then. That's not very long, is it?"

"But that's my point—you don't want it to be a long time, you want it to be the right time."

"What are you talking about?"

"Look, you're in love with her and she loves you back, right?"

"Yuh, but we're still getting to know each other and we're both still trying to get established in the city."

"You're established," Barry said, with surprising emphasis. "You're the editor of *Beekman Place*."

"*An* editor..."

"You're teaching college in Philadelphia and you're a published writer."

"All stories—no books."

"The books will come. Your position at *Beekman Place* will make a big difference there—you'll see. You also live in one of the more beautiful apartments in New York. I'd call that being established."

"But the down side is I haven't found anything for next year when my contract at school ends and Cheri also has to freelance and basically count every penny."

"The two of you could save a lot by living in the downstairs apartment."

"That wouldn't be right."

"Why not?"

"I wouldn't feel right about it. Come on Barry, we've discussed that already. But over and beyond all that is that while I love her a lot I'm still getting to know her and she's still getting to know me."

"OK, I see your point. You don't want to rush, but you don't want to delay either."

"Four months is delaying?"

"Don't get so hung up on chronological time. I think in every relationship there's a window of opportunity when the man can propose and the woman can accept and not feel humiliated that he waited too long to ask. Otherwise a woman's anger begins to accumulate and at a certain point it becomes too late, they get too angry to recover and they take it out on you in one way or another."

"You have a pretty dark view of the opposite sex."

"I'm serious, Elliot. I hate to say it, but I've always wondered if that wasn't what went wrong with you and Lianne. You two were living together for over a year but you never proposed…"

"So that gave her the right to fuck somebody else?"

"I'm not saying that, not at all."

"Look, Barry, I'm grateful for your interest, very grateful for that and for everything, but Cheri isn't Lianne, the present isn't the past and our window has just begun to open—it's still got a long ways to go—I'm sure of that."

Barry turned his head and appeared to be watching the game again. Elliot finished his beer, turned his own head and said, "Now what about you? What's going on in the women department with you?"

Barry forced a laugh and said, "What is this, quid pro quo?"

"No, I'm just curious, that's all. I don't care just about myself, you know, I happen to care about you."

"Well, I *was* pontificating a bit, before. Are you going to pontificate back?"

"Probably a little."

Barry laughed. "Then since you make it so irresistible, I'll admit that yes, I've finally met someone."

"Really? Who is she?"

Barry got up from his chair and paced a few steps while Elliot hit the mute button.

"I've met someone who's extraordinary, someone kind and warm and talented and sensual who I think is just right for me."

"Wow. So what's her name?"

Barry turned and paced a few more steps. "You're probably going to think this is ridiculous but I just don't want to jinx it by mentioning her name."

"What?"

"No, seriously, this sort of thing hasn't happened to me a lot, hasn't happened to me at all, ever, so it's making me kind of superstitious."

"So where'd you meet her?"

"At a party. We met at a party just like you and Cheri did."

"Was it at Lillian Davis's?"

"Could be. Look, Elliot, I really don't want to talk about it when it's so new and hasn't even been consummated yet."

"So you're going to deprive me of the chance to give you advice," Elliot said laughing.

"That does seem a bit unfair. But right now, because it's so early, there aren't any problems to discuss. I'm not confused at all about what I feel and since she's not married or engaged to anyone I'm going to go right after her."

"That's great. It's good to hear you talk this way."

"But I'm sure *some* problems are bound to develop and when they do I'll come knocking on your door. And then, of course, when things work out you can find out who she is."

"And meet her?"

"Yes, you'll see her for the first time."

He wasn't exactly sure why he did it, but shortly after Elliot left Barry began playing "Ghosts." Ghosts was a game where he shut off the TV and paced around the living room leaving only the night lights from outside to come through the opened shades. Usually, while he paced, he kept the TV on, not only the picture but the volume too. Then (often) he would drink when he paced, sometimes holding the glass of wine or vodka while he circulated around his living room until he exhausted himself enough to pass out in his room. When he played Ghosts, however, things were quite different. He would drink as well, but *before* he started pacing. Otherwise he would spend too much of his attention on not spilling his drink in the dark. The nearly complete darkness was a necessary condition for Ghosts. The whole idea was to become more aware of things as you attempted not to bump into them. It began with the Lazy Boys but there was also a coffee table and sofa, a desk and a number of other chairs to avoid. The point was that while trying not to collide with them he felt the reality of things more deeply, felt the ghostlike presence of the furniture's souls, or at least of the inhabitants who used them. Gradually, if he played long and well enough, that awareness spread and he could tune into the furniture in his mother's apartment below him. Sometimes, before Elliot moved in, it was excruciating to hear the faint but unmistakable half whispered singing that came from his mother's bed. He could feel her essence so clearly then, the beautiful innocence that had somehow survived in spite of time, in spite of his father and Benjamin Walters and the courts and everything else that had conspired to torture and kill her.

Of course it was painful, the very essence of pain, to feel such things and yet without feeling it, once in a while, often only after he'd felt many other things and seen many other images (including, last time, an image of Jordan in bed in the Motel 6, that nearly doubled him over) he felt his own soul would turn to furniture too, a chair so cold that no music could ever emerge from it. Since Elliot moved in, these sensations were less intense, as if Elliot's presence literally muted the ghostlike music. It was a tradeoff, he would feel much less pain, but also less direct contact with his mother. The problem would be solved when Cheri moved in with him, into his mother's apartment. If Elliot still wanted to stay (and he hoped he would understand and would stay) Elliot could have his apartment, the upstairs one where he was now playing Ghosts.

Of course he also continued to have thoughts—sometimes even reports from his police—while he played Ghosts. The thoughts never completely went away—they seemed to revolve in a dark netting inside him.

Well, tonight he'd given Elliot a chance, he thought as he walked past the blue velvet chair. It was Elliot's last chance and he didn't know it, which might not be fair, but for God's sake he'd had her for four months. If Elliot loved her, as he did, it would be more than enough time. Elliot was bright and very sensitive about some things, but he didn't really go as deep as *he* did—neither in his understanding of literature nor of women. That was why he ultimately wasn't right for Cheri, as Elliot, being an essentially fair man, would eventually understand, himself. Yes, sooner or later Elliot would realize that he, Barry, had actually done him a favor by taking Cheri from him simply because it would be obvious that she was more deeply fulfilled with him. He would want that, wouldn't he? It was what he should want and being an idealist, Elliot *would* want it—probably sooner rather than later. Hadn't Elliot just said they were just starting to get to know each other, he thought, as he slipped past the sofa. There, unwittingly, was the bald admission of failure. Four months and they're "just starting to know each other"! Four months and they still had "a long ways to go"! But he knew he had penetrated to her spiritual essence in his first visit alone with her in her apartment, the afternoon when she made him cookies and walked outside with him among all the Christmas shoppers (including the little bastard who bumped her) on their way to Washington Park. He could never forget the images from that day. Her thrilling blend of naiveté and nervous sexual energy so eternally feminine as Goethe would have undoubtedly said of her, the very essence of the secretive but innocent woman she was. And you are and remain innocent if someone who really knows you loves you as he really knew and loved her. It was dark and terrifying to be loved by someone who really had knowledge of you which was why she was resisting him to the extent she was—but it was ultimately irresistible. He knew that and so did his police.

...Everything was in order suddenly, as piece by piece things were falling into place. It was like a quiet avalanche of order, like climbing up a winding and difficult mountain trail strewn with slippery rocks and sharp thorns and filled with bees and mosquitoes until suddenly you reached a clearing, a vista that revealed the land and water below stretching out and shining for miles.

There were still a couple of clouds, serious clouds that partially obscured this vista. One was the Elliot cloud—that he might not react to losing Cheri the way he hoped. The other cloud—moving closer to the Elliot cloud and actually fusing with it at a couple of points, was the Louise Leloch cloud. Because he couldn't deny he was lusting at times for her ever since he met her at Lillian's and to justify what he had to do—the boldness and purity of his vision—he needed to face up to that lust and "own it" as the TV therapists would say. Why? Because to carry off his plan with Cheri he had to be focused completely on her and not be inhibited by any free floating extraneous desires. Cheri had to become, in effect, the first woman he was ever faithful to and the only way to be a hundred percent sure of that, or his capacity to focus exclusively on her would be to see Louise again and test himself with her. It was an unlikely scenario, he realized, his chances of even seeing Louise again were small, but at the stakes he was playing, what did he have to lose? He was always preaching risk to Elliot—even fifteen or twenty years ago when they were kids on the playground—to the point where Elliot once called him his "risk master." Now it was time for the risk master to take a risk. He had her number; it was a simple question of calling her for an interview to be scheduled for the second issue of *Beekman Place*. Elliot might not like the idea of a profile of someone in show business, purist that he was, but he'd eventually be convinced once he'd see their sales rocket. It was also unfortunate that he'd led Elliot to believe the interview would be with Eric West. But he could explain that away and eventually smooth it over. Yes, he should call Louise tomorrow morning or afternoon before she entirely forgot him. If she did refuse him that would clarify his path as well, and clarity was what was most needed now, his police all agreed on that point—and so did he.

24

"Of course I remember youuu…" she'd said, extending the *u* to a comical degree and then letting him hear her trademark giggle. "We sat next to each other at Lillian's and had that fascinating talk about babies and immortality. 'Art is the last illusion,' you said, right?"

"Right," he said, laughing a little himself.

"See how well I remember? I'm not as dumb as they make me look in the movies."

"I'm very impressed."

"You're the publisher of a magazine, too, that's just about to debut, a literary magazine."

"A literary and film magazine," he said, deciding that sounded better but hoping he wouldn't have to tell her too many lies because when he was nervous, as he was now, the quality of his stories suffered. "I'm extremely impressed by your memory," he added. "That's actually one of the reasons I called you, though I didn't really expect to get you on the phone."

"Why wouldn't you get me? Who else would answer my phone?"

"I thought your secretary or someone like that."

"Eric and me always travel alone when we come to New York. We like to keep it simple. That's why we never have any help staying with us in our New York apartment. That's a no-no. Otherwise, they end up selling stories about us to the tabloids."

"I see your point. Well I certainly won't do that."

"Oh no, of course not. I know what a great intellectual you are."

He was stunned by her compliment for a moment but managed to say thank you. "I was hoping, though I know it's a long shot, to try to schedule an interview."

"I'm sure that'd be cool," she said, cutting him off. "But Eric's in meetings all day today, and tomorrow we're off to LA."

"No, no, I was calling about interviewing you."

"Me? Really?"

"Yes, I thought I told you that at Lillian's. Of course I'd be deeply honored to interview Eric West at some point, who wouldn't, but I wanted to interview you as an example of a terrific young actress and rising star. I think your story would fascinate our readers."

"Wow, I'm really flattered. I don't know that I have that much to say. My career's been pretty much just showing off my body so far. You could blink and miss the *acting* I've done."

"I'm sure you have lots to say," he said, trying to contain his elation at how easily everything appeared to be working.

"Well, I do have a few free hours this afternoon. What would we do about pictures?"

"I can send a photographer the next time you're in the City or fly one out to L.A. at your convenience."

"OK, I'm starting to like this, Barry."

He liked the way he was talking, too, boldly and without hesitation—the way Bobby Fischer played chess.

He had to admit he was excited when he got off the phone— exhilarated and almost hyperalert—as he sat at his desk and wrote out a list of twenty five questions for Louise Leloch, potentially a Pamela Anderson who could act, some said. It was just incredible how things like this happened in New York, really incredible.

Next on the agenda was selecting what to wear. Of course, the temptation was to go with a jacket and tie but he knew it was a mistake to dress as if you were intimidated by the famous. That would be a sure sign he didn't belong. Much better to underdress but with some imagination or elegance. Since he didn't know enough about clothes to dress with real imagination he decided on casual elegance—his silver wine drinking shirt from Italy that Elliot liked so much and a pair of black pants and black Italian shoes. Hadn't Cheri even said she liked it once as well? Yes, he was sure she had.

He felt that familiar Cheri pang in his heart then (and would feel it he knew for the rest of the day), as if he were about to betray her and suddenly thought of canceling the interview. But he shouldn't doubt himself so easily. He had a solid plan, both he and his police agreed on that. It's true there was something bizarre, even surrealistic about it, but that was only because Louise was a star and in his life he'd had very few collisions with the world of celebrity, and none as far as one on one meetings with a woman as attractive *and* famous as Louise.

It was amazing the dividends that *Beekman Place* was already paying. Really, it was as if he were dreaming. And they were going to continue to pay off even more, year after year, as the magazine grew in stature. Elliot was right to have pushed him to do the magazine six years ago. He hadn't seen it at the time, not in the clear way he saw now.

Yes, one had to live life aggressively, without second guessing or self doubt. You made your plan first, you thought it through, as he had done and then you attacked. Though it was almost certain that nothing would happen with Louise, that in any event Cheri would ultimately prevail, he still had to follow through on his plan to know for sure, didn't he?

…On the phone he was focused and aggressive but unfailingly polite. He'd suggested a number of restaurants for the interview but she said she didn't want to risk dealing with the paparazzi.

"Eric pretends not to care," she said, "but it really pisses him off when these lies about us come out in the sleaze rags."

"Of course," he said, "Who wouldn't be angry?"

"And let's face it, because he's so famous and also, well, an older man, (although he's the youngest man I know in energy and spirit) they pounce on me every time I'm spotted with someone around your age and write these awful stories about my cheating on Eric which just about tears my heart in two."

"That's awful."

"So if it's OK with you I'd rather do it right here in my apartment so long as you promise not to take any pictures of me I don't approve."

"Of course not. I won't take any pictures at all during the interview. What about a tape recorder? Would you like me to tape it or not?"

"Yah, I think I'd rather you tape it. I'm not exactly the world's best speaker and sometimes I blurt out things I wish I hadn't and then Eric gets upset. So if you tape it and type it up and promise to send me a copy, I can read what I said and get a chance to edit out the stupid parts which will probably be about half of it," she said, laughing.

"Of course," he'd said, though he didn't even own a tape recorder and had to take a taxi immediately after the phone call ended to look for a place that sold one. Luckily she'd made him laugh on the phone which helped him relax. It was only when her doorman said, "Yes, Mr. Auer, she's expecting you, the elevator's to the right," that he began to feel nervous again.

It was an impressive Park Avenue apartment—not enormous—but certainly big enough. As in a fairy tale, the door was open for him but no one was there.

"Come in, make yourself comfortable," she said a moment later from behind a wall, "I'll be right out."

He looked around furtively—still acting like a criminal, his police noted. The furniture was elegant but not ostentatious. There was a roomy sofa and big soft chairs, as if they were catering to Eric's older producer friends, he thought, with their big, soft asses. There was also off-white, thick wall-to-wall carpeting on which the great director no doubt dicked Louise from time to time. But the only tip-off that this was a multi-millionaire's apartment were the paintings judiciously placed on the walls. Originals by Chagall, Modigliani, and Diego Rivera. There was even a small etching by Picasso, and one by Giacometti, too. It seemed the "cowboy director" (who really grew up in Fort Lee, New Jersey) favored the European masters. There was no American, much less any western art, in sight. How our apartments do reveal us, Barry thought with a little laugh. But shouldn't he be writing some of this down for the introduction to his interview? No, he would remember, he was sure of it. At any rate, he didn't want to be seen scribbling away like some third rate stringer when Louise finally made her entrance.

A moment later she walked into the living room wearing skin tight blue jeans and a low cut pink blouse that revealed a generous view of her extraordinary cleavage.

"Hey, Barry, thanks for coming," she said, extending her hand then leaning in for a hug and peck on the cheek. He could smell her perfume—expensive and delicious.

"Thank *you*," he said, feeling her, no doubt, artificially enhanced breasts brush against his chest. He was surprised by her height until he realized she was wearing very high heeled black shoes.

"Your apartment is beautiful."

"Thank you."

"And your art is amazing."

"Most of it's back in L.A., but we left a few good ones here."

"I'll say."

"Eric's been collecting a long time. It's all his taste. I don't know much about art but he's trying to teach me. Do you need to set up or...?"

"Oh, for the interview? No, my tape recorder is very discreet, very diminutive—you'll barely notice it, see?" he said, taking it out of his jacket pocket and holding it up.

"It *is* small."

"So you'll barely notice it."

"Do you want to just sit on the sofa then and put the recorder on that glass table in front of it?"

"That should work fine."

"Fabulous. Now I just have one more question for you: would you like a drink now and some really super hors d'oeuvres left over from a little dinner we had last night? I've already had some drinks so I'm way ahead of you."

"A drink sounds good. I'm trying to diet so I'll pass on the hors d'oeuvres, but thank you."

"Are you sure? Woody couldn't stop eating them last night."

"Woody Allen?"

"Yes, he and Sun Yi were over last night."

Now I'm supposed to want the hors d'oeuvres, he thought, so I can eventually shit the same food that Woody Allen ate. He told her he'd stick to his vodka tonic, then sat down and tried to stay calm while she disappeared again to fix his drink. It nearly rocked him—the painful beauty of it—that somehow Cheri knew what he was doing and was even somehow there in the room judging every minute that he spent with Louise. Yet, a part of him was relieved to know he could feel this much, relieved that it proved to him he really did love her. Wasn't that enough of a test, he asked his police? He waited for an answer but they were mysteriously quiet.

When Louise returned, her breasts were half visible as she bent down to give him his drink.

"OK, I'm all yours," she said, as he tried to keep his eyes raised to an appropriate level.

"When did you know you wanted to become an actress?" he said, turning to face her (she was only a few feet to his right on the pale green sofa), "and how did you know it?"

"Wow, what a question," she said, smiling even more broadly at him. "That's pretty deep. I think I always knew, I mean, I think I was 7 or 8 and had a part, OK, the lead, I admit it, in my school play and it just gave me a feeling I never got in any other way."

"What was that feeling?"

"Oh, just the fun of pretending I was someone else and making it all seem real. And then of course the applause was nice. The first time you hear it, there's nothing like it on earth," she said with a smile that revealed her straight, gleaming teeth and that made him erect a little for the first time since he'd been there. This ambivalent discovery, in turn, made him increase his concentration on the interview. He absolutely couldn't try anything stupid with her as he'd been doing with other women recently. It was out of the question.

"Did you ever study formally?" he quickly asked, "and if so, at what point in your career?"

She looked genuinely introspective. It was strange to see a woman with such outrageous tits look pensive, but there it was.

"No, I can't claim to have studied with anyone formally. Of course, I learned a lot from a lot of different actors and actresses and then when I met Eric, especially from him. I mean—who wouldn't? He's one of the world's great directors."

"Of course."

"I remember a talk we once had early in our relationship. I don't think he'd mind my telling you this," she said, swallowing the rest of her drink. "I'd asked him if he thought I should study—join an actor's studio or whatever, and you know what he said?"

"What?"

"He said, 'You don't need to study, baby. You're a natural. If you studied, they'd just fuck you up.' Wasn't that sweet of him? I think it's the greatest compliment I ever got. Especially since it came from such a genius."

Barry nodded and said something supportive, reminding himself to keep well hidden the contempt he felt for West's movies. One day, sooner rather than later, when his novel was published, his work would bury that fake cowboy's.

"Who are some of the actresses who've influenced you? I mean your approach, to acting…." It was such a typical question that for a moment it embarrassed him.

"Oh there're so many. Meryl Streep is great, Eric loved working with her and he loves Julia Roberts, too. And you know who else Eric and I always loved is Angelina. She can do it all, don't you think? And then, of course, we both loved Marilyn. She was the greatest, right?"

"Definitely," he said, though he was barely listening. He felt he was in a movie himself, not acting in it, but photographing it and not as the photographer exactly, but more like a magical camera floating invisibly in space. An invisible camera with a little tape recorder inside it that kept asking questions.

"And what about actors? Have they influenced your work as much as actresses?"

"That's a really interesting question, Barry. Let me think…I think we've all been influenced by Jack and Marlon and by Bobby DeNiro. Of course all those guys are geniuses and I'm, well, I really feel that I'm just starting out. So far I've just been kind of a tit queen but I aspire to be much more. I guess that's why being interviewed like this is making me kind of nervous."

"You're nervous?"

"A little. I mean, you see the expensive breasts but underneath them beats the heart of a hick," she said, repeating her joke she'd said at Lillian's party.

They both laughed, then he said, "I thought you were wonderful in Eric's last movie."

"*Rainbow Café*?"

"Yes," he said, hoping he sounded sincere since he hadn't seen it.

"I love being in Eric's movies 'cause they have so much substance and, and . . . meaning, don't you think?"

"Of course."

"He gives me a chance to really act because he really believes in me. At least, I think he does."

There was a silence until he said, "Have you ever thought of doing any independent films?"

"Yah, sure, I think about them all the time. I was even going to be in one by…well I shouldn't mention the director's name."

"Why not?"

"Cause . . . some bad stuff happened."

Barry raised his eyebrows to show he was interested. "You're being very mysterious," he said.

"Well, this director thought he was in love with me. Least that's what he said."

"I'm sure he was."

"Nah, it was more like he was in lust for me. He started writing me these crazy letters and making lots of phone calls and naturally Eric noticed and got upset, so I had to withdraw and there went my independent movie."

He nodded. His erection was back but he wasn't worried. It was like his own independent movie he was directing. He wouldn't do anything stupid again. He was a pawn then but now he was a king and Cheri was his queen he would be faithful to.

"I'm sorry it didn't work out."

"Don't be," she said, although her eyes were tearing up. "I'm so lucky. I mean look at this," she said, gesturing with her arms to indicate her apartment. "And I have a beautiful home in Beverly Hills and a house in the south of France."

"Really?"

"Yah. Eric doesn't talk about that one so let's keep it off the record, OK?"

"Of course."

"And then we have an apartment in Paris, too, even though we only go there one or two times a year. I guess I always make a fool of myself in Paris 'cause I can't speak any French. It irritates Eric no end."

He decided he wasn't going to reassure her about that and instead said, "You have an amazing life, don't you?"

"Believe me, I pinch myself all the time. I know how lucky I am. You think I think I deserve this? What have I done? Just married the right guy I guess," she said, laughing, as she put her empty glass on the table.

"Now all I really need to be happy is a baby and we're working on it...or I am. If I could only convince him to have one more. Eric already has a lot of kids you know...well he's had a lot of wives."

Once more they laughed in unison. It really was like they were performing a concert together or a play.

"I guess that's what keeps him so young."

Sure, thought Barry, that and his daily thermos of Cialis.

"I remember your talking about wanting to have a child at Lillian's," Barry said.

"That sounds like me, always blurting out private stuff to people I've just met. Eric hates that about me, he's warned me many times to stop it but I can't seem to help it—especially when I'm a little tipsy, like I am now, screwing up this interview."

"Don't worry, you're doing great."

"See, my only problem is I worry about him 'cause so many women want to have affairs with him and a lot of them are more beautiful and smarter and more talented than me and wouldn't bug him about having a baby, either. Do you see what I mean?"

He hesitated, not knowing what to say, while she finished another drink. When she put the glass down on the table it sounded like a wind chime and made him long for the outdoors.

"Did I say the wrong thing? Am I talking too much again?"

"No, not at all."

"It's just that you've gotten so quiet," she said.

"I'm just listening to you, that's all."

"That's a wonderful quality, Barry. Women really like that, 'cause they don't meet many men who ever really listen to them. Even Eric doesn't really listen to me much. Sometimes I think he'd like it better if I never talked at all. Anyway, all I'm trying to say is sometimes I get nervous being married to such a great and desirable man. You know, some people have said he's the new Orson Welles. Did you know that? They used to compare him to Robert Altman but now they compare him to Welles, you see what I'm talking about, and I'm just a Hollywood body that's never even had one of his kids—like three other women have. Can you understand what I'm feeling…Barry?"

"Of course, but I don't really think you have anything to worry about."

"Thanks, but I do worry. Most nights I have to take pills just to get to sleep."

"Really?"

"'Fraid so. Well, now I'm definitely talking too much."

"Don't worry, I won't print that."

"Oh thank you, darlin'. You're a true prince. Please don't print any stupid stuff I say, OK? 'Cause, you know, half the time I really don't know what I'm saying."

"Of course," he said, but he could barely hear her because his police had their night sticks out and were screaming like sirens. He tried to look away from her then. He looked just to the left of her but that was too close, too tempting, so he looked up at the ceiling hoping to see Cheri's face—the constant sun he needed to locate.

Meanwhile, Louise was slurping the rest of her drink, or maybe starting a new one while she continued talking.

"You really are a prince," she said, "you're a really special prince to look out for me this way."

"Thank you," he said softly, with his eyes still averted in what must have been at least a vaguely comical way from the point of view of anyone watching, except no one was watching, not even the police.

"I think you really do understand what I'm feeling, don't you? You know what I'm going through."

"Yes."

"When he leaves me alone at night, or even sometimes in the afternoon like he did today, it's like I die a thousand deaths imagining him doing some woman, maybe even a hooker. I mean, everyone wants him so he could probably get any hooker for free. I'll feel it then like it's gripping me by the throat and then a rage will go through me.... You look surprised but it's true, I'm ashamed to say it's all true. I'll feel rage even though I don't have any proof that it's anything more than my mind working overtime, being overstimulated and turning on itself....Well, OK a few times I really did have proof, I mean I figured out the code in his appointment book, I'd smell the woman's perfume on him (I have a very sensitive nose, maybe cause it's the only part of me they didn't reconstruct, much). Once I even kind of had him followed . . . and I'll think 'Jesus, I didn't ask for any of this, I didn't ask for this,' you know."

He heard the glass go on the table then heard her crying and once again didn't know what to say.

"Give me a hug, will you, Barry? OK? I really need one."

They moved closer to each other, then she was in his arms, breasts against his chest, his arms covering her like a tent.

"It feels good in here," she said, "really good."

The next thing he knew her tongue was in his mouth, then he didn't think anymore, just felt her tongue. He wanted to close his eyes but kept them open unable to resist the sight of Louise Leloch, bona fide Hollywood sex symbol, kissing him. He only wished he'd brought his camera so he could photograph her. Meanwhile, her tongue was making a series of complicated loops and probes all very skillfully executed, and he had to concentrate to be able to respond properly. He could hear her breathing, could feel her breasts—finally he closed his eyes. But the moment he did, he saw an image of Cheri's face with the hopeful, slightly frightened expression in her eyes as she handed him the pineapple juice and cookies in her apartment. It was the exact moment when he not only knew she liked him, but was hoping, in spite of himself, for love from her, real love, the kind that could transform them both.

He waited till one of Louise's deep probes ended and then pulled away from her.

"What's the matter?" she said.

"I'm sorry, I can't."

For a second she looked like she'd just been shot. "What?" she said. "Are you kidding?"

"No, I can't. There's someone I love, so I can't."

"Sweetie, I love someone, too. What do you think I've been talking about all afternoon?"

He shrugged, in spite of himself. Looking down, he was surprised to discover that one of his buttons was missing from his shirt. She must have torn it while she was massaging his chest.

"You know how much I love Eric, right?"

"Yes," he said, "of course I know."

"I can barely say two sentences without talking about him. I mean, this was supposed to be my interview but it ended up being all about him just like all my other interviews."

He looked up from his shirt and saw that she was watching him closely.

"Well," she said, straightening her own clothes, "this is a first. I thought you were going to say you were gay or had some kind of injury or something."

He didn't appreciate her remark. How dare she say that to him? Although it was true he was physically intimidated by her (who wouldn't be?), especially when he thought about all the actors she'd already had with their artificially enhanced dicks and other body parts.

"No, I'm enormously flattered, but . . ."

"Don't say any more, OK?" she said, holding up one of her hands. "I heard you the first time. It was just a mistake I made—it's no big deal."

"OK. Well, would you like me to finish the interview?"

"I'd like you to go now, Barry, that's what I'd like."

"All right then, if that's what you want."

"And I don't want you to print that interview, all right?"

He looked at her. Something in her tone of voice frightened him, reminded him of her deep pockets and powerful connections.

"OK then, I definitely won't."

"I'd feel much better if you'd give me the tape right now. Then I think we could be friends and there'd be no more issues between us."

He felt another jolt of pain at the thought of handing over the tape and closed his eyes again for a second. Cheri's face, the same image he'd seen before, was still there and his police were nodding in agreement.

"Here," he said, handing her the tape. "Here's the tape," he said, thinking that Cheri had saved him again, and he had to see her and make her his, that she was the key to everything, the key to the ten thousand doors he felt shut against him.

25

She lay next to him in bed, holding his hand and smiling in the half light of early morning.

"That was exquisite," she said.

"Yes it was," Elliot said. He gave her hand a little squeeze and she giggled. Then they lay together without speaking for a while.

She'd been right not to talk about her past or Barry. Thank God she'd kept her mouth shut and just believed in him and now this magnificent morning surprise seemed like a reward for her good judgment.

"What are you thinking?" Elliot finally said, squeezing her hand again as if their bodies were performing a post-coital fugue.

"Just wishing we could lie together like this all morning."

"So do I. You can imagine how much I feel like taking a train to Philadelphia and teaching all day."

"Well, think of me on the train and maybe it will go by faster."

"I always think of you. I always feel like you're with me no matter where I am," he said, leaning over and kissing her forehead, then her lips.

He wanted to ask her to marry him then, but said nothing, in part because he wanted to get the ring first to give to her when he proposed and also because he really did have to hurry now or he'd miss his train. Tomorrow he'd do it, right after he bought the ring. He'd take her out to one of their favorite restaurants and ask her there or later at her place or maybe, at his apartment at Beekman Place, though there was always the possibility of Barry somehow interrupting, so perhaps her place, small and cramped as it was, really was better. He decided he'd deal with these logistics on the train, saving a little time also to review for today's classes.

Usually, when Elliot left, she got dressed and fixed breakfast in fairly short order, or if she and Elliot had already eaten together, she'd proceed directly to her shower, her make up (which was always modest) then finally get dressed. She was not the type to spend any significant time on her wardrobe as some of her friends like Gretchen did—selecting then discarding a variety of outfits before a final, tortured decision was made. She supposed she was a tomboy that way. Always had been. Not that she didn't like getting dressed up from time to time—especially for Elliot—but that left to herself she was perfectly happy to just wear jeans or old clothes—the clothes she wore when she painted each morning had a way of staying on her all day.

Today, however, she decided she wouldn't rush through her morning rituals and would wear something nice after work, and something really nice when she and Elliot went out tonight. She also decided to take her time, instead of rushing, that she wouldn't even call Gretchen right away with news of her bedroom success. She'd definitely call her today, though, because Gretchen deserved to know, given all the advice she'd given and all the time she'd listened on the phone.

She smiled as she brushed her teeth, thinking of her morning with Elliot. Remembering the look on his face when she came excited her again and she wished he were here and wondered if she'd eventually end up masturbating while she closed her eyes and thought of him, but then thought she probably wouldn't. She really was eager to paint—especially when she simultaneously felt so calm and so full of energy.

"Hey, Barry."

"Hi," Barry said, wondering where all these "heys" he'd been hearing from Elliot lately were coming from. "Back from your class?"

"Yep."

"Where are you calling from?"

"My apartment."

His apartment, Barry thought, with a flash of ironic anger.

"So what's up?"

"Just checking in, wanting to see how everything's going with the magazine."

"Everything's going fine. I have a final meeting with Paul about the cover."

"Cool."

"Anyway, we're right on schedule to go to the printer next week and have the issue come out at the end of March, just in time for our annual April 1st *Beekman Place* party."

"You sure it's a good idea to link the magazine to April Fool's Day? We leave ourselves open to a lot of jokes."

"Absofuckinlutely. It's much worse to appear like we take ourselves too seriously. I'd rather be accused of rape than pretentiousness," Barry said, making Elliot laugh.

"It's a paradox, isn't it?" Barry continued. "The most serious people feel they have to prove they don't take themselves seriously, that they haven't lost their sense of humor. Plimpton was a master of that and look what it did for *Paris Review*."

"Good point, I can't deny it. I guess I'm being a little myopic . . . it comes with being an academic."

"We're lucky no one else—no other literary magazine anyway— has thought of an annual April Fool's issue and party. This way we've staked our claim to it; it will always be associated with us and we'll own it. Do you see?"

"How did the interview with Eric West turn out?"

"Very well—surprisingly well. I predict it will get us a lot of press coverage. It certainly will separate us from all the literary rags that just publish stories and poems, n'est-ce pas?"

"That's true."

"So I'm feeling pretty good about things, I have to admit," he said, thinking he sounded convincing enough and that there was plenty of time to tell him about West's change of heart later. Besides, Elliot wouldn't care. Stodgy classicist that he was, he'd never wanted the piece in the first place.

"It's scary. I'm feeling pretty good, too," Elliot said.

"Well, you should."

"Yes, I do. I have some news of my own to tell you."

"Oh?"

"I'm going to ask Cheri to marry me."

Barry dug his nails hard into the palm of his left hand. "That's incredible . . . . That's great news. When is this going to happen?"

"I think probably tonight. I bought a ring today in Philadelphia."

"When did you have time for that?"

"There's a jewelry store four blocks from my school. I did it during my break between my office hours and my class," he said, laughing.

"Wait, wait, don't tell me any more over the phone. I'm coming down to your place with a bottle of wine to hear the rest."

Only then did he release his nails—didn't even bother to look at the marks they made—went instead to his refrigerator, checked out the white wines but nothing was good enough, saw a bottle of champagne then remembered that he'd bought it for Cheri and himself and decided he couldn't drink that with Elliot, that Elliot didn't know much about wines anyway and took a California white with him downstairs.

He thought of nothing but having the right smile when he'd first see Elliot, because the wrong one could reveal everything. He didn't even prepare a speech, not even a line. Knew he would first say congratulations and shake his hand or hug and then the right words would come—but a smile would be harder to control.

The odd thing is he didn't remember the words he said—they were like clothes he'd worn two days ago that he couldn't recall. But he did think he knew what his smile looked like, that he would always know that, and also that he'd passed his smile audition, as it were, must have.

He remembered his toast, too, and Elliot's wide, guileless smile. Then, after the toast Elliot said, "I know I don't have a permanent job or even any prospect of one. And Cheri doesn't either, but I just don't want to wait any longer. I guess I followed your advice. You think I'm crazy?"

"Of course not," Barry said, thinking it's me that's waited too long—but I'm not going to wait any longer.

"Of course your congratulations are premature. She could very well say no," Elliot said, with typical Elliot modesty.

"I doubt that. That won't happen," he said.

They talked some more about it for at least ten minutes he thought. It was as if he were improvising in a jazz duo. First Elliot would solo on drums and then he'd answer back on piano—as if they were trading fours just like Paul Motion and Bill Evans did when they played together in Evans' best trio.

Then the piece ended and he said, "Where are you going to pop the question?"

"I don't know. Maybe when we're at the restaurant or more probably afterwards."

Barry turned away and paced off a few steps. He closed his eyes for a second—willed his smile back—then turned towards Elliot, though he kept his head at a slight angle away from Elliot's eyes.

"Are you going to stay at her place tonight as usual?"

"She feels more comfortable there for some reason. So, that's where it'll probably happen."

"Well, after she says yes . . ."

"She may not," Elliot said, holding up his hand to make a kind of stop signal. "She may not want it now or ever."

"I'm sure she will and then you can celebrate the next morning."

"Unfortunately not."

"You don't teach two days in a row, do you?"

"No, but I have a so-called important department meeting. C'est absurde, n'est ce pas?"

Barry laughed. "So you have to take the usual morning train to Philadelphia just for that? You can't call in sick?"

"It'll look bad. They already don't like it that I'm commuting from New York. They take that as a kind of slap in the face, so no, I can't really take the chance. I'm already on slippery ground there."

"Well, so be it. You can make up for it the next day."

"Oh, I will."

"Elliot, it's really great. I'm very touched."

He shook his hand again then said, "By the way, to transition from the grand to the trivial, for a moment, I somehow misplaced my copy of the keys to my mother's, to your apartment. I'm afraid they may be lost, so I was going to go out now and get a copy made, then come right back with them if that's OK?"

"Of course," Elliot said, handing him his key chain. Barry saw the key to her place on it—a little golden key like a miniature magical instrument. All the way to the hardware store he carried them in his right hand, looking down at her key, thinking that it would always be his, that he would have her key forever now.

26

He made a list, then immediately put it in his back pants pocket and buttoned it so it couldn't get out.

Things to bring:

> Her key
> Your keys
> Sleeping pills
> Credit cards
> Map of Pennsylvania
> Cell phone
> Change of clothes
> Ativan
> Pot
> ID
> Passport
> Fake ID
> Rope
> Gun

He got out of the subway on Christopher Street and started walking towards Grove Street. It was a gray, heartless sky. It didn't matter. He wouldn't let it matter—his police were asleep or at least inaccessible. He walked purposefully through the streets with his head up as if he were running down court on a fast break expecting a basketball to be thrown to him. He didn't stop once to duck behind a dumpster or a tree as he had when he'd followed her before in her neighborhood. Those days were done now, just as over as heartless gray skies discouraging him, because he had a secret weapon now, he had Cheri inside him beating like a little sun, warming him, and brightening his view. He started hearing the old Brian Wilson song "Warmth of the Sun" when he was two blocks away from her and Elliot had already been on his train for eleven minutes.

"But I have the warmth of the sun . . . ," he sang to himself, or maybe, more accurately, just heard it inside his head. Such a beautiful song—the way the melody went was a stroke of genius—yet it all came from a stoned, simple minded Beach Boy. Amazing how often, especially in music, talent avoided the intelligent and permeated the otherwise average mind. Perhaps if he'd had that kind of natural talent, everything would have been different. It was hard to say.

It didn't matter. Everything was different now and what wasn't different already, soon would be changed and then *stay* changed forever. In less than five minutes he would sing a different song, "Across the Universe" by John Lennon. There were good songs today by people like Cat Power and James McMurtry and even Coldplay, but the old songs were the best. He was already hearing a line from it, "nothing's gonna change my world, nothing's gonna change my world."

He was behind the dumpster directly outside her building. Her shade was up but he saw nothing. What if she'd left already? But that was unlikely only twenty minutes after Elliot left her apartment, with no job of her own to race to. Very unlikely but still possible.

But where would she have gone? For a few seconds he imagined her on her way to his apartment to confess her long repressed desire for him. "Help me leave Elliot, Barry. I'm about to make a big mistake," she whispered in his ear during their first, intense embrace.

Of course that hadn't happened. His police were laughing at that one. What had really happened instead was an image from future time had invaded the present through some kind of covert attack and filled his mind for a moment. His police were right to laugh now, though they wouldn't be laughing for long.

He looked up again—scanned her two other windows with the shades up, but saw nothing. Of course there were many more pedestrian answers that could explain it. She could be in the bathroom, perhaps taking a shower after her morning sex—it wouldn't matter, it would all be different for her after they finally became lovers. Then again, he thought, she might have run across the street to the little grocery/news store to buy a *Times* and some milk. He looked over his shoulder in the direction of the store but didn't see her.

Anyway, he was anticipating too much. Nothing had happened that should or could disrupt his plans. He stood up, looked around himself briefly and then headed towards her apartment.

He opened the door to her building on the first try. A smooth, firm turn to the right and he was in, alone at the foot of the stairs. So far, brilliant luck, he had to admit. He decided to walk, figuring the chance of anyone seeing him on the stairs was less that way, as people always chose the elevator over walking. She lived on the third floor—it wouldn't be much longer and he'd see her. He was assuming now that she was home and wondered why he'd ever seriously thought otherwise. He had to stay focused in the present. He had to be ready to act immediately and felt his gun again deep in his bag just before he put the key in her door.

It was like stepping into a white dream or a desert or dream of a desert and he felt an instant sense of disorientation, like vertigo. He looked to his left and right, holding his gun, and knew instantly that she wasn't home. Her apartment was so tiny and innocent. There was just the bedroom, in which she still painted, the little bathroom, and the kitchen area where she'd once fed him cookies and pineapple juice. He crouched down and waited behind the refrigerator.

Then he had an awful thought. What if she went to Philadelphia with Elliot because she'd said yes to his proposal and just didn't want to be separated from him? It was possible just because it would be such a wildly romantic thing to do and Cheri was a terminal romantic. But Elliot had probably proposed last night and they'd already had hours to celebrate—he had to accept that, found he could even picture it vividly enough to startle him—Elliot's sperm dripping from her pussy—plip plop plip like notes of soft music.

Also there were plenty of reasons why she wouldn't go, not the least of which was that deep inside (deeper than Elliot could go when he fucked her) she couldn't deny her love for him, Barry, (he would never be Gordon to her).

He waited and listened but heard nothing. After a few minutes his legs ached and he stood up, still staying behind a side of the refrigerator. How long could he remain like this? How long could he really stand to wait when his mind was burning with so many plans and visions? She really had thrown him off by not being home when he'd never considered in all his plans that she wouldn't. Perhaps before he looked at her apartment she spotted him through her window that she happened to look out of then, maybe just to check the weather. Or maybe while he was looking up at her, she was walking out her door, spotted him by the dumpster and turned away just in time. He got the sense, the last two times he met her on the street "by accident" that she was a little nervous or ill at ease, as if she wanted to get away from him quickly. It broke his heart to remember, but she acted that way the one time he visited her in her apartment. She was ill at ease then too and eager for their meeting to end, even as she fed him juice and cookies, her attraction to him no doubt making her nervous.

He got up, bag in hand, and walked out of the kitchen to her bedroom windows, looked out, but saw nothing. He swore under his breath, then walked back to the kitchen. He felt hungry and opened her refrigerator. It was a collage of health food—yogurt, pomegranate juice, green tea, granola, flax seed oil, orange juice. But where was his pineapple juice, where were his chessmen and sugar cookies? He opened up a couple of cabinets without success. It was the refrigerator of a woman who's taken up dieting. It was for Elliot. Did he mean so little to her then that she forgot to replenish the cookies and pineapple juice again for one of his future visits? Did she really not expect him to visit—really have no idea, then, how he felt? But perhaps the diet was for him.

He paced off a circle in her kitchen then stopped stone still as he heard a key turning in the door. Finally he unfroze and made it back just in time to his spot behind her refrigerator.

He heard her walking then—the music of her step. He half expected her to be whistling or singing some upbeat tune but she didn't. *Come into the kitchen*, he thought, *come into the kitchen*, but she went into the little bathroom instead and peed, which made its own kind of music. He listened till the last note then took out his gun, got up from his crouch, and tiptoed forward. He couldn't wait any longer. She might make a cell phone call at any moment. He had to startle her before she could think to use it.

He was near the bathroom now to the side of the door. He pictured her wiping off the last drops of urine and began to erect. Then the door opened and—he could never explain to himself what happened next—he leaped, seeming to float through the air like a praying mantis in an insect ballet. When he landed he already had his hand over her mouth, stifling most of her shocked scream (the way he had with Jordan) while the other hand held the gun. Next he spun her around so she could see the gun, see that he meant business, but she continued to scream and struggle.

Finally he forced her down on the bed, turning her around and planting both knees on her shoulders the same way he'd sat on Love Hunt in Exton. It made him shiver for a moment to see Love Hunt's face so clearly, though he had to remember it was only a memory. It made him say "open your eyes" so he could be saved by Cheri's face (unless he imagined he said it). "Open your eyes and look at this," he said, pointing the gun at her. Her eyes grew large like Little Orphan Annie. It was as if he'd electrocuted her.

"Don't say a word until I tell you to, capiche? Don't make any noise and I won't hurt you. OK? Nod if you understand."

She nodded the way a little princess would nod and he felt his heart nearly break again.

But she had been a rambunctious little princess, even a rebellious one.

"What are you doing?"

"No more talking."

"Please don't hurt me, please . . ."

"I won't ever hurt you. I love you."

"Let me go then. Just let me go."

"You'll understand later."

"I'll never understand . . . . Elliot will never forgive you. You're ruining everything."

"This is bigger than Elliot, much bigger."

"What are you talking about? What are you doing? What are you going to do to me?" she said, like a quasi-hysteric.

"I'm going to change your life, in a good way, in the best way."

"I don't want to have my life changed. I'm going to marry Elliot, don't you understand that? I love him, I'll always love him."

"*Always* is the most illusory word."

"What are you doing with the rope? Are you going to kill me?" she said, and as if in sympathy, her hearing aids began making a wounded, whistling sound.

"Of course not."

"Are you going to rape me?" she said, and then started to cry.

"Of course not," he said, but she continued to kick and struggle, making the hearing aids go off again until he finally tied up her arms. She was a lot more difficult than Love Hunt, which surprised him.

Then when he gave her the pills, she bit him. He had to pry open her mouth with both hands to be able to force them down. He held his bleeding finger tightly while he waited, pointing the gun at her the whole time with his other hand and reminding her not to scream, or talk, just to be still—but she continued to cry and beg. It nearly made him cry, but he didn't capitulate. They were very powerful pills—knockout pills. When she finally was almost asleep, he took her coat from her mini-closet, untied one of her limp arms, put the coat on her, and began to walk outside. Again, despite the difficulties involved, he chose the stairs.

I'm living like Bobby Fischer again. But what if you do run into someone on the stairs, muttered one of his half-sleeping police. He decided he'd make a joke about her drinking too much. If anyone asked if she were all right, he'd make a joke which he rehearsed in his mind three or four times.

But he didn't run into anyone. People were at work, he'd forgotten that. They were either at work or too lazy to use the stairs.

Outside it was gray and raw and still heartless. He figured he'd draw some looks the way Cheri was shuffling along half asleep like a zombie, but people walked with eyes straight ahead of them like faithful New York soldier/zombies. A half block of this and he was in the car buckling her up (he remembered she looked at him in a half pleading, drugged-out way) before she passed out. She never took drugs (he knew that) so they affected her strongly, as he knew they would.

At first, while she was sleeping he kept reviewing what happened in her apartment. Then suddenly he felt a tremendous urge to turn on the radio—feeling an almost palpable craving for music—but didn't want to risk disturbing her sleep which he hoped would last until they were inside his Exton apartment. That's when the challenge would really begin.

He was passing through Philadelphia now looking for the highway exits. It was dangerous territory, full of police, which made his own police wake up with sirens blaring. It would be a full time job just to keep them quiet, keep Cheri asleep, and his car not over the limit (though he yearned to speed) until he'd finally reach Plum Point Drive.

She was lying down on the same bed Love Hunt was on in almost the same position. But he wasn't sitting on her arms. He thought of it, but couldn't bear to hurt her or even to disturb her sleep, and so he watched, holding onto his gun the whole time.

The rest of the day passed through several periods, each one with its own distinct light and color. Not that he saw it directly with his Venetian blinds pulled tight and the curtain drawn across the sliding glass doors at the end of his living room that led out to the back yard. No, he could only see the shifting, gradual darkening indirectly—sense it more than he saw it.

She woke up groggy, and at first without any idea where she was or why she was tied to the bedposts. When she saw the rope and focused on him with his gun, she let out a quick half scream the way someone does when they awake suddenly from a nightmare.

"What are you doing?"

"Watching you, I've been watching you for hours."

"What are you doing, Barry? What? Why am I tied up?"

He paced off a few steps, turning away from her and looking down at the floor.

"What are you going to do now? Have you thought of that? Have you really thought about what you're doing?"

"I've thought about you and Elliot, too. I've thought about everything long and hard and the end result of that thought process is to be here."

"Why?" she said, crying for a few moments. "Why have you done this? I just don't understand why you're doing it."

"It was the only way."

"The only way for what?"

"The only way to spend the kind of time with you we both need. If I could have done it any other way, I would have."

"Done what? What are you talking about?"

"I've already told you—we have to change our lives."

"My life *has* changed. I want my life the way it is now. Don't you understand, I'm going to marry Elliot. I'm very happy now."

"I know you think you are. I know you're very earnest and don't mean to deceive me. I believe that."

She shook her head in frustration. He could see little tears forming in the sides of her eyes. Then she focused on him—looked right into his eyes while she spoke.

"Can you just tell me where we are? Can you tell me what state we're in?"

"We're both in a state of anxiety, but it will pass."

She shook her head. She hadn't liked his joke. He looked for more tears but didn't see any.

"I had to take you to a special place. We both need to be away from New York, capiche?"

"Are we in New Jersey?"

"I said a *special* place," and he laughed at his own joke, hoping she would laugh too, but her expression held firm.

"Do you remember the day I came to your apartment to see your work?"

He waited for her to respond but she said nothing.

"The day you fed me your sugar cookies and pineapple juice, and then walked with me to Washington Square?"

She nodded or half nodded.

"That's when I knew I had to take you to a special place. That's when this day was born."

"But you're throwing away everything, don't you see?"

"I'm throwing away nothing."

"The magazine you've worked for—we've all worked for—your friendship with Elliot, your lifelong friend and . . ."

"I'm throwing away nothing because I'm trying for everything. It's you who needs to do the same thing."

"So what is your plan? What do you imagine is going to happen now?"

"Can we just let things unfold on their own for a while?"

She shook her head and looked at him incredulously. He noted that he'd never seen that expression before and liked it.

"No matter how much you let things *unfold*, you can't make me stop loving Elliot or make me fall in love with you. You're a very intelligent guy—obviously you know that."

"Thank you."

"For what?"

"For calling me intelligent. It's the first nice thing you've said to me today."

"Do you enjoy the compliments people give you at gun-point?"

The remark stung him—it was the first time she'd made him angry—but even his mother did that. He would forgive her—he wouldn't even show her he was hurt. That's what people who loved at the highest level did.

"As I said before, if there was any other way I could do this, I would. But the gun is necessary for now."

"No it's not. You could put it away and we could talk."

"And if you ran for the door?"

"You could stop me, we both know that. For Christ's sake, I'm tied up."

He looked at her to see how sincere she was. Her hazel blue eyes were clear like a clear lake or sky.

"OK. I'm going to trust you. I'm going to put the gun in my pants pocket. I'm going to make a Kierkegaardian leap of faith."

"Thank you," she said.

He nodded at her in acknowledgement. He wanted to be on top of her. To pull down her skirt and see what kind of underpants she was wearing, which he'd once thought about for almost a whole day not too long ago.

"So how much time do you think we're going to spend here?"

"I'll know, I'll know and then we'll know."

"You realize that within twelve hours or so Elliot's going to call the police. He's expecting me to be home tonight. He's expecting to stay over at my place."

"I've thought of that. I brought a laptop. If you like you can send him an email eventually, or if you don't I will, telling him you're all right. You see, I don't want Elliot to suffer. This isn't about meting out punishment, suffering and retribution. It's important that you understand that."

"So what is it about? Trying to change what I feel about Elliot and you?"

"Those aren't the exact words I'd pick but they're a lot closer. Maybe if you started to think of this humble little place in the middle of nowhere as your school, your life school where a new life does ultimately await you."

She looked hard at him and then tears sprung to her eyes again.

"Do you believe you can teach people to love people they don't and unlove people they do?"

"In the kind of education I'm talking about, I do. I think you can learn what love really is and when you do the most amazing transformations are possible once the total mind, especially the unconscious, is involved. It really is amazing."

"Can't you just let me out of here? I won't tell anyone what you did. I'll just move away and . . ."

"No. It had to be you," he said, half singing the words. "You can't pick the people you love any more than you can pick what kind of eyes you have."

"I think you did pick me—but you don't have to. I think it was some unconscious compulsion having to do with Elliot. I think you could unlearn to want me very easily."

"I don't think so."

"I'm not beautiful, I'm not brilliant, and I'm half deaf. I'm just a regular struggling person. I'm not an intellectual like you. I can barely understand it sometimes when you and Elliot talk."

"I can't unlearn what I feel. It's too late for that as it's too late for so many other things."

"Why is it too late? Nothing really bad's happened yet—except you've scared the shit out of me. If you just let me leave you'll still have your life—your magazine, your future, and even Elliot, because I won't say anything, I promise."

He gave her a curiously serious look and for the first time she felt her head lighten as if there was real hope.

"Of course you'd tell him."

"No, not if you untie me and let me go now. What would there be to tell? You haven't done anything bad yet, everything can still be saved."

He sat down on the bed and she shrank away from him.

"I'm not the Hunchback of Notre Dame, am I? I'm not going to contaminate you, either."

"Sorry."

"To answer your question—I am trying to save everything . . . worth saving. I'm trying to save both our lives and in the process Elliot's too, but you don't see that yet."

"No, I don't. I'll never see that. That doesn't make sense, it just doesn't make sense."

He got off the bed and took a few steps before turning and looking at her as if he'd just passed through a revolving door.

"Did you ever stop to think that everyone you see is a ghost? Yourself included."

"What?" she said dully.

"Whatever we look like now is an illusion because we're all going to get old and look like (and then actually become) a different person—so different from the younger version as to make our current incarnation a ghost—something illusory or insubstantial. The only person I've known who wasn't a ghost was my mother because even when she was dying she still looked like her young and beautiful self. You know why? Because she truly loved me. She was truly capable of love and she loved me which is how I know that love is the anti-ghost, the true fountain of youth, capiche?"

"I'd agree with that," she said, somewhat relieved that his conversation had at least taken a hopeful turn. As long as he wasn't agitated, was instead, as he seemed now, relatively tranquil, she figured there was a chance that nothing awful would happen.

"The problem is that love like that is so rare, that you have to search for it so long and so relentlessly and so alone. You look puzzled, but think about it, who is going to help you in a world full of ghosts? Ghosts are essentially helpless when it comes to this. They can't do a thing where love is involved—that's why they're ghosts."

"So your definition of a ghost is someone who can't love?"

"It's not a question of my definition. I didn't invent the world, I just describe it. First I observe it and then I describe it—in my mind first, of course, before I finally put it on paper. That's what writers do, n'est-ce pas? And I am a writer more than anything else. Even more than I'm the publisher and editor of *Beekman Place*. I'm a writer first. Ask Elliot, if you don't believe me. He used to read me when we were children or teenagers. But teenagers are really children, aren't they? If only she were alive you could ask my mother. She was my greatest reader. But then mothers always are because they read you with love in their hearts—if you're lucky enough to have the right kind of mother, as I was lucky, while it lasted."

"When did she . . . ?"

"Die. It's OK. That's what happened. She died and left me alone although I have a father who's probably alive somewhere, but I'm not sure. I used to think of him as a king when I was young but the king deserted me. Anyway, my mother went and died on me though she was still so young and beautiful looking when she died, which wasn't even a year ago. Wait a minute, maybe it was little longer, I should know this, of course, I should be able to rattle off the statistic but my view of time is so different now . . . . Chronological time is virtually meaningless to me now, the lie of measuring time by clocks and calendars."

"What should we measure it by?"

"By our memories, our hearts. We only die when there's nothing left to remember, when there's nothing left to think."

"That's a really interesting way to look at it."

"Don't say that if you don't mean it. We have to have complete honesty in our communication—otherwise, everything I've done with you so far is meaningless."

"I understand," she said soberly, as if chastened. "But I did mean it."

They exchanged a quick smile. It wasn't any longer than the light from a firefly—on and then off again—before it disappeared, but she felt a slight clearing in her head. She saw now what she had to do. It was a delicate balancing act to empathize enough with him to convey a certain kind of respect and appreciation that she knew he craved without making him think he could sleep with her.

"What are you thinking about?" he said.

"What you said about memory and time."

"Do you want to know what I've been thinking about?"

"Sure, yes."

"What kind of underpants you're wearing."

She tried to look away from him. She could feel her face redden. A moment later she thought she might have said "oh" but wasn't sure.

"Did you know I once spent an entire morning, actually almost a whole day and night, imagining what kind of underpants you wear? And the conclusion I came to is that you wear simple white cotton ones like a boy might wear, maybe also some yellow or pink ones. Was I right?"

"That's personal, Barry."

"Of course. All things about people are personal, no question about it. So you're not going to tell me? You're not going to solve the mystery that I devoted so many hours of my life trying to solve?"

She looked down at the bed. Her wrists were beginning to ache.

"Of course, you know, I could easily find out."

"Please, no."

"I'm just saying. You were unconscious for a long time while you were with me and I had a lot of opportunities to find out a lot of things but I didn't. I could have looked while I was tying you up, for instance, but I didn't. Do I get any credit for that?"

"I appreciate that."

"You can simply tell me the answer, you know. You don't have to show me. Just tell me what color."

She considered telling him but was sure he'd make her show him anyway.

"Let's talk about something else," she said.

He laughed. "You're pretty brave to say something like that. Especially under the circumstances," he said, pointing at her. "You speak as if I were the one tied up. I like that, you have guts. I think that's a positive quality if you handle it well. I really do. I, myself, have guts, too, though I haven't always handled it well. I suppose you think bringing you here the way I did is an example of my not handling it well, right?"

"Yes," she said softly.

"And then talking about your underpants that way. What a mistake that was. Admitting how long and intensely I thought about that and yet if you could somehow be inside my head, or just know the thoughts in my head like watching a kind of videotape I think you'd understand and forgive me. Why? Because I didn't think about it in a dirty way as you might imagine. Far from it. My thoughts were . . . poetic really . . . I mean that. They were lyrical and filled with love. It was one of the first days, maybe *the* first day when I realized that I really loved you on the highest level. So now that I've made my confession, now that I've revealed so much of myself including the context of my fantasies, would you still deny me the answer to my question, my simple question about the underpants you're wearing today?"

"They're white . . . I think."

"You *think*?"

"They're white."

"I knew it! You see how well I know you."

She tried to say something but only nodded.

"Some women would find that a very attractive quality in me. You look puzzled. Not that I can guess the color of your panties but that I'm capable of concentrating on you enough to realize things about you. Some women I've known are grateful for that kind of attention . . ."

"I'm sure lots of women have liked you," she said, trying to ignore the pain in her wrists which had come back again.

He paced off a semi-circle and when she saw him again he had a quizzical kind of smile on his lips.

"Did you know I could have made love to Louise Leloch?"

"The actress?"

"Yes, that Louise Leloch. The one you saw at Lillian Davis's party. The one I interviewed for *Beekman Place*. And do you know why I chose not to? Because of you."

"Me?"

"Yes, you."

She shook her head as if in disbelief, as if she were deeply interested, believing the longer he stayed in a light, almost surreally self-congratulatory mood, the better.

"You have trouble believing it? Well, it's true. I interviewed her for the magazine in her apartment in New York—you knew that, n'est-ce pas?"

"Yes, I'd heard about it."

"Elliot told you, right? I knew he would. Anyway, she has a beautiful apartment on Park Avenue in the mid-fifties filled with all kinds of art . . . a Picasso, a Renoir, a Giacometti."

"Wow."

"Yes, 'wow' indeed. Anyway, I was very professional in the way I conducted the interview. I concentrated on her acting, her film decisions, her aesthetic influences and didn't ask any gossip-mag questions and I guess she liked that—that I took her seriously as an actress and person. So, soon she started giving me drinks and more drinks and told me her husband was away for the afternoon—you know who she's married to?"

"Eric West, the director."

"Yes, Eric West the *world-renowned Academy Award-winning* director. And then she started getting, how shall I say, playfully physical with me, touching me and then hugging me, doing the things, you know, that women . . . do to let a man know they want to make love . . . . Well, I won't lie and say I wasn't tempted, especially certain parts of me," he said, with that same strange little firefly-sized smile about his lips. She felt her face redden again when he said it, wishing that it wouldn't turn red like that but it seemed to have a mind of its own. Maybe if she made some kind of comment, said something, anything, it would help, but she couldn't think of anything to say.

"In fact, certain parts of me were extremely tempted a number of times, but I never fully responded to her passes. You know why? Do you know why I turned down Louise Leloch? Because the image of your face was burning in my mind the whole time. Your face—which is more beautiful than Louise's—infinitely more beautiful and filled with your innocence and enthusiasm and capacity to love. It wouldn't let me. At one point, it even fused with my mother's face and that's when I knew I was protected, made invulnerable from lust by the power of love. My love for you and your, still unconscious, love for me."

She stared at him and nodded, just like a little child learning a sacred truth about her parents' past, he thought, or perhaps learning the secret of Christmas.

"It's amazing how divided people are. Did you ever think of that?" he said.

"No, yes. I have thought about it, I mean, from time to time."

"We all walk around with other people inside us, don't we? Like we're all part children, for instance and part adult."

"Sure, I see that, I agree with that." She thought of Elliot calling her "his baby"—thought she might cry then or scream but fought it off. Then she decided she'd use that image (and any other future images of him) to make her stronger if she had to fight off Barry, if he really did try to rape her or worse, although that wasn't happening now and she knew she should try to stay positive and as much as possible act normally.

"There are other kinds of divisions, too," he said, "many other divisions. I was just giving a for instance."

"Oh sure, of course," she said, as if she were following his argument closely. She decided that was the best way to keep his mind off sex, to act like he was making intellectual history with every remark he made and that she alone was his only witness. You couldn't kill your only witness if you were making history, could you?

"Then there's the good person and the evil person inside us.

Stevenson was on to something big with Dr. Jekyll and Mr. Hyde. I mean, we're all Jekyll and Hyde, don't you think?"

"Yes, I see what you mean."

"Stevenson's using them metaphorically but really not, I think, in one sense. Because we all really do transform, at times, into different people we carry around inside us. *But . . .* there are certain people . . . people like you who aren't really divided, who are whole the way children are whole, capiche?"

She didn't know what to say. Probably it was better to agree with him but then the conversation might suddenly stop and that was what she feared the most.

"You look puzzled," he said. "Puzzled into silence. You've probably never thought about this very much."

"No, probably not."

"Why would you? Why would an innocent and undivided person think about this? It's simply not part of your world, is it?"

"Not the way you describe it, no."

"In my case I even give this other person inside me a different name."

"What is it?" she blurted.

For the first time she saw something like fear in his face.

"No, no, I'm not going to tell you that. That's not anything you need to know."

"No, of course not."

"I've probably already told you too much already. Don't you think so? Has it damaged your opinion of me, what I've said so far?"

She looked at him incredulously for a moment, then quickly said, "No, not at all."

"All right, then, I'll tell you something else. I don't know why I'm telling you all this but I feel a strong desire to."

"Go ahead."

"OK. There are other people who are in there all the time too."

"Really? Who are they?"

"They try to regulate what I do, in a way. Sometimes, I have to convince them or appease them or just sneak by them to get to do what I want to do. Just to get from point A to point B. I call them the police. There's more than one of them but I think of them as being the same, like a chorus in a Greek tragedy."

"What do your police think of what you're doing now, with me?"

"They're allowing it because they know why I'm doing it."

"Why are you doing it?"

"Because I love you, and this is the only way. I told you that—my answer isn't going to change."

27

He was the only person she'd ever seen who she could really say had "steely blue eyes." His name was Dan Morisson, but to herself she called him "Steely Dan." Just before he spoke she saw the slightest hint of a smile.

"We found him."

"You sure?"

He nodded with a slight look of irritation.

"How'd you do it?"

"We don't discuss that, Miss Hunt. Here," he said, handing her a manila envelope. "What we know about him is all in our report."

"What's his name?" she said as she took the manila envelope, clutched it almost angrily, as if she were once more forced into contact with *him*, Gordon.

"His name is Barry Auer. Like I said, what we know is in the report, including the balance of your payment."

"Let me settle now. I want to pay it all now, OK? I brought my checkbook."

"Certainly, Miss Hunt."

Her hand trembled slightly while she wrote the check and she worried that he saw it, but when she looked up, his steely eyes were looking out his office window.

"Here," she said, handing it to him. He didn't look at it.

"Thank you, Miss Hunt," he'd said as she turned to go. "There's one more thing," he added, Columbo-like, as she'd started towards the door. She turned and looked at him.

"You have the information you requested, so our job is done, and what you do with that information is your business. But *if* you decide to do something that might involve further contact with him . . . well, I strongly suggest that you don't, that you work with the authorities instead, or call us again and work with us. Do you understand? This is a dangerous man, remember that."

"Yes," she said, nodding her head superfluously, she thought, like she was some kind of horse. "Thank you, very much. I appreciate that."

Then in the next moment it hit her just like the late winter sun in her eyes when she first left the building. It wasn't going to be enough just knowing what she knew (it wouldn't even be enough to convince the police). It wouldn't be enough unless she tracked him down and made him do his own dance for mercy. She was glad she had a gun now—the one she'd bought outside the bar on 12th Street from that skinny but tough looking black dude. (Question: Since the gun dealer was doing something illegal, why did he dress so ostentatiously, like a pimp in that long fur coat that could only call attention to himself? Criminals were like actors that way—attention junkies who could never resist attention even when it threatened them.)

She remembered how the second she got to the car she'd read the report (only two and a half typed pages) over and over—fascinated, appalled. It was only factual information, yet it seemed like lines of poetry revealing his twisted, inner self. It told his name and address, the fact that he had no known job but also no criminal record. It also mentioned his hefty bank account, which figured since he had a home in New York ("Auer resides at 30 Beekman Place, an expensive district in the east side of Manhattan" it read) as well as the place in Exton on Plum Point Drive near where she'd seen the boy with the Eagles jersey, and also nearby the oddly lighted pool that gleamed in the distance like some kind of extraterrestrial park even in winter.

508 Plum Point Drive—it was only a few miles (though out of the way) from the detective's office. "Auer appears to spend the vast majority of his time in New York City," he'd written. But there was a chance he could be in Exton now, and even if he wasn't, she wanted to see the place where he'd violated her—with his gun and blindfold and hideous weight—then made her pray to him. She felt her jaw clench when she remembered it as she turned the car towards Exton as if she really had no choice where she was going—as if that had been predetermined all along.

It had gotten dark. The Exton late winter dark that obliterated almost everything, eating it up like a black shark. She turned her lights on, only then noticed the snow on the ground and trees. How could she not have seen it before? Or maybe she saw it but didn't notice it. It was like her night with Gordon—she must have seen warning signs about him, but they didn't register or not strongly enough, not in her conscious mind at least. For a moment she pictured those signs huddled together trying to push through the door to her consciousness. But they hadn't been powerful enough to push through. They weren't an army of signs, after all, more like a little band of three or four and they weren't strong enough to do it. Instead they froze there at the door, or else simply evaporated.

What was she doing? She wasn't thinking straight. Instead of concentrating on what she should do next, she was scaring herself with her own train of thought—a train that Gordon had derailed ever since that night.

Finally she turned on to Plum Point Drive. It was too cold and dark even for a ghoul like Gordon to choose to stay in Exton—not when he lived in an opulent Manhattan apartment in the warm, rich city with millions of potential victims to choose from. She grit her teeth as she imagined him in bed with another woman, torturing her no doubt in a soundproof room high above the streets.

It was probably good that he wouldn't be in Exton (Detective Steely Dan would certainly think so), but small matter if he wasn't—she'd go to New York soon, maybe even today, and find him there. He wouldn't get away without paying. Besides, she couldn't be sure he wasn't in Exton. A ghoul like Gordon probably loved the dark and cold—it was ideal torture weather. Hadn't he called himself Mayor Bat? And bats loved the dark. Like vampires and zombies, they thrived in it.

28

They heard the noise at the same time. She tried to pretend she didn't hear it, but he saw her eyes get big, and immediately he sat on her again.

"No," she said. She couldn't tell if she screamed or not before he covered her mouth with his hand.

Then he let out his own half scream when she bit him. He withdrew his finger that gleamed in the half dark like a sword as he checked it for blood.

"Don't ever do that again," he said as sternly as he could, while he increased the pressure on her mouth and shoulders with his knees. He hated to do that to her, but there was no choice. He saw tears forming in her eyes then, increasing as if they were fucking and multiplying. Then he eased the pressure and listened again to the sound outside.

He heard steps—what else could it be—like high heels against the pavement that reminded him of Renee. Odd how a woman's shoe was so much louder than a man's.

"Don't make a sound," he said, regretting that he'd freed one of her arms. He looked around the bed for the rope while he listened but couldn't find it, as if the rope had slithered away like a snake.

The steps were getting closer. They sounded almost cricket-like—like a human cricket.

He thought of taking her into the closet with him and shutting the sliding door in case she tried to make noise again, but worried that she'd make too much noise on the way there. The ceiling was soundproof as well as two of the walls, but he couldn't do anything with the windows that he thought of as sound tunnels, amplifying his life in the room.

Then the unimaginable happened—there was a knock on his door, repeated three or four times like a woodpecker on a tree. He had to point the gun at Cheri again, had to place it a few inches from her head even though she looked so shocked and frightened—just like he'd electrocuted her. In the time since he'd rented this place, he'd had very few visitors. Just the landlady once and another time someone with a petition they wanted him to sign. Maybe it was someone like that again—although his other visitors had come in the late afternoon or early evening, certainly not in the dark like this human woodpecker who was knocking again.

He felt anger surge up in him that he should be scared like this at night, that he should be violated in this way, and would have loved to answer the door, gun in hand, and make the woodpecker outside feel some of what he was being forced to feel. Except he couldn't do that. Couldn't risk leaving Cheri alone even if he were able to retie her other arm and pad up her mouth again, both of which he could probably do in a half minute. It was still too risky. He could lose everything that way.

Then the bell rang—vibrating like an electric organ inside him. When he recovered from the shock of the sound of it, he listened more closely than he'd ever listened to anything as if each part of him had transformed itself into an ear. He thought he heard the person saying something, muttering outside his door. Was it Elliot? It sounded like him, just like him, but that was impossible, wasn't it? To think like that was an invitation to madness he couldn't give in to. Yet the resemblance was uncanny. How can something happen that can't happen? He thought of Jordan for a moment. Then he looked at Cheri's face, half fearful, half hopeful, and renewed his listening—the way he used to listen to the sounds in his mother's apartment in Beekman Place, listening and hearing the secret music from her empty apartment like Roderick Usher, communing with the dead.

Finally the bell stopped and the knocking did, too, and a moment later the music of the high heels retreating on cement and Cheri cried softly, respectfully, so that he didn't have to punish her and he was back in the present again.

But it hurt him, her crying, as if she'd bit him in his heart.

"You act so disappointed, as if your last chance just got blown away. . . a sin of the wind. . . . Am I really so repellent to you? Why can't you see this as your *first* chance, as our first chance to really be together?"

She turned her head from him and closed her eyes. The crying continued.

"It's not that I don't empathize with you," he said, as he got off her shoulders and made a gesture with his hands to emphasize this latest empathetic gesture. "If anything, I feel too much for you, to the point where it clouds my judgment."

"If you empathize with me so much, why don't you let me go?" she said, turning to face him. He thought before he answered her. It was her fundamental question.

"This is too important for both of us. Why can't you see that? All our lives have been pointing to this day, this night. Haven't you ever felt 'when will my life begin?' I mean one 'lives,' one performs one's routines, one moves through time and space like a human or a zombie, the two often overlap, have you noticed? When what you're waiting for, what you're secretly living for is for life to begin. Real life, real love, real feeling, not the endless progression of fake programmed feelings that people call 'love' but something powerful and almost deadly like an ocean or a tornado ripping through you. That kind of feeling, that kind of life. Don't you want to feel that just once? The death of death, the birth of life."

She looked closely at him. "But shouldn't I get to play a role in how I want my life to begin? Shouldn't I get to choose the details of my own life?"

He smiled. There was something so adorable about her type of innocence that it often made him smile, even laugh out loud when he was alone and thinking about her.

"My Cheri amour, of course you have a role in choosing. Of course it's your life this is happening to and no other. But sometimes we have to defer to something stronger than us."

"The way I'm 'deferring' to you now that you've tied me up?"

"Ha, ha, good one. I didn't know you had a sarcastic sense of humor. I didn't know that sarcasm was a part of you—that sarcastic cells flowed through your bloodstream. You see how I keep learning new things about you? That's why it's so important that we give in to the greater force and learn more about each other while we can. Notice I say 'we' because although I love you with every fiber of my being, I also have to be humble so I can learn about you, capiche? Do you understand? Are you beginning to understand?"

"About why you have to tie me up and point a gun at me and sit on me?"

"That isn't what this is about."

"Then why don't you stop it? My body could use the break. It's sore. I'm sore. It hurts me and scares me a lot."

"Do you think I enjoy doing that?"

"Then why do you do it?"

"I do it to keep you here. To keep your attention focused on us and the vision you need to see—not just with your eyes but with your heart. I can tell by the look on your face that you don't understand yet, that it all sounds like gobbledygook to you but you'll see, in time. I'm very confident about that, and you can't kill my confidence."

"But in the meanwhile, if I'm quiet will you stop hurting me?"

"Yes, of course I will."

She looked away from him for a moment and the muscles in his heart seemed to constrict. It was unbearable to lose contact with her eyes, surprisingly unbearable.

"If I could just feel that you won't do anything to me physically against my will it would mean a lot."

"Of course, I won't."

She raised her head and looked at him tentatively.

"Why are you looking at me that way, with so much fear and uncertainty? Why don't you believe me?"

"Because, I mean, you already have done things to me physically…against my will."

"And here I thought I'd been behaving like a perfect gentleman. Why the incredulous expression? I haven't touched you in any bad places, have I?"

Her face reddened again, almost as if she were having sex with him and he felt an instant sense of reward.

"I didn't mean that," she said.

"Not that I haven't been tempted," he said, staring at her breasts and then moving down to her thighs.

"I didn't mean that. I never accused you of that. I mean when you sat on me, that was against my will and then the gun . . . ," she said, biting her bottom lip to keep from crying.

"I thought I explained about that. You were fighting me then and I had to restrain you to keep you focused. You're much calmer now."

"Then can you untie my other arm?"

He looked at her uncertainly. "I think you've earned my trust enough for that," he said, still holding the gun and watching her face closely as he untied her left wrist.

"There, how's that?"

"Much better. Thanks. Who do you think that was at the door?" she said.

"Some person with a petition or a collection jar. Maybe it wasn't a person at all. Maybe it was a ghost with a petition."

He laughed and she tried to force a smile.

"I'll tell you a little secret about our dear departed ghost," he said, still smiling.

"What's that?"

"He's got a lot of company."

She smiled quizzically. He could tell she didn't understand.

"Because the world is full of ghosts," he said, but she still looked confused—innocent and confused. "Meaning most people you meet are already dead," he added.

"I don't understand."

"They're either dead or the living dead. Most people are zombies actually. Does a zombie *know* he's a zombie? No, they think they're alive, of course, and that's the grand illusion of the world, and the great irony of the world, too. 'Cause what could be more ironic than a zombie thinking he or she is alive when they're really dead? Yet that's what millions of them—hundreds of millions of them—think."

She stared at him. Her skin had whitened almost the way it did when they'd struggled earlier.

"How do you know for sure who's a zombie and who isn't? How can you tell for sure someone who's alive, but maybe very depressed, from a zombie?"

"Oh, you can tell all right. By the way they look and the way they smell. Zombies don't feel any emotion, you know—just need. They only care about what they're addicted to—food or drugs and maybe TV, otherwise they're completely uninterested. For their addictions they'll kill or do anything, but for everything else they're uninterested."

"How long has it been since you realized all this?"

"About zombies? I began to realize it after my mother died. After she died the scales fell from my eyes and I began to realize a lot of things."

"How long ago was that?"

"Pretty soon it will be the first anniversary of her death, very soon in fact, maybe even tomorrow. But my mother was not a zombie. Just the opposite. It's that her death made me realize that other people were—*many* other people. You know what else about zombies?"

"What?"

"They don't even like to have sex. Sure, some of them double as prostitutes but that's just so they can get drugs. But as a rule, they're not interested in fucking, it just diverts them from their purpose."

She nodded but it was an insincere kind of nod—his police told him that. It was the first thing they'd told him in hours. Then she looked down at the bed.

"You look upset. What happened?"

"Nothing...I just don't like that word, I guess, the 'F' word."

"You don't like the word or the fact that it was me saying it?"

"I don't know...both, I guess. But it's no big deal."

"It is a big deal. Your feelings are a very big deal to me."

He looked at her intently. Couldn't she tell how sincere he was being? If only she knew how hard he was trying *not* to fuck her—not now at least, when she was still afraid of him. His resistance was nothing short of heroic yet all she could do was criticize him, albeit in her adorable, erection-inducing way.

She had a different look in her eyes now. She had the kind of face that couldn't hide anything. He looked deeply in her eyes. It was their best moment yet because the world and all the zombies in it disappeared then and there was nothing left but their two souls. The only other time he'd felt that way was with his mother (maybe also a few times with his father when he was very young), but now he knew he could feel it again and that made everything worth it.

"Is there something you want to tell me?" he suddenly said.

"I'm still scared."

"Even though I've untied you."

"You still have the gun."

"But I'm not pointing it at you anymore, n'est-ce pas?"

"Are you sure you couldn't just drive us back to New York and go back to the magazine. You put so much work into it and the first issue hasn't even come out yet."

"This is more important than the magazine. We're more important. Anyway, I don't intend to abandon the magazine or anyone in it, including Elliot. Elliot will accept what happened with us. I know he will. Remember I've known him a lot longer than you."

"If we went back to New York now, I promise I'd never say anything about what happened, not to anyone. We could still get back in time so Elliot wouldn't suspect anything."

"No, it's too late for that. I could never pretend. Our souls just touched a moment ago. We both know that happened...I think there's something else you want to tell me. I sense it."

She looked at him for a moment. He could sense something cracking in her like a little earthquake in her soul.

"OK, there is something . . ."

"Tell me, tell me now."

"I'm extremely scared now because, because I was raped once."

"What?"

"I was raped. There's no other word for it."

"Tell me who it is and I'll personally dismember him part by part."

"It happened in Ohio, years ago when I was in college."

"Did you know him?"

"Yes. It happened on a date, but I don't even know where he lives now. I don't want to know or even think about him. I never even told Elliot."

"Don't worry, I'll find out. I'll hire a detective and he'll find out and tell me and then I'll personally hunt him down and make him pay big time for what he did."

"I appreciate that but what I'm trying to say is this situation that I'm in now is scaring the shit out of me."

He winced. He didn't like her using a word like that. It was a violation, like drawing a mustache on the Mona Lisa which that stupid artist did. Was it Duchamp, Dali? Of course they weren't stupid, they were both probably geniuses—stupidity and genius got so easily mixed up. Anyway, he knew what he meant. He assured her that she had no reason to be scared of him, but he could see that she still was which excited him a little but upset him even more.

"Rape is the opposite of what I want to happen to you, to us," he finally said. "You've got to understand that about me. I want us to make love, I want that desperately but I want you to want it when we do. Otherwise it would be meaningless."

"And horribly cruel."

He didn't say anything. Instead he looked towards the window, suddenly wondering if that person who interrupted them—the human woodpecker—was still hovering around, contaminating his space.

She opened her eyes and realized she'd fallen asleep, maybe for a long time. The measly reassurance he'd given her must have relaxed her just enough, although it never would have if he hadn't also drugged her. She saw him standing near her, then closed her eyes and remembered in a flash how he'd done it in her apartment, gun in one hand, pills in the other. But weren't they already out of her system by the time they'd gotten to this place? Hadn't she slept during the whole trip? She opened her eyes again.

"How long have I been asleep?"

"A long time, for hours."

"How many hours?"

He laughed. "Three, at least. Maybe four."

"Four hours?"

"I'm not a person who pays that much attention to clocks. Don't you think we'd all go crazy if we did? Just looking at them or even worse, listening to them, gives me the creeps. Seeing or hearing our lives ticking away like that."

He continued talking but she stopped listening. Her wrists hurt, her arms and whole body hurt. The ropes were still on, boring into her like some animal that had been dully biting her for hours.

"Anyway, if I have to choose between watching a clock or watching you, it's no contest."

"There aren't any clocks here."

"That's true. I'd have to go out to the kitchen to find one and I didn't want to leave you. I've been in a dreamy state watching you sleep. Without intending to, you've put me in another world and I didn't want to leave it for a second."

I hate you and want to kill you, she thought, but only nodded. Then her phone rang.

"What's that?" he said, almost squatting on his knees in bed like a catcher. "That's your cell phone, isn't it?"

"Yes."

"Don't answer it."

"How could I?" she said, or maybe she just thought those words and mumbled them to herself.

"Where is it?" he said. He seemed nervous again, almost disoriented like he was when they heard the knocking on the door.

"It's in my pocketbook, on the floor," she added, nodding slightly with her head as if he somehow might not know where the floor was.

"So, you took your phone along?"

"I didn't know I had it."

"That's all right," he said, in an oddly cheerful voice. "We can't be blamed for what we don't know, although we often are."

He was on the floor now going through her bag like a wolf picking at bones, she thought. He finally found it just as it stopped ringing, then held it, staring at it with a kind of fascinated repulsion as if it were a beautifully rare but poisonous spider. Then he looked up at her.

"Don't worry, I'm not going to take your cell phone. I don't want your cell phone, just your cells. That's a joke, don't look so concerned."

"Barry, do you think I could use your bathroom . . . just for a minute?"

He seemed dumbfounded as if she'd just asked him to give her an explanation for the origin of life. A moment later she thought he appeared to be visualizing the bathroom in his mind, as if checking it for potential ways to escape. Finally, the strange little half smile she'd gotten to know reappeared. "Go ahead, feel free to. It's a good thing I have a key to the bathroom, otherwise it'd be more difficult to let you go there . . . unsupervised. But this way it won't do you any good to lock the door—so by all means, go ahead."

Can I close the door? She wanted to ask him, but didn't. She decided she got her way more often when she just asserted herself, that that was the way to keep intact the tenuous boundaries that still existed between them.

"Can you help me untie the ropes on my ankles?"

"Oh," he said, walking over to the bed posts to begin working on them. She noticed that he still kept the gun a few inches from him, however.

She didn't want him to know how good it felt to have the last ropes off. She wouldn't give him the satisfaction, nor would she even say thank you, she didn't think. *Thank you* for letting me go to the bathroom—preposterous! Nor would she ask him if she could shut the door while she urinated—she would just go ahead and do it.

"Thanks," she heard herself say, softly but distinctly, as she got off the bed.

"Of course," he said, with his half smile still intact. "Just turn to your right."

She shut the door, at least, without hesitation and immediately felt she entered a lightless tunnel or some place under the earth. She felt along the walls, all the while barely able to contain her urine and then she found the switch at last and sat down while the stream seemed to fly out of her.

When it was done there was an awful silence. She had the feeling that he was listening to her but at least he hadn't come in. She pulled up her underpants and heard an anxious voice saying no more than two or three words.

It was Elliot! Barry must have been playing her cell phone message. So the call *was* from Elliot, and she felt herself suddenly buoyed by hope. He worried about her, he loved her. *Of course* he was trying to find her.

Again she told herself not to act as if she'd heard anything, or was feeling a surge of hope. Their eyes met for a few seconds before she looked away towards the room. He was still holding her cell phone, gripping it as if it were a baseball.

"Don't worry, I'm not going to take your cell. I'm going to put it back in your pocketbook."

She paused on the threshold of the room and nodded. Maybe she shrugged. She was remembering Elliot's voice on the phone again, imagining how he was suffering now and something broke in her, made her know she had to do more than she was doing now, even if it involved a huge gamble. Otherwise, she couldn't forgive herself.

"Are you going to tie me up?" she said, looking at him again.

"Do you have any other ideas about what I should do with you?"

"I can think of something," she said, putting a hand on her hip.

He looked at her. "Would it be the same thing I've been thinking of, dreaming of, every day and night since the moment I met you?"

"Could be."

He walked over to her and she tried not to tremble. The next thing she knew he had his arms around her but was so far keeping his hands in relatively polite places.

"What's that sound?" he said.

"It's my hearing aids. When you press against them, even a little, it sets them off."

"I'm sorry."

"That's OK."

He kissed the top of her head.

"I know you don't love me yet," he was saying. "I know that will take more time. But are you starting to feel closer, are you starting to understand?"

"Yes," she said, "or I wouldn't want to do this."

His hands slid down and gripped her buttocks.

"Wait," she said, and he removed his hands. "No ropes, OK, and no pointing the gun at me."

"Of course not. I love you. I was only waiting for this. You do really want to do this, right? Because I can wait, a long time if necessary, until you do."

"I do want to. I'm starting to see things your way."

"It would be cruel to try to trick me or to pretend something you don't feel."

"I do feel it. And you're right, I was always attracted to you, though I tried to fight against it. The only thing is, I'm really hungry. Can we go get something to eat first?"

"There's no need to. I have food here. I bought it when I knew you'd be coming."

She trembled and tried to cover it with a smile. "Can we eat first, then?"

"OK, we can do that."

"Also, it's kind of cold here."

"I'll turn the heat up," he said, taking a few steps away and flicking a switch on the thermostat. "The beauty of these small apartments is they heat up right away, just like a hot woman."

"Where's my coat?" she said, ignoring his remark.

"Don't worry. It's in a safe place in the closet. You worry too much. I want to give you things, not take them away, capiche?"

The phone rang again. He looked at her angrily. "I thought you shut that thing off."

She looked at him and shook her head side to side like a pendulum.

"Where is it?"

"It's in my pocketbook," she said, while it continued to ring. It was Elliot, she knew. It seemed to ring with an impassioned music. That's why Barry was angry and even more scared. He was still standing as if frozen, staring at her.

"Where's your pocketbook?"

"*You* put it in there," she said, a little more boldly than she meant to. "Remember?"

He brushed past her into the bedroom, and shut off the phone.

"I'm sorry to snap at you," he said, in what she'd once thought of as his normal voice.

"That's OK," she said.

He came towards her and hugged her and she felt herself stiffen and shake simultaneously. It was worse than hearing chalk scraping against a blackboard. It was more like being hugged by a huge black widow spider. Then the spider kissed her, first on her forehead, then half on her cheek, half on her lips, while she shook.

"What's the matter?"

"I thought we were going to eat first."

"Yuh, OK," he said, "you excite me so much I forget."

She could feel her heartbeat while she forced a smile.

"I got pretty hungry while I was lying in bed all that time."

"I'm sorry," he said sincerely, though he was staring at her breasts.

"I'm still feeling cold, too, can I put my shoes on?" she said, taking a step away from him into the bathroom.

"Aren't you feeling the heat yet?"

"No, I'm cold."

"I'll get the shoes," he said, walking past her so she could feel the gun in his pocket as he brushed by her side. She stepped back into the living room and looked at the front door fifteen feet away from her.

"Here," he said, handing her her sneakers.

She bent down to put them on. "Can I put my coat on?"

"You act like you're in Alaska."

"Please," she said.

"What won't I do for you?" he said, as he opened the sliding doors of a closet in the hallway near the front door.

He came back with a coat that wasn't hers.

"That's not my coat."

"I know. It's warmer than your coat," he said handing her a dark brown, fur overcoat. "Yours was more of a jacket. This will make you warmer. Go on, try it on."

"Can't I just wear my own coat?"

"No. Your coat stays where it is. I want you to wear this one."

"But it won't fit."

"It will fit you fine."

"Whose is it? One of your girlfriends'?"

He looked down at the floor for a moment. "No, it belonged to my mother, but I want you to wear it now. Go on, put it on. Do you want me to help you?"

"Are you sure?" she said.

"Sure that I want to help you? Yes."

"Sure that you want me to wear your mother's coat."

"No one else ever has but, yes, I'm sure. It's a measure of how much I think of you that I want you to wear it. The coat, anything of hers, is sacred to me, because my mother was such an extraordinarily beautiful person on the outside and on the inside."

She was putting the coat on now, trying to fit her arms through the sleeves that she could already tell were too small, while trying to keep eye contact with Barry lest he feel insulted or hurt that the coat didn't fit her.

"Elliot will tell you," he suddenly said. "He'll tell you about my mother. He was very fond of her, I think he loved her, too. It was impossible to know her and not feel love for her."

The coat was tight on her shoulders and chest and comically short in her arms, but of course she wouldn't say anything.

"There," he said, as if he'd just climbed to the top of Mt. Everest. "You look beautiful, like an angel. I always dreamed of meeting a woman who'd deserve to wear her coat, and now I've finally found one."

"Thank you," she said softly. She saw tears in his eyes and for a moment almost felt moved herself.

"I'll tell you what else. For a long time I wondered what to do about my mother's apartment. I couldn't bear to give it up, but I couldn't bear to have anyone live there either."

"But Elliot lives there," she blurted.

"That's different. I meant I couldn't bear to have another woman live there, until I fell in love with you . . . . Besides, Elliot knows it's a temporary situation—that I was just helping him out. He's spoken to me a lot lately about wanting to get his own place."

She turned away and took a couple of steps towards the kitchen before stopping with her back to him.

"Ah, you're hungry. My little angel is famished. OK, we'll eat a late supper with what I have here, some pretty good French cheese and artichoke hearts and quite a good merlot. What do you say—we'll eat a last supper before we make love."

"Sounds good," she said.

He turned and opened the refrigerator and she snuck a look at the front door again. He took out a big plate with cheese, artichokes and fancy crackers on it and placed it on the table next to a bottle of red wine. Then dinner plates and silverware, glasses and napkins appeared. He was focused on his task, stopping to smile at her only once.

She was half watching him, half watching the door. She had to stay focused on her goal but she couldn't tip her hand either. It was a question of picking the optimum moment from the diminishing number of moments before the end of the meal. Like picking one sea shell among the hundreds at your feet to take home with you with only ten minutes or so to decide. Difficult, almost impossible to choose, of course, because the moment would not be perfect any more than the sea shell would. It was simply a question of picking the best available one before the unthinkable would happen—which she'd ruled out. She'd rather die than let that happen, she decided.

Somehow she was sitting down opposite him (so far not touching) putting food in her mouth without shaking, feeling like a human camera, recording everything, waiting.

"You're not saying very much," he said.

"Too busy eating. I was really hungry."

"Drink your wine. It's a good merlot. You'll like it, I'm already on my second one."

She picked up the glass. She'd have to have a little or he'd get suspicious, so she opened her lips and swallowed. He was watching her.

"It's good, n'est-ce pas?"

"C'est très bon," she said.

He smiled. Conversationally he was easy to please, at least in the mood he was in now. He seemed delighted by their little exchanges in French and so she played along with him while they ate their food and pretended to drink more than she did while he finished his second glass of wine and started on his third.

Then it happened unexpectedly. One moment he was talking about his mother with his mouth full (not because he was oblivious to manners but because the subject was too urgent for him to wait), then about time and memory and what Proust had to say about them in relation to love when he suddenly took a sip of wine and got up from the table saying, "Excuse me. I've got to use the bathroom for a minute. I'll be right back."

Did he say a moment or a minute? She kept still and nodded, might have even added "of course" once he started to walk away from her. Did he take the gun? Probably—she didn't see it anywhere.

Shut the door, shut the door, she said to herself, hoping the wine would relax him enough that he'd do it out of habit, especially if he were going to do more than pee. She listened more closely than she'd ever listened and thought she heard the door close. Then she thought of her cell phone, pictured it in the bedroom in her pocketbook, followed by a picture of her coat in the closet—but there was no time to get either. She ran as quickly and as lightly on the carpet as she could, pausing at the door to turn the lock and open it as quietly as possible, then left it open as she ran out into the black night in his mother's coat.

She turned left, running furiously then turned left again. "Get off his property," she told herself, which meant his parking lot, "now cross the street." Would she even be able to hear him if he were running after her? Would he wait, realizing she couldn't hear until he caught up with her and then shoot her so that his gun would be the last sound she'd hear on earth?

She crossed the street heading towards a neighboring house when she half heard his awful bellow, "Cheri, Cheri, come back!"

29

He knew there'd be trouble the second he saw her—attractive but skinny, with dark circles under her eyes and a slightly crazed look in the eyes themselves.

Why had he let her in? It was because it was a woman's voice so he pressed the buzzer—violating Barry's rule, not to mention common sense. It was also because he was so worried about where Cheri was (he'd called her three times without success and had just decided to go to her place) that he couldn't think straight. Maybe he thought the woman whose voice he heard clearly over the intercom but whose name he didn't recognize knew something about Cheri's whereabouts. Still, Barry had warned him more than once about buzzing in people he didn't know. "You're in New York now, not Boston or Philadelphia. This is in a lower and darker circle of hell. You can't forget that, capiche?"

But he had forgotten and now the woman was pointing a gun at him.

"What are you doing?" Elliot said, holding up his hands as if he could catch the bullet if she shot it. He backed away from her into the living room.

"I want some answers, Gordon, no more bullshit, OK?"

"I'm not Gordon, I don't know any Gordon."

"OK, I'll call you by your real name—Barry. Barry Asshole, that's your name, isn't it?"

"You're making a mistake. I'm not Barry either. I've never seen you before, never. I'll show you my ID."

He was still backing away and had nearly bumped into the sofa just in front of the large picture window.

She squinted her eyes while she stared at him. "OK, you're not Barry, but you're living in his apartment so you do know him, don't you?"

"I don't understand. I'm sure this is all a horrible misunderstanding."

"I'm not misunderstanding anything, buddy. I spent a lot of money and drove a lot of miles to track down Barry Ballless, so I don't thing there's any mistake on my part."

"Put the gun away, OK."

"I don't think so. I'll make the gun decisions. You answer my questions, then I'll be glad to never see you again."

Elliot nodded.

"He's your landlord, isn't he?"

"No," Elliot said.

"Then what are you doing in his apartment? You his friend or his lover?"

"I don't understand, what did he do to you?"

"Kind of what I'm doing to you now, only for a whole night. He also hit me and choked me and photographed me naked at gunpoint among various other tortures."

"I don't know anyone who'd do anything like that."

"But you do know Barry Auer, the cosmopolitan pervert, don't you? Shall I describe him to you—he of the gleaming green eyes and raven black hair and just about the same height as you. Sounds like someone you know, or think you know, capiche?"

"I do know a Barry. I still think this is a mistake."

"No, the mistake is all yours. Especially if you don't tell me where he is."

"Where did this happen?"

"What?"

"What you say happened to you."

"In a little apartment in a little town in Pennsylvania."

"The Barry I know doesn't have any apartment in Pennsylvania."

"Not that you know about. Maybe you don't know him as well as you think."

"I've known him over twenty years."

"Yah, but he's not into torturing men. They fight back better."

"I still really think it's a mistake," he said, but his voice was shaking a little and he could feel his heart beat.

"I saw your face when I described him. I saw your face go white when I said 'capiche.' He likes using foreign words, doesn't he? He always tries to remind you how well-traveled he is and then about all the famous people he knows. He's a writer, too, now how'd I know that?"

He started to feel dizzy then.

"I can't really comprehend this."

"Yuh, well comprehend it. The things you're hearing about actually happened to me, OK?"

"Can I sit down?"

"No, you're doing fine standing. You're a stand-up guy, aren't you? Look how you're standing up for Barry."

"I'm just very upset," he said, gripping the air conditioner. "I'm upset because I don't know where my fiancée is."

"Does Barry know her?"

"Yes, but . . . it's not the same Barry. It couldn't be."

"You sure? Why don't we visit him now and find out? He lives in the apartment on the second floor, doesn't he?"

He looked at her, wondering if she knew about Barry's money and was trying to get some. Even if she didn't know before, she knew now.

"He's not home. I've been calling him to find out about where my fiancée is. I'm very worried about her, can you understand that?"

"Listen," she said in a somewhat softer tone, "I don't want to put an awful thought in your head, but it seems that you can't find your fiancée and you can't find Barry either. Any possibility they might be together?"

"He's known her over five months and nothing's happened." Elliot felt a flash of anger. "If he did all these awful things to you, why didn't you call the police?"

"I never said he was stupid. He met me at a bar. I think he drugged me and I passed out in his car. He took me to a place in the middle of nowhere, told me his name was Gordon and after he was done torturing me, he blindfolded me and dropped me off at a train stop in the middle of the night—just like I was a sack of trash."

"So how'd you find out he lived here?"

"Because I didn't just roll over and accept what happened to me, OK? He didn't count on that. I hired a detective and he found out."

"So what is it you want to do now? You want to kill him and end both your lives? What is it you're really after?"

She seemed nervous and for a few seconds looked down at the floor.

"I don't want his goddamn money, if that's what you're thinking."

"What is it you want, then?"

"I want him to feel a little of what I felt. I want him to go through some of what I went through."

Elliot nodded. "And you don't see the tremendous potential for violence that could happen? Then you'll both be criminals and if you were to actually shoot him and me, you'd go to jail for the rest of your life. You don't want that, do you?"

"I want to see his apartment, that's what I want right now."

"How can I do that?"

"You have the keys to it, don't you?"

"No."

"You're lying, buddy, and just when I was starting to trust you."

"I can't give you what I don't have."

"Oh yuh? Give me *your* keys then. I'll bet somehow one of them opens his door."

"Why do you think that?"

"You already said you knew him and I remember he said he was going to call his best friend in all the world after he got rid of me. I bet that friend was you."

He could see her tightening her grip on the gun.

"Come on, you're hesitating. He who hesitates is lost."

"You're not going to shoot me if I don't give you the keys."

"You don't really know that, do you?" She moved back a few steps. "Now put them very carefully on the sofa, OK. The one by the picture window, then step away from it, moving towards your dining room nice and slow because I *will* shoot if you don't do what I say."

"No you won't. You won't shoot me."

"But I will. Come on, we're talking in circles."

"I just wish you'd stop saying it."

"I wish a lot of things too. Come on, we're wasting time."

He took out his keys and put them on the sofa that echoed the one upstairs where he'd sat when Barry first showed him the "amazing view of New York" as part of his sales pitch to get him to move here. He was thinking about Barry and had to admit he was always more than slightly uncomfortable with all the attention Barry paid to Cheri, not to mention all the questions he asked him about their sex life and worse still, perhaps, his surprise visit to Cheri. He saw again the unmistakable expression of love, love even more than lust, on Barry's face when he looked at Cheri the night the three of them rode in the taxi to Lillian Davis's party.

"Come on, you lead the way to his place. Then you let us in."

"How do you know I won't scream for help?"

"First, because I think you're starting to realize that what I'm telling you is true. Second, because if you do, I'll shoot you."

"You're not going to shoot me."

"Yes, I will. I'm a pretty crazy woman right now and I'm also very angry."

. . . It was like walking on the moon, or some kind of dream walk through a fine snow. She opened then quickly shut the door and told him to sit on the sofa while she started picking up various objects in the living room and staring at them as if she was farsighted.

He could smell Barry in the apartment and felt guilty for violating his home. Then he thought of Cheri and thought he would scream for the time he was wasting when he could be en route to her apartment to look for clues about where she might be.

"There's nothing here," he said.

"I'm going to look in his bedroom so I need you to get up from the couch. You lead the way."

He walked past her, thinking of lunging at and tackling her, but walked instead into Barry's room—neat and minimalist in its décor. She opened his closet door and his bureau drawers, slamming them shut after seeing nothing but clothes. Then she saw the gold framed photograph of Barry and his mother on the bed table. She picked it up and for a moment Elliot was afraid she'd smash it.

"That's him. That's the creep who tortured me."

Elliot took a few steps towards her but stopped when she spoke again.

"Who's the woman?"

"It's his mother. They were very close. She died about a year ago."

She nodded. He saw that her hand was shaking a little as she put the picture back. Then she opened the bed table drawer. She was looking at something again.

"Was his mother's name Cheri?"

"What are you talking about?"

"Whoever it is, he's pretty fond of writing her name."

She handed him a piece of paper. On one side were the words "Cheri D'amour" repeated all over the page.

"It's a song by Stevie Wonder he wanted to get. That doesn't prove anything."

"Look at the bottom of the page."

He saw the word "Exton" with a line through it followed by the words "leads to Eden." It made no sense to him.

"Remember I told you about that little town in Pennsylvania he took me to? That town is Exton."

He turned the paper over. There was an ink drawing of a bird carrying a stick figure on its wings headed towards the sun. In the lower right hand side was the apparent title in Barry's small, slanted handwriting, "The Flight of the Cheri Bird."

"Your girlfriend's name is Cheri, isn't it?"

"Yes," he said. She was looking at the drawing again. Her back was to him but he no longer thought of making a break for it.

"Here, look at this," she said, handing him a fragment of a photograph that had been cut out with scissors.

It was a photograph of Cheri in his favorite yellow dress. He stared at it uncomprehendingly until he realized it was from the night at the restaurant when they went out with Barry and Gretchen. Barry had cut everyone else out but Cheri from the picture, even himself.

"Is that Cheri?"

"Yes," he said. "I'm really worried about her."

"Maybe I can help you find her, if you want to go to Exton with me. I can take you to his place."

"Let me get my cell phone first."

"Oh, and guess what else I just found," she said, turning away from the bed table and waving a small card in the air.

"What is it?" Elliot said.

"Something he took from me that night, my ID."

30

At first he had run after her but it was too dark to know which way she went. He stood for a moment unable to see and uncertain if he heard the sound of Cheri running or just some leaves blowing along the ground. He looked around. There was still snow out— enough to mute the sound of her steps. For a moment he thought of the night he chased Renee. Once again he was holding a gun, staring into the dark trying to find a woman who was fleeing from him. But he had known nothing then. He was like an ignorant ape who hadn't known love. Now he knew what it was and that changed everything.

He got in his car. It was a long shot, but the only one left. She couldn't hide in the woods all night. He backed out of the parking lot, took a right towards the highway where the stores were, where it would figure she'd go for help. He opened his windows.

"Cheri," he said in a loud short voice like a dog barking. "Cheri!" He looked on both sides of the road but didn't see her. Could she already have gotten to the highway? He didn't think so. Then he had a terrible thought. What if someone had stopped and given her a ride. He felt the desire to protect her, didn't she know she shouldn't get in a stranger's car?

He had another awful thought. What if she'd simply run to the nearest neighbor? They could already be calling the cops then. He reached the highway, looked at both sides of it and turned around, deciding to try the other part of Plum Point Drive.

It was like chasing the dark in the dark. Nothing would show up unless it was in the little patches of snow that still dotted the sides of the street. It's always night or we wouldn't need light, Thelonious Monk had said.

It was because he had let himself go—given into his instincts, to eat, drink, and then go to the bathroom, lowering his guard as he slowly surrendered his vigilance. And then gave in to convention by closing the door while he peed which allowed her that long, silent, running head start.

"Cheri," he hissed, like a wolf would hiss, he imagined. "Cheri."

He drove past his building complex, his headlights on full, craning to see both sides of the road almost as if he'd already had his head half severed by a quietly efficient guillotine that somehow allowed him to rotate what was left like some ineffectual owl.

"Cheri," he bellowed. "Cheri," then he didn't say it anymore. He drove another mile up the hilly road then turned around, wondering vaguely if she'd taken her cell phone, if she'd already called the police.

It was all over now—everything. His dream of a lifelong love with Cheri and a lifelong friendship with Elliot. The dream of making the best literary magazine in America—gone before a single issue had come out. He wouldn't be the next Fitzgerald. He wouldn't have a Zelda, a book, or a baby. He would have nothing, be married to nothing. Before, he had his mother and once even the King and now he had nothing. He had guarded her urn so carefully and took it everywhere with him, but then he lost that, too. Lost it on the night with Jordan when his life essentially ended. Everything after that was really counterfeit, one long odious illusion. It was all doomed because of Jordan, even now he could see her face more clearly than he saw Cheri's.

He was sitting in the Lazy Boy in his living room. Already his chase after Cheri seemed a long time ago. He felt like a wolf with his teeth knocked out, head battered in, the pain persisting in it in a dully constant way.

He heard a phone ring. He saw himself spinning like a top, then went into the room while it was still ringing and traced it to her bag on the floor. It was her cell—all that was left of her. He pressed the talk button but said nothing. "Cheri, are you there? Cheri," he heard a voice saying. It was Elliot. He felt himself reel, holding onto the bed for support. Then he hung up—pressed the end button and took the power out of the phone. That voice and the images from his past with Elliot went through him like a shock. He saw the two of them walking along the Charles River after the party where he'd talked to Elliot about his mother. For a moment he wondered if he'd somehow been electrocuted, but then he sat down on the bed, drew in air, realized it was impossible, or at least hadn't happened, nor had he had a heart attack or a stroke. His stroke, his heart attack, was the loss of Elliot, permanent this time like his loss of Cheri. In an irony of economy, he'd realized both his losses as soon as he heard Elliot say her name. Of course any future career was gone, too—just like the phantom magazine that had miscarried. And beyond all that his mother whose ashes he'd even lost—left in Los Angeles—the city where his life had really

ended, the city where he'd thrown his own life into the garbage at
the same time he'd thrown away Jordan. But that was too horrible
to think about.

Time passed—he could be certain of that. Once you crossed
into hell, as he had, it was always just a question of time before you
finally understood what life was—that zoo of loss. Hell was where
you were ultimately left to wait, animal-like like he was, for the police
in your cage.

He got up from the bed in a start. Someone was knocking on
his door, or rattling his cage, he couldn't be sure which. He went to
the door and opened it without asking who was there, then staggered
backward, as if electrocuted a second time.

"Where's Cheri? Where is she?" Elliot's face was like a white
rock, the eyes small but invincible, like jewels.

"I don't know where she is," he finally said.

"What did you do to her, Barry?" Elliot said, moving into the
apartment while he retreated from the hallway. Only then did he
notice a familiar-looking woman hovering behind Elliot, crouching
monkey-like as if at home in the shadows. But that was impossible.
Elliot didn't know any of the missing women, not Renee or Love
Hunt, or the whore in Madrid, or Jordan.

"Nothing happened," he said, holding up his hands. They'd never
had a physical fight, but he felt one coming. As kids, he was stronger
and the assumption between them was that he was the better fighter.
He'd even stuck up for Elliot two or three times on the playground.
But it was different now—this was a different Elliot—Elliot white
rock.

"What do you mean, nothing happened?" Elliot said, pointing
a finger at him. "You took her here, didn't you? That's kidnapping,
Barry. What did you do to her?"

"Nothing. I took her here because I love her and I thought she
loved me, but I never touched her. Never. She just left a little while ago."

"You mean she ran from you before you could rape or kill her.
Which was it going to be this time, Barry?"

"No, neither."

"You think you're above the law, don't you? You think you're
Raskolnikov and can do anything you want to anyone."

He shook his head, then looked away from Elliot's eyes and tried
to identify the shadow woman but she was gone—or maybe she was
never really there.

"Elliot, I loved Cheri with all my heart."

"You don't love anyone. You just want any woman I have 'cause
you're jealous and you're sick. You're incapable of loving anyone but
yourself, don't you know that?"

He closed his eyes. It was like swords passing through him to hear this from Elliot.

"That's not true. I loved you too, Elliot. I always did." He waited before saying softly, "Can you forgive me?"

He heard nothing, then finally opened his eyes. No one was there. He was staring at his door which was locked from inside—as forlorn as a piece of the moon. Was Elliot ever there? He could understand that he left to look for Cheri but how did Elliot close the door without him hearing it? How did he lock it from the inside and still leave?

He paced off a circle (one of my last circles, he thought), then stopped abruptly.

"You did this," he said to his police, half expecting them to hiss or cackle at him for being fooled by the hallucination, but they were gone, too. Had he killed them or were they only hiding from him temporarily, as they'd been doing lately?

He got up from his bed. He'd been sitting in the same spot where he'd tied up Cheri. So he hadn't changed as he'd promised his police, not even after Jordan. No wonder his police were so merciless and had put him in his cage. Why hadn't he seen this before? He went to move but couldn't. Somehow he had a gun in his hand (had he got it from a drawer in his desk?) but his gun was useless, couldn't help him leave his cage. His choices had shrunk to two. He could wait actively, like those animals that paced in their cages, filled with the illusion that they could avoid the police, or he could wait passively, like those animals that lay down in their cages to die. Either way, the police would come, because they always kept their appointments. There was only one thing left to do and now that he was alone, he could do it. [Elliot, or the Elliot ghost had picked the wrong character. He was Kirilov, not Raskolnikov.] He would never let *them* take him. He was glad now that Cheri had outwitted and outwilled him. Why should she have to witness this like a zombie bride? Because it was too late to wait any longer.

Then for a second he couldn't find it. Another spin cycle, another session as a human top before he finally found the gun again on the bed by the pillow. It had a strange, forbidden taste, like something he'd always wanted. Without hesitation he put it deep inside his throat and fired.

31

They were on the highway now, where he did nothing but stare at it as if trying to spot a child who might be walking beside it. Fortunately, Susan seemed content to drive, saying very little, so that he heard only the noises of the car. He'd tried Cheri's cell three more times without success, the first time from her empty apartment where it looked like a couple of pieces of furniture had been moved but otherwise showed no overt sign of struggle. Susan had been all business there, too (she'd put her gun away by then), searching through the bureau drawers and stacked canvases.

"I like her paintings," was her only comment.

There were still no obvious signs of a break in, no trace of blood anywhere either, but everything looked a little off, and he told her that. Also, he saw that Cheri's coat was gone and her pocketbook too, but, of course, that figured.

He shifted his position in the car. "How much longer till Exton?" he said. It still sounded like a foreign word to him.

"Seventy five, eighty miles. We're making good time."

He nodded and gripped his phone again that he'd been holding the whole trip.

Exton. He still didn't wholly believe that Barry had a place there he didn't know about, much less that he could have kidnapped Cheri and be holding her there, as Susan had intimated. He saw Barry's face again on the bench of their 8th grade baseball team, the day they'd first really talked. He saw them walking together through Harvard Square with Lianne—yes, he knew Barry was attracted to Lianne, but nothing had ever happened, though how could he be sure of that now? He saw the tears in Barry's eyes listening to Mahler's Second Symphony in Barry's Tappan Street apartment, saw him and Roberta discussing the upcoming trial then went back in time to the night he and Barry walked along the Charles River, both half drunk as he'd told Barry he was too close to his mother. No, it couldn't be possible. Still, six years had passed without seeing him, and time sometimes treated people cruelly, twisted and misshaped them like sculpture gone awry. Hodge had tried to tell him that, he remembered.

He started to think about Cheri again, seeing the same images he'd seen throughout the trip. Her smile—childlike, open, yet a bit secretive, the night they met at the loft party in Tribeca. Then the look in her eyes just before they kissed at 30th Street station in Philadelphia, followed by her expression when she took off her shirt, the first time they made love. It was a dance of pain and anxiety in his mind, yet he guarded these pictures, knowing he couldn't speak of them, or of Cheri, to Susan, and probably could never speak of them to anyone. He could only guard them even as they tortured him and then submit again to the endless speculation about Barry, looking for signs—words of his that might either prove his innocence or guilt. On the side of innocence was the fact that until yesterday, nothing bad had happened to Cheri, nothing that she'd ever told him about, anyway. On the side of guilt, there was nothing concrete besides Susan's experience (about which there might be many mitigating circumstances he would never know without hearing Barry's side of the story). But there was also Barry's mysterious unannounced visit to Cheri and then certain expressions he'd seen on Barry's face for a split second when he wasn't aware he was being observed. A jealous look at the loft party the night he'd first introduced them repeated almost exactly a week or so later. Then that unmistakable, shocking look of longing he'd detected in the cab on the way to Lillian's party, itself a close repetition, now that he was forced to remember it, of Barry's expression the night at the restaurant with Gretchen just before Barry managed to kiss Cheri goodnight on her cheek.

"How many miles now?" he asked.

"Fifty five or sixty."

He nodded. He'd been leaning forward slightly like a jockey rigid with concentration. Now he leaned back, closed his eyes and saw Cheri's face. A moment later he felt an extraordinary tightening in the atmosphere as if there might be an earthquake, then the feeling condensed rapidly, though it was just as intensely concentrated as before. It was as if time were about to burst like the splitting of a grape.

He opened his eyes. His phone was ringing and in the next moment he was speaking to Cheri. She told him she was all right (they both thanked God), that she was in Exton at this kind couple's house that had taken her in, then, finally, that she had indeed been Barry's prisoner.

32

It was a lovely May Sunday in Philadelphia. Cheri was sleeping in and he was puttering around their apartment in the Chatham—the same building (albeit in a different, larger apartment) that he used to live in before he moved to Beekman Place.

After Barry's suicide, they decided to live together right away—before they even had a definite wedding date. On balance, he thought that things had gone as well as could be expected between them. Within a month they moved out of their New York places to Philadelphia. He'd stayed with her in her studio almost every night before they moved, though, of course it was very crowded, but staying in Beekman Place, even for an occasional break, was out of the question.

He'd thought she'd miss New York, but she never said she did. The first month she did go to Manhattan about once a week to show her work to galleries or to see friends like Gretchen, and once to cover something for the *Voice*, but now she took the train in only once or twice a month. Probably she'd missed some writing gigs she didn't tell him about, but he didn't think she'd missed anything professionally important, and possibly, nothing at all. She still kept in touch with Gretchen, who'd come to visit once (one of Cheri's happiest days). They'd spent most of the day together and at night the three of them went out to eat.

The night after Gretchen's visit, Cheri told him about her rape. He didn't understand at first and thought Barry had done it. But she told him again that nothing sexual had happened between her and Barry, that this was something that happened to her in graduate school in Ohio, years before she met him. His understanding came quickly then. He felt more sympathy for her and his appreciation of her courage deepened as well. He was thankful that she told him, though it was painful to hear. They were going to be married and such things had to be told. A few days later, after they'd listened to a Bill Evans album together, she told him she was pregnant. He remembered embracing her so tightly it made him laugh. Later he felt moments of panic followed by exhilaration again as in a fugue, until it began to level off into a steady feeling of happiness accompanied by a heightened sense of anticipation or concentration, as if he always had to remember something.

Thank god he'd still kept his job. He still had one year left on his contract and from what he could glean his chances for staying on at least a few more years were reasonably good ("We're going to try to extend you," his chairman said, as if he were made of springs) and probably were enhanced by his moving back to Philadelphia where he could attend more school functions and do the crucial socializing that, unfortunately, counted so heavily in academic job decisions. He'd told his chair he was engaged, with a wedding planned for early June, and had even had lunch with him and Cheri in the faculty dining room. The lunch went well and his boss seemed very fond of Cheri. While he felt slightly nervous about his job, he didn't think he would panic if it didn't "get extended." He somehow knew he would find a job now that he would soon become a father.

Many times he'd reflected that if just one of a seemingly interconnected series of events hadn't occurred, Cheri might not have been saved. While not transforming his lack of religious conviction, it did make him think quite often about Hamlet's line "there's a divinity that shapes our end, rough hew it though we may." He also thought a good deal about Susan. If he hadn't handled the situation the way he did when they first met, she, too, might have shot him. Yet she ended up being an invaluable ally who not only drove him to Cheri and later helped extensively with the police after Barry's body was discovered, but was as well an ongoing source of understanding and solace for him and Cheri.

For a while he thought Cheri and she would become friends, but that gradually faded in part because of their dissimilar interests, and in part because after a period of reconstructing events with Barry and trying to understand them (an experience he and Cheri both went through together like intense collective cramming for a final exam) Cheri wanted to stop talking about Barry, and Susan was then an eternal reminder.

He himself still wanted to talk about it, though not enough to disturb Cheri's newfound level of fragile tranquility, especially important now that she was pregnant. He realized that in the years ahead, unless she brought him up, he would never intentionally mention Barry again. Sometimes, especially when his anxiety about fatherhood increased, he toyed with the idea of seeing Dr. Hodge, but too much time had passed and he'd lost his belief in Hodge. Other times he thought of talking about it (and what happened to Barry) to Annette, but that seemed difficult and vaguely futile as well, and so he never really explained much the two times they had lunch.

He walked into their room where Cheri was sleeping, feeling somewhat tempted (a temptation he'd given into before more than once) to look through his memory box again that was well-hidden in his closet and once more read the letters Barry had sent him in his youth. To his right was Cheri sleeping, to his left was his memory box—the treasure chest of his past. For a moment he felt he was part of an invisible game of tug-of-war, but then he walked, tiptoed actually, towards the bed and looked at Cheri—his bride to be in a month, the mother of his child.

How lucky he was to watch her sleeping—her blonde hair in a pattern her dreams had helped form, her profile that still revealed most of her thick sensual lips and made him remember the laughing, liquid eyes closed now as she rested from the world. Yes, he had pursued the Lawrencian vision Barry used to talk about. He'd wanted both the platonic love of a best friend (Barry) and the sexual love of a woman, and he'd thought that without having both in his life something would always be missing. But now, looking at Cheri, he felt that maybe she was all he needed, that this was as full and complete as reality could get, and that maybe if Barry had had a child, or at least been able to love a woman, everything would have been different.

He felt tears coming to his eyes then and he closed them as if to protect himself or else, perhaps, to help the tears flow. But when he closed his eyes he saw an image of Barry sitting on the floor next to him in his Tappan Street apartment. Roberta had just given them cookies a few minutes before and now they were listening to Mahler's "Resurrection" symphony. In his memory, Barry closed his eyes because the music was so heartrending. Meanwhile, in the present, in Philadelphia, Elliot opened his eyes and shuddered.